RANDOM DEATH

As Lesley Egan:
RANDOM DEATH
THE MISER
A CHOICE OF CRIMES
MOTIVE IN SHADOW
THE HUNTERS AND THE
   HUNTED
LOOK BACK ON DEATH
A DREAM APART
THE BLIND SEARCH
SCENES OF CRIME
PAPER CHASE
MALICIOUS MISCHIEF
IN THE DEATH OF A MAN
THE WINE OF VIOLENCE
A SERIOUS INVESTIGATION
THE NAMELESS ONES
SOME AVENGER, ARISE
DETECTIVE'S DUE
MY NAME IS DEATH
RUN TO EVIL
AGAINST THE EVIDENCE
THE BORROWED ALIBI
A CASE FOR APPEAL

As Elizabeth Linington:
CONSEQUENCE OF CRIME
NO VILLAIN NEED BE
PERCHANCE OF DEATH
CRIME BY CHANCE
PRACTISE TO DECEIVE
POLICEMAN'S LOT
SOMETHING WRONG
DATE WITH DEATH
NO EVIL ANGEL
GREENMASK!
THE PROUD MAN
THE LONG WATCH
MONSIEUR JANVIER
THE KINGBREAKER
ELIZABETH I (Ency. Brit.)

As Egan O'Neill:
THE ANGLOPHILE

As Dell Shannon:
CASE PENDING
THE ACE OF SPADES
EXTRA KILL
KNAVE OF HEARTS
DEATH OF A BUSYBODY
DOUBLE BLUFF
ROOT OF ALL EVIL
MARK OF MURDER
THE DEATH-BRINGERS
DEATH BY INCHES
COFFIN CORNER
WITH A VENGEANCE
CHANCE TO KILL
RAIN WITH VIOLENCE
KILL WITH KINDNESS
SCHOOLED TO KILL
CRIME ON THEIR HANDS
UNEXPECTED DEATH
WHIM TO KILL
THE RINGER
MURDER WITH LOVE
WITH INTENT TO KILL
NO HOLIDAY FOR CRIME
SPRING OF VIOLENCE
CRIME FILE
DEUCES WILD
STREETS OF DEATH
APPEARANCES OF DEATH
COLD TRAIL
FELONY AT RANDOM
FELONY FILE
MURDER MOST STRANGE

RANDOM DEATH

LESLEY EGAN

PUBLISHED FOR THE CRIME CLUB BY
DOUBLEDAY & COMPANY, INC.
GARDEN CITY, NEW YORK
1982

All of the characters in this book
are fictitious, and any resemblance
to actual persons, living or dead,
is purely coincidental.

Library of Congress Cataloging in Publication Data

Random death.

I. Title.
PS3562.I515R3   813'.54
AACR2
ISBN 0-385-17862-X
Library of Congress Catalog Card Number 81–43279

First Edition

Again, this one is for
Margaret Van Tine
because of the Lonely Unicorn
and the interest we share in
the Unknown

Ah, Fortune, what god is more cruel to us
than thee! How thou delightest ever to make
sport of human life!

Horace, *Satires*

Penetrating so many secrets, we cease to
believe in the unknowable. But there it sits
nevertheless, calmly licking its chops.

H. L. Mencken, *Minority Report*

CHAPTER 1

It was raining again. This was going to be a wet winter in southern California. Since the official beginning of the rainy season two months ago in September they had had four heavy storms. In the big, square, communal detective office on the second floor of Glendale Police headquarters, the tall windows streamed grayly, and all the strip fluorescent lighting was on.

At his desk next to Delia's, Varallo was reading a report. Leo Boswell was typing one a couple of desks away, cussing now and then at the typewriter. Everybody else was out somewhere. Delia was listening to Mrs. Grace Phillips.

"I tell you, Miss—what did you say— Riordan, that poor girl never had a chance. See, she opened up to me, I heard the whole story. She never had a damned chance. Raised on a farm some place in Kansas, for God's sake, and never seen a town bigger than the wide place in the road she went to school—runs away to Hollywood on the bus with the idea she'd get the swell modeling job next day, people always said she was pretty enough to be a movie star—my God!" Grace Phillips was a hard-faced blonde by request somewhere in her fifties; she looked as if life had used her hard, but she had her head screwed on the right way and had kept a sense of humor and a warm heart. "Haven't we all heard the story before!"

"Yes," said Delia. "Did she tell you anything about Jerry Rubio?"

"Oh, you know his name. Maybe I'm not telling you nothing you don't know? Well, the cops are smart these days." Grace Phillips stubbed out her cigarette in the ashtray on Delia's desk. Her expression was brooding. "These poor damned silly kids. Yeah, she told me the whole story, she needed a shoulder to cry on— I told you she'd just got hired at the place I work, Chris's Night Owl Cafe on San Fernando, and middle of the evening it's usually slow, there was just me and her. Look, she wasn't a bad kid, Miss Riordan— Rosalie—she was just silly, and young, and she got took."

"Like a lot of others," said Delia.

"Yeah. Yeah. She just didn't know which way to turn—she lands here last year, and with the money running out, she couldn't get a job, and this guy gets hold of her. Rubio. Over in Hollywood. She never set out to be a hooker, it was him roped her in. Working for him. I thought I'd be blowing the whistle on him, but you know about it already, hah?"

"About Rubio, yes. What did Rosalie say?"

"Well, she was into it before she hardly realized, see, and she didn't like it no way. She'd been brought up right, she wanted out as soon as she got in. She'd tried to get away before, and he beat her up. He kept her pretty short of money, but she managed to squirrel some away, and she come over here about three weeks ago, like I say got the waitress job at Chris's, and a cheap room, and was kind of laying low. I don't know how Rubio found her, could be she'd said something to one of his other girls about where she was going. My God, when I come to work last night and Ollie—that's the owner—tells me she's got murdered, I like to died! I said right off, it's that Goddamned pimp found out where she was, and Ollie says prob'ly the cops'll want to talk to me. My God, I felt sorry for that girl, I did. She was only nineteen. She was a damned little fool maybe, but I guess most of us have made mistakes, ain't we?"

"Most of us," said Delia wryly. "Did she know where Rubio was living?"

Grace Phillips shook her head. "If she did, she never said. She said he showed up every day to take most of the money she'd got from the johns. She'd had a room on Harold Way in Hollywood. He paid the rent and left her some eating money, was all. The poor damn little fool. Only nineteen. It must have been him killed her, wasn't it?"

Delia said, "Probably. We don't know yet." As a matter of fact, Jerry Rubio's prints had showed up in the shabby cheap apartment on Everett Street, and there was sufficient physical evidence to show that he had probably not intended murder, just a severe enough beating to scare Rosalie back to his little stable of hookers. "This fills in a little," she added, though what Grace

Phillips had to say was largely redundant. "Thanks very much for coming in, Mrs. Phillips."

"Got to help the cops. That poor damn girl." She got up, a square hefty woman, and picked up her raincoat from the back of the chair and put it on slowly. "Do you want me to sign a statement or something?"

"If we want one, we'll let you know, thanks," said Delia. There would probably be enough evidence to nail Rubio legally; and equally probably there would be a plea bargain, a reduced charge, and he'd spend a couple of years in and come out to prey on more silly women.

She watched Mrs. Phillips out with a mental sigh. Now there'd be another report to write, in case the DA's office decided it needed testimony from Grace Phillips. She didn't immediately reach for a form to roll into her typewriter. It was twenty past two, three and a half hours to end of shift on this late November Thursday, and she was feeling bored and stale. Since Rosalie King's beaten body had been found by her landlady yesterday morning, and the lab had turned up Rubio's prints and long record with the LAPD, there was an all-points bulletin out on him and his car, and it was just a question of time before he'd be picked up. It was just the latest little sordid job to be worked, not remotely interesting. They also had a hit-run they were never going to get anywhere with, and the paperwork on the latest suicide was just about cleaned up. Delia yawned, looking at the steady gray rain streaming down the windows.

Sergeant Joe Katz came in with Detective John Poor. They sat down at their respective desks and Katz said, "I wrote the last report."

"All right, all right," said Poor, and rummaged in his desk for forms and carbon.

The phone rang on Varallo's desk and he picked it up. "Sergeant Varallo . . . oh, hell. Where? All right, we're on it." He looked over at Delia. "We've got a new homicide."

"Fine," said Delia. "The more the merrier. Give me five minutes and I'm with you." She got her handbag out of the bottom drawer and went down the hall to the ladies' room. Shrugging into her raincoat, she got out powder puff and lipstick, eyeing herself in the mirror impersonally.

All those long years of proving herself as an LAPD policewoman, the long hours of studying, acquiring all the useful extra skills to help her make rank—the fluent Spanish, the courses in police science—most of the time working the swing shift, which just made everything more difficult—she had deliberately cultivated the plain-Jane effect. No-nonsense Riordan, poker-faced Riordan, all out to make rank and the great career. Neil had tried to tell her how foolish that was—how foolish all of it was —and of course he had been quite right. About that as well as other things. Now, when it was too late, forever too late, and there was nothing ahead of her for the rest of her life but the sordid thankless job, she was at least looking different: a small compensation. She had let her dark brown hair grow, and it was professionally cut and styled, in loose waves halfway to her shoulders, showing its chestnut lights. She was using more makeup, and her wardrobe had expanded to something more than the plain dark dresses and pantsuits, and included some good jewelry. She powdered her nose, touched up her lipstick, and fastening the plastic rain hood reflected that she might almost pass as still twenty-nine, instead of a year and a half older.

These last two and a half years had dragged by uncertainly, now speeding too fast, now moving in slow motion. A lot had happened, but very little that had happened to her had been good.

She finished buttoning her coat and opened the door to the hall, to face Detective Mary Champion just coming in. "Damn," said Mary, looking at her, "I thought we could take a coffee break together."

"There's a new body," said Delia. She liked Mary, who was a plump fortyish grass widow with a teenage daughter and a breezy disposition. She had come to them from eighteen years on the Santa Monica force, wanting to be nearer her ailing mother. One of the things that had happened in the last two and a half years was that the crime rate in Glendale—conservative, quiet, bedroom-community Glendale—had shot up to unprecedented heights, and, however reluctantly, the city fathers had had to part with the wherewithal to upgrade the police department. Not before it was time, they had acquired sixty new uniformed men and a fleet of new squad cars; there were five more men in the lab and two policewomen in the scientific investigation unit; six more detectives added to the former strength were now nominally divided into a Robbery-Homicide Bureau, Burglary, and Narcotics, with detectives Ben Guernsey and Mary Champion aided by a couple of policewomen forming a Juvenile Division in a cubbyhole of an office downstairs. Varallo had made sergeant. Lieutenant O'Connor, to his annoyance, had been given the dignity of his own office, a closet-sized room behind the communal office, and he and Leo Boswell constituted the Narco Bureau. As the gregarious soul he was, O'Connor resented the isolation and was as often to be found in the big office as his own; and in practice, being still shorthanded for the normal amount of work on hand, they still filled in for each other regardless of the type of crime to be worked.

"Damn," said Mary again. She ran her fingers through her short graying hair, setting it in wilder disorder than usual. "Well, I'd better fortify myself anyway—another hour and we'll have the Mata Haris in with the latest. It is to be hoped. The things we get into. Well, see you around."

"How's it shaping?" asked Delia.

"By what it looks like, we'll be hauling in half the student body," said Mary cheerfully. "The lieutenant's fit to be tied. These kids." She brushed by Delia into the ladies' room.

In the lobby downstairs, Varallo was belting an ancient trench coat. "It's coming down cats and dogs," he said unenthusiastically. "I'll drive." He opened one panel of the double front doors for her and clapped his hat over his crest of tawny-blond hair. "I hope to God we don't get too much more of this or we'll be getting more landslides up in the hills. What a climate."

They made a dash for the parking lot and his year-old Ford sedan. Some while ago, he had got tired of the cramped space in the Gremlin, and now the children were older and Laura's car not always reliable, they had needed something bigger. He fished out keys. Delia asked, "Where are we headed?"

"Address on South Glendale. I don't know what it is, the squad just called in a shooting. All we need." He started the engine.

The address was two blocks this side of Chevy Chase on Glendale Avenue, and the pounding rain had kept any potential crowd from collecting. There was a drugstore on the corner, offices and a few stores up from there. The squad was parked in the red-painted curb zone outside the drugstore. The ambulance was ahead of it, and the two paramedics and Patrolman Steiner were standing under the awning over the drugstore door. There was a white-smocked clerk in the doorway looking shaken. In front of the other three men was a boy about twelve, just standing there. As the Ford pulled up behind the squad, Steiner came over. They all, by tacit agreement, joined up under the awning.

On the sidewalk just in front of the door to the drugstore was something under a blanket. There were splotches of red on it rapidly darkening in the pelting rain.

"Look, we didn't know how you'd want us to handle it," said one of the paramedics. "It's always, don't move the body, don't touch anything—and God knows she's dead all right—but this damned rain— I said we should move it into the ambulance, but Jack says you'd jump all over us—"

"So let's have a look." Varallo squatted and lifted the blanket, Delia looking over his shoulder.

She couldn't be more than ten or eleven, a thin little girl with dark hair; her face was untouched, and she had been a pretty little girl with neat small features. She was wearing a blue pullover sweater and a dark skirt, a red coat and ankle-high black boots.

"My God," said Varallo. What could still be seen of her clothes was a mass of blood, torn intestines spilled out; she had been nearly cut in two.

"Yeah," said the other paramedic. "A shotgun, what it looks like."

"I heard the shot—it must have been the shot," gabbled the clerk. "I don't believe it—just a little kid— I don't believe the things that happen these days—"

"The other kid says he was with her, he saw it happen. It was a car going past, somebody stuck a gun out the window. I tried to get him into the squad," said Steiner. "Maybe he's in shock—"

Delia went up nearer to the boy. He was a nice-looking boy about twelve, in nondescript shabby clothes, rubber boots, an old raincoat. "Can you tell us your name? We're police, we have to ask questions about this."

He nodded his head once, jerkily, without looking at her. His eyes were glassy. "Richard Gilmore. She's Connie—she's my sister."

"Where do you live?"

"Maple Street. Just—up a ways. We were going home from school. Just walking—walking along. I never even noticed the car—till there was this big bang—and Connie—and Connie—" He sagged, and one of the paramedics caught him and took him over to the ambulance.

"I heard the shot," said the clerk. "There wasn't anybody in, I was putting out some stock. I heard the shot— I knew it was a shot, and I ran out to look, and saw this poor kid—sure, it had to be a car going past, there wasn't anybody on the street but the kids—"

"Did you see the car?" asked Varallo.

"Now how could I? It was maybe fifteen seconds before I got to the door—nobody on the street for a block, all this rain, and not much traffic, but cars both ways in the next block, not right out in front, nothing to say which car— God! Just a kid! Some one of these louts all doped up maybe—a hell of a thing—"

Varallo said to Delia, "Not very practical to try for photographs. She didn't move after she was hit, and she wasn't hit from far off. It was most likely a car on this side of the street, heading south. Let's see if the boy's all right. They'd better take her straight to the morgue." The blanket and what it covered was already sodden black with rain.

The boy looked white and sick, but they thought they'd better get him home. He said his mother would be there, she didn't work.

It was a modest frame house on an old block. Part of the thankless job was breaking bad news, and it was never easy. Mrs. Gilmore was a pleasant-faced woman in her late thirties, with untidy brown hair, and a warm voice. The boy hurled himself at her, shaking, and she held him, patting him automatically as she listened to Varallo, her eyes glazing, her tone at first merely bewildered.

"Connie—but she's only eleven," she said. "How could Connie be—shot? I don't understand—how could Connie be shot? In the middle of town? It's just silly—" But of course eventually she took in what they were saying. She didn't quite break down, but she probably would sooner or later. Delia asked questions and called her husband; he worked at The Broadway in the Galleria. They stayed until he got there, answered his few numb questions. They had got the clerk's name, the only other witness. Varallo took Delia back to headquarters to write the initial report.

"You know you'll just be wasting time asking questions down there," she said, as he pulled up in the parking lot.

"We do have to go by the book," he said rather savagely, lighting a cigarette. He hadn't shut off the engine, waiting for her to get out. Eyeing his handsome regular profile, Delia thought academically that Laura was lucky: a good man, Varallo, and a good police officer. "No, we probably won't get a damned thing, but we have to ask and look. When the boy's calmed down, see if he can give us anything at all on the car."

"Yes," said Delia, her hand on the door. "Tell Laura I'll be there at six tomorrow night."

"And thanks very much," said Varallo. "We appreciate it."

"No trouble." She got out and shut the door, and he took his foot off the brake, heading back for the scene. It would be a waste of time asking questions down there because obviously no one else had heard the shot; nobody had rushed out to the street except that clerk. Any pedestrians, and they would have been few and far between on that block on a day like this, had been too far away to hear the shot, be attracted to the scene; the people in the stores and offices shut away behind closed doors and windows. They would have heard about it now, from the clerk; they'd be ready to ask excited questions, but they wouldn't have any answers.

Connie Gilmore. Eleven. If there was any answer to that, it would be the answer that so often turned up: the meaningless, motiveless violence.

Delia came into the lobby, and heard O'Connor's rough bass voice from the open door of the Juvenile office across the hall to the right. O'Connor was used to having a finger on all the current cases, though he wasn't technically supposed to be concerned with homicide these days. She went over and looked in the door, stripping off her coat.

It looked like an interesting little conference. O'Connor, broad and bulging and as always needing a shave at this hour, was sprawled back in a desk chair, the outline of the .357 Magnum very visible in the shoulder holster. Mary Champion was taking notes briskly, a cigarette in one corner of her mouth and one eye screwed up against the smoke. Detective Ben Guernsey, sandy and stocky and cynical-eyed, was leaning back fiddling with his unlit pipe and watching the two girls sitting in front of his desk. One was blonde and one was dark, but aside from that they looked like any two average high-school girls in today's uniform, the jeans and dun-colored pullovers, the boots, the messy hair styles—one frizzy and short, one a lank mid-parted tangle—the chipped red nail polish and pale lipstick. And that was no small achievement, for as a matter of fact they were both policewomen. If only just. Wanda Hart was a six-month rookie just twenty-one, and Ruth Sawyer had been sitting on the switchboard in Communications only six months longer than that.

"This Dutchy keeps coming up, Lieutenant—most of the kids seem to know about him, the ones into dope. He's the main contact, it looks like."

"At least half a dozen of the kids have told me he can get you anything you want. But you have to go through one of the seniors—"

"Oh, for God's sake," said O'Connor. He ran a hand through his curly black hair. "Back to the roaring twenties. Knock twice and ask for Joe."

There were always a few of the kids into drugs, and the ongoing problem on most high school campuses; but the situation at La Crescenta High had got out of hand in the last six months and the principal and a delegation of parents had descended on headquarters demanding action. The usual routine of locker-searches, questioning, arrest and the inevitable probation, was worse than useless; it was the source, the suppliers, who were important; and the dirty fuzz, interfering with their innocent fun, would never get the time of day from the kids. It had been Mary Champion who had remarked that kids only talked to other kids of the things important to them; and O'Connor had thought that one over and come up with the not unprecedented idea of using the *agents provocateurs*. Of all the females on this force, only Wanda and Ruth were young enough to pass—with judicious attention to dress and manner—as eighteen-year-olds; and they were young enough to be enjoying the play acting, even when it meant going back to school. Only the principal knew their true identities; and they had been collecting information all right, if nothing particularly solid yet. These idiotic kids, they had reported after the first week, even the straight ones who didn't go in for dope, seemed to think it was interfering with the other kids' civil rights for police to bust the sellers and suppliers.

O'Connor caught sight of Delia at the door, got up and came over. "Has that Rubio got picked up yet?"

"I don't think so. Vic and I were just out on a new body." She told him about Connie Gilmore. He didn't comment, just dragged a hand down over his bulldog face and scowled. "How are your Mata Haris doing?"

"Nothing definite enough to move on, damn it. Eventually, I hope."

Delia went on upstairs. Joe Katz was still there, his desk spread with paperwork; the burglary rate was way up. Gil Gonzales, their newest detective, was hunched over his typewriter batting out a report with two fingers. Lew Wallace was on the telephone. Delia took her coat down to the ladies' room, came back to her desk and rolled a report form into her typewriter.

Katz looked up and said, "Is Charles still down there with the kiddies? Fun and games. I want to kick around some ideas with him on these damn break-ins— Listen, Tracy was just in when the shift changed." The Traffic shift changed at four o'clock. "I suppose it'd be something for Robbery-Homicide— I'm not used to being all divided up yet. Damn nuisance. He said to tell you you'll probably be getting a visit from this preacher, he told him to tell the tale to the front office."

"What's it about?"

Katz shrugged. "I didn't ask details. Some trouble at this church—started out as vandalism, and now some attempted robberies. You'll be hearing."

Delia filled in the date on the report and headed it properly HOMICIDE: CONSTANCE GILMORE. With her hands on the keyboard, a sudden black wave of depression engulfed her, and she thought bitterly, but what was the use? There could be a hundred reports written—it was all futile—there'd never be any leads to the anonymous shotgun blast fired from a car, the random snuffing out of innocent life. If the job had taught her anything, it had to do with that little word *random*. Because the majority of the events they were dealing with on the job were just that—random and meaningless. There was no pattern, no discernible cause and effect, and above all no reward for virtue or inevitable punishment for evil. And so much of it was not so much evil as stupid; and no swift judgment brought on that either.

Omar Khayyam rounded it out so neatly:

> 'Tis all a Chequer-Board of nights and days
> Where Destiny with Men for Pieces plays:
> Hither and thither moves, and mates, and slays,
> And one by one back in the Closet lays.

Which might be charming poetry, but wasn't true at all because there wasn't any planning or management about it, about anything; things happened blindly, reasonlessly, in a blind and reasonless universe.

She roused herself to start the report. If there was nothing left to her but the thankless job, at least she could do it efficiently—and that was a reasonless conclusion too, if it brought no reward but an indifferent one.

It was five-thirty then, and she finished the report five minutes after the end of shift at six o'clock. Varallo would have gone straight home. The ladies' room was empty. From force of habit she powdered her nose, arranged the plastic rain hood becomingly. Which was even more reasonless. Suddenly seeing the humor of it, she smiled at herself in the mirror, touching up her lipstick.

The rain had let up slightly, but it was slow driving down Brand Boulevard to Los Feliz, through the dreary Atwater section to the wide intersection at Riverside Drive where you always got held up. At last the light changed, and she made a left at the first narrow side street, a block farther on turned onto Waverly Place. It was a dark block, only a few lights showing; and at the big Spanish house at the end, as she pulled into the open garage, there were no lights at all. There was no one in the house to welcome Delia Riordan home now. Now, or ever again.

Varallo didn't, of course, get anything at all talking to people along that block of Glendale Avenue. He hadn't expected anything; but they had to go through the motions. At five of six he gave up and started home. At least it was his day off tomorrow.

Up on Hillcroft Road, Laura had put the garage light on, and the door was open. He closed it, and on his way to the back door spared not a glance for the climbing Alida Lovett growing up the trellis alongside it. The rain would be good for his roses, if there wasn't too much rain, but thank God roses didn't need much attention in winter, besides the necessary pruning in January.

The kitchen was warm and comforting after the cold rain. Laura was setting the table in the dining room; she came to kiss him. "Poor darling, you feel frozen. Go and toast your toes—there's a fire going in the front room. Do you want a drink before dinner?" Her bright brown hair was a little untidy, her cheeks flushed from the stove.

"I feel as if I deserve one." And then, of course, the children discovered he was home and came running. He picked them up one by one and hugged them—amazing how solid and energetically squirmful they were, and even more amazing how they seemed to grow day by day. It wasn't at all possible that solemn blonde Ginevra would be five in January, or that Johnny had been three last month. Ginevra had a new coloring book he had to admire, and Johnny demanded to be read to. Laura vetoed that firmly.

"You know that's after dinner, Johnny. Daddy's tired, he wants to relax now. After dinner there'll be stories before bed."

"Bean stalk?" asked Johnny hopefully.

"Yes, yes."

"When do they get over wanting to hear everything a hundred times?" wondered Varallo plaintively, and started to make himself a brandy and soda. "Delia said she'll be here at six, by the way."

"Nice girl," said Laura warmly.

"Though if it's still pouring like this it'll hardly be a gala evening."

"You needn't try to back out of it now. A little culture will be good for your soul, and I do like to be taken out to dinner occasionally." They had tickets for the local symphony's popular concert tomorrow night; and where once their friendly neighbors, the Andersons, had always been available as baby-sitters, they didn't know the new people in that house at all. Old Mr. Anderson had died of a heart attack last year, and Mrs. Anderson moved to live with her daughter. These days Delia often came to stay with the children when the Varallos wanted a night out.

He wandered into the living room with his drink. Gideon Algernon Cadwallader, with the usual feline instinct for comfort, was curled up in front of the fire, sound asleep. Varallo sat down in his own big armchair and was immediately clambered on by Ginevra and her coloring book, while Johnny crawled happily after a mechanical truck.

O'Connor drove home to Virginia Avenue muttering to himself about the stupid kids, and left the car in the carport ahead of the driveway gate. He opened that, tentatively bracing himself for Maisie's playful pounce; but she wouldn't be out in this downpour. Out just long enough, probably, to bring large dollops of mud into the house. He opened the back door and went through the old-fashioned service porch to the kitchen. Katharine was stirring something on the stove, his beautiful dark Katy, whom a lout like O'Connor, dragged up in the orphanage, never had deserved.

"You do look a sight," she said, kissing him soundly. "You come home half an hour early tomorrow so you can shave again and start out looking civilized at least."

"Why, where are we going? I don't want to go out anywhere."

"It'll be very good for you, and I didn't tell you till now because I knew you'd raise a fuss. We're going out to dinner with Vic and Laura and on to the symphony pops concert."

"I don't understand symphony music," said O'Connor. "I'd rather stay home."

"All nice simple popular music, darling—you'll enjoy it once you're there. Look, dinner'll be half an hour. You fix drinks for us beforehand and you'll feel better."

"Oh, hell," said O'Connor. He stripped off his tie and started down the hall past the living room, and young Vincent Charles, who had turned three last month, scrambled up from his fleet of toy automobiles and shrieked, "Daddy! I got a new blue car! I got—" The enormous blue Afghan hound Maisie, stretched out the length of the couch, leaped convulsively and uttered a shrill bark.

"Quiet!" said O'Connor. "Oh, hell, I didn't mean you, Vince. All right, let's see your new car." Dogs. Symphony orchestras. Those stupid Goddamned kids. He damn well needed a drink before dinner.

Delia went around switching on lights, checked the mailbox just in case—but she seldom got any mail except the routine bills—and looked doubtfully into the freezer on the back porch. That had been one trial about living alone; she'd never learned to cook, never done much cooking, and she hadn't the time or inclination now. She usually ended up putting a couple of frozen entrees in the oven. She took out a package of salisbury steaks, one of au gratin potatoes. She thought there was some of that bottled salad dressing left.

The rain was pouring down steadily. It would be nice to relax over a drink before dinner. But she didn't know whether she'd be going out again, and if she had to drive up into Hollywood she wouldn't have a drink.

Before she turned on the oven she went down the hall to the phone. That was the routine every night—to find out what sort of day it had been for Alex. To find out if she'd be going to see him.

Of course, of course, it had had to be the sordid thankless job, for Alex. Alex Riordan, losing his first wife after twenty years of childless marriage, marrying a girl half his age only to lose her in childbirth a year later. Delia knew very little about her mother. They had managed somehow, she and Alex, with a succession of housekeepers, until the year he was sixty-five and Delia was thirteen. He'd been full of plans for her first time of entering the junior target-pistol competition—he'd started her with a gun on her seventh birthday. Then, just two days before his official retirement, he had gone out on his last call— Captain Alex Riordan, Robbery-Homicide LAPD—and taken the bank-robber's bullet in the spine. That had been a bad time for a while, and then they'd found Steve—ex-Sergeant Steve McAllister, LAPD, just short of twenty-five years' service when he lost a leg in an accident: a widower with a married daughter in

Denver. The three of them had been together for fourteen and a half years—the new leg hadn't hampered Steve from manipulating Alex's wheelchair, and Alex had always liked to cook. Of course, of course it had had to be this job—for Alex. She was all he'd ever had.

This job—to pretend to be the son Alex had never had.

Neil had seen that from the first, and hadn't he tried to make her see it—stubborn, blind, foolish Delia, resisting him all the way. She and Isabel Fordyce had been best friends all through school, and Neil not really the superior elder brother—a friend, until he was something else. How desperately she had held out against him, blindly committed to the all-important job for Alex —and how they had hated each other, of course, of course—the two strong characters.

And it hadn't been until two and a half years ago that she had, in one devastating moment, realized the truth: that the little victory she had won was worse than meaningless. Neil coming to say good-bye and good luck—and she had known, starkly, that she had nothing at all in return for that sacrifice of resisting him. In the years of study and hard work on the job, intent on making rank, all her friends had been neglected and drifted away. There just hadn't been time to keep up with friends; there'd been nothing but the job. She hadn't even talked on the phone with Isabel for a year, before that last time of seeing Neil; and a month after that she'd had her last letter from Isabel— Isabel so happily married with three children now: the note telling her noncommittally that Neil had married a Spanish girl he'd met in Ecuador. He'd been directing that archaeological dig there for the University of Arizona, for a couple of years.

So it came to her, blindingly, that it had all been for nothing. A piece of stupidity. The promise of a meaningful life, a woman's life, exchanged for a mess of pottage. And most frighteningly, she had suddenly seen her two idols, Alex and Steve, as two rather commonplace men of narrow interests and little knowledge outside the dreary job.

So all that was left to her was that job. It was nothing of any importance to her as a woman. That, she saw so clearly now: all the trumpeting about equality was simply silly, it was Canute trying to order the tides, because to any woman the first importances were a husband, a family—anything else was second best. Anything else was essentially an unimportant job, compared with the most important job, the most demanding of all—the children, the next generation.

But if all that was left was the sterile job, it was something. Alex was proud of her; Alex and Steve loved her.

And that had gone from her too. Life changed between seconds, like the patterns changing in a kaleidoscope—and suddenly you were somewhere else. In a completely different pattern.

It was eighteen months ago that Alex had had the massive stroke. He had been in the convalescent home ever since, bedridden and helpless. Still alive, still—sometimes— Alex. There were good days and bad days. Sometimes he didn't know her at all. Sometimes he did, and could understand her; he liked to hear about the current cases she was working.

When it was evident that he wasn't going to come home again, Steve had gone back East to live with his daughter and her family. He said he wanted to enjoy his grandchildren while they were still small. That was understandable, of course. He wasn't much of a letter writer; Delia heard from him, a brief scrawl, perhaps once in three months.

But now there was Hildy. Miss Hilda Gunnarson, the RN on duty in Alex's section of the convalescent home from three to eleven. Big, buxom, warm, competent and friendly Hildy. On her days off there was the slightly more impersonal and brisk Mrs. Mentor.

Delia dialed the familiar number, and the familiar comfortable voice answered.

"No, you need not come, Delia—he would not know you." She retained still a little accent, after twenty years in this country. "It has been a bad day, he has been sleeping mostly. We will see about tomorrow."

"Yes, thank you, Hildy."

Alex was all right, in good hands. And she could have a drink before dinner, and get on with her latest library book.

The night watch came on— Bob Rhys, Dick Hunter, Jim Harvey. There were the usual heisters roaming around, and they had a call to a liquor store at ten o'clock. It sounded like the same pair that had pulled a couple of jobs over the last two weeks. The liquor-store clerk was shaken; he agreed to come down and look at mug shots, but didn't know if he'd recognize either of them. They hadn't got a smell on that pair, only vague descriptions.

They'd just got back from that when they got a call to a coffee-shop on South Central. There was a man and a woman there, both highly upset and barely coherent.

"Listen," said the woman, "he just walked in—we were just closing, it was eleven o'clock—he just walked *in* and shot her—my God, Alice—is she dead? She can't be dead—he just walked *in*—"

CHAPTER 2

On Friday morning Delia came in a few minutes early, and found the night-watch report centered on Forbes' desk. She was reading it when Katz, Boswell, and Poor drifted in, and then Wallace and Gonzales. Jeff Forbes came in on their heels; he was yawning and looking tired. "The baby kept us awake half the night. Joan says if her fever doesn't go down this morning, she'd call the the doctor. I hope to God it isn't anything serious. Anything new down overnight?"

Delia passed over the report. "Nothing for you," she told Katz.

"Praise heaven for small favors."

"Another heist—doesn't sound like the same one as on that other liquor store or the pharmacy." There were always the heists, and seldom any useful leads. Of those on hand now, the loner on three jobs was described as wearing a stocking mask; there was just nothing on that; and on two jobs last week, they had vague descriptions of a young Latin type. None of the victims could identify any mug shots. "I don't suppose," said Forbes through a yawn, "the lab can give us anything on the homicide yet."

He and Gonzales were both nominally assigned to Robbery-Homicide; Delia told them all that had showed up on Connie Gilmore, and they said the expectable things. "I want to talk to the boy again some time today—it could be he can give us something on the car, when he's calmed down a little."

"And maybe not, too," said Forbes. "Meanwhile, I suppose we'd better do some routine on the new one."

Gonzales said he'd check with the lab, see if they'd turned up anything. The night watch had, of course, left them addresses. Forbes called the Magnolia Cafe down on Central and got an answer; the owner was there, and eager to cooperate.

It wasn't a very big place, sandwiched between a record shop and a drugstore, but its front was brightly painted spanking white with orange trim, and the menu posted in the front window was spotless. The CLOSED sign was showing just below that, but as Delia and Forbes came up to the door a man inside was already unlocking it, gesturing them in. He turned out to be one of the owners, Robert Orley.

"My God, what a thing!" he said. "What a thing!" He was about forty, a little over middle size, slightly paunchy and dark. He eyed Forbes' height and muscles with abstract respect. "See, usually I wouldn't have been here at all. My partner, Tim Owens, he's a bachelor and always takes the night shift, on three to eleven—short-order chef." He waved them over to one of the booths, by the big front window. There was a long counter, and one line of booths. One relic of the lab men was still visible, the chalked outline of the body about halfway down the long room between the counter and the booths. "But Tim's been sick in bed with the flu the last three days, I had to fill in—it's been a little rough. I tell you, I was never so shook in my life—what a thing! Not a soul in the place, we could've shut half an hour before, and the girls were just getting their coats and so on, ready to leave, I'd just gone over to put up the CLOSED sign when he walks in— I didn't see the gun, I started to say we're closed, he just rammed by me and started shooting—my God—it couldn't't've been five seconds, and he never said a word, he just turned and ran out—and Alice lying there and blood all over—"

Alice Bailey, he told them. A nice girl. She had worked here about a year, a good reliable girl. "I told the detectives last night, she had an apartment on Arden—they took her handbag —she's got a sister lives in Sunland, I think. I don't know anything about her boyfriends, but it doesn't seem likely—but on the other hand, the guy must have known her? She must have known him? I mean, nobody would just walk in and shoot somebody they didn't know, would they?"

It did happen, of course. The nut might do that. Any variety of nut.

"Could you describe the man, Mr. Orley?" asked Forbes.

"Well, hell, I don't know as I could. It was so fast, see. He goes by me, he fires the gun before I get turned around—"

"Once, or more?"

"I don't know, I guess four or five shots. And he runs out—it wasn't five, ten seconds. The only thing I can tell you, he wasn't young. He could be maybe in his forties, around there. He had on an old raincoat and a sort of slouch hat. That's all I could say. Maybe Ada saw him better. Well, Ada Tarbell, she's the other waitress."

"You'd never seen him before?" asked Delia.

He shrugged helplessly. "I don't think so— I don't know."

"He didn't touch anything, as far as you saw?"

"No, the detectives last night asked about that—he never got farther than three feet inside the door," said Orley. "He just stood there and shot at her, and turned and ran out—damnedest thing you ever saw—it couldn't have been five seconds!"

Ada Tarbell's address was an old California bungalow on Harvard. She welcomed them in eagerly, to a very neat and clean living room full of nondescript old furniture. She was in her forties, a tinted blonde, a little too plump.

"I just can't get over it!" she told them. "Alice! Such a nice girl—a real good worker, and ambitious—she was only twenty-three, you know that? Honest to God, I was never so shook in my life. Jim made me take one of those sleeping tablets, I was so strung up, but it didn't seem to do much good. That fellow just walking in and shooting her!"

"Did you know her pretty well?" asked Delia.

"Well, yes, I guess you could say—not that we ever had an awful lot of time to talk—you can see that. We do a pretty steady business at the cafe, a lot of businesses around and people coming in for lunch, coffee breaks. I been working there nearly two years—see, I wouldn't take an outside job till Chrissy was old enough to be alone after school, but she's nearly fifteen now and a good responsible kid. And we could use the extra money. Jim—my husband—he drives a bus for the city. Well, Alice had been there about a year, she used to work at a cafe on Broadway but it went out of business last year, you know how they tore down a whole couple of blocks of buildings, where that new shopping plaza's going in, what they call Galleria Two. Well, boyfriends— I do know she wasn't going steady with anybody, how could she, hours she worked, and she was taking a course at the Glendale Beauty College, mornings. She was a serious girl, ambitious like I said. She went out with a couple of different fellows, a Harry and a Roy, but it wasn't anything seri-ous. Her sister Marian, she's married and has a little girl—"

"Could you give us a description of the man?" asked Forbes.

Ada Tarbell hunched forward in her chair and her tone was suddenly fierce. "You'd better believe I can! I can see why Mr. Orley hardly got a look at him, because he came right in past him, and it was all over so fast—but I was standing right by the counter where the register is, see, I'd just put my coat on—and Alice was just walking down from the ladies' room at the back. I know it wasn't long, maybe not ten seconds, but I was looking right at him—when he stood there shooting—he fired about five or six times—and I got a good look at him. A real good look. It's like that face kind of got burned into my mind, you know? He was about forty-five or fifty, sort of stocky, say about Mr. Orley's height, call it five foot ten, and he had a real dark complexion— I mean, he was a white man but a sort of olive complexion, you know? And he had a round sort of face, and he was wearing horn-rimmed glasses, sort of a square shape."

"That's very good," said Delia. "We'd like you to look at some pictures, Mrs. Tarbell."

"What you call mug shots? Sure, I'll be glad to do that. If you got his picture anywhere, I'd sure spot him. Mr. Orley said the cafe'd be closed over the weekend, I could go now and look."

She had an ancient VW bug, and followed them back to head-quarters. Delia saw her settled down in Records, poring over the books, with Policewoman Helen Campbell keeping an eye on her. If she didn't pick a shot in their collection, it might be worthwhile to take her downtown to look at LAPD's infinitely larger collection; she seemed very sure of herself.

Forbes had gone upstairs. Delia went down the hall to the lab and found Gil Gonzales still there, waiting for prints to dry. He heard what she had to say absently, fingering his neat line of moustache.

"This is about all we've got for you," said Rex Burt, coming up with a handful of glossy 8 × 10 prints. "Rhys told the night watch there wasn't any point dusting for latents, the guy hadn't touched anything. Ahearne thought it might be a .32 or some-thing smaller, but we'll see when the doctor sends the slugs over."

They looked at the stark black-and-white prints. The photographs hadn't been taken to flatter the corpse, but they could see that Alice Bailey had been a pretty girl. She'd had crisp curly dark hair, pert features, a very nice figure. Sprawled gracelessly on the worn cafe carpet, in her plain waitress' uniform, raincoat thrown open to each side, and a plastic rain hood still clutched in one hand, she looked pathetically young.

"Gene and Ray went over to the apartment," said Burt. "There wasn't much in her handbag—keys, cosmetics, Kleenex, usual junk. We towed her car into the garage, it's an old clunker of a Chevy—you want us to go over that?"

"We'll let you know," said Gonzales. It was ten-thirty by then. He and Delia went over to Alice Bailey's apartment, a cheap small apartment in an old building on Arden, and found the lab men poking around. "You want the full treatment?" asked Gene Thomsen. "We found an address book." He handed it over. The apartment looked anonymous, ordinary; it was clean and neat. There was a humdrum collection of clothes in a small closet.

"Boyfriends," said Gonzales, flexing his wide shoulders as he riffled through the address book. "I suppose we'd better see the sister, see if she has any ideas."

"Yes," said Delia. "And the people at the beauty college. But it hardly sounds like a boyfriend, Gil."

They split up to save time, back at the office. She went upstairs to the ladies' room before taking off again, and passing the office she found Forbes just putting down the phone. "Hell," he said, throwing his lank length back in the desk chair, "Joan says she's taking the baby in at two o'clock, the doctor wants to see her. I hope to God it's nothing bad. You never realize what a worry kids are until you've got one of your own."

At the Glendale Beauty College Delia talked to the two proprietors, Mrs. Scanlon and Mrs. Westfall, who were shocked and incredulous. They hadn't known Alice Bailey except as a student, casually, but they said she'd been a good student, hardworking and serious—she'd have been a very good beauty operator. The seven girls who had shared morning classes with her hadn't known her well either, but said the same things. None of them knew anything about possible boyfriends, any of her friends at all.

And it didn't look likely that the fellow Ada Tarbell described so graphically had been a boyfriend.

By then it was twelve-thirty, and she went back to head-quarters, left the Chevy in the lot, and walked half a block down to the bright little cafe in the middle of the next block. There, sharing a table by the window, she found Katz, John Poor, and Mary Champion just ordering lunch. She sat down beside Mary, told the waitress to bring her a tuna sandwich, and accepted a cigarette from Poor.

"I swear to God," said Katz gloomily, "I don't know what the citizenry expects. That damned self-righteous editorial in the *News-Press* the other night—talk about bricks without straw. The burglary rate going up every month, and it isn't once in a hundred cases we pick up any smell of a lead, let alone the physical evidence. All that expensive lab equipment, and what the hell good is it? The last time I dropped on a burglar through a latent print was last year some time. Never even any clear patterns, they just wander around doing what comes naturally—" He sniffed, and his thin dark face wore a suddenly thoughtful expression. "Though speaking of M.O.s, if I'm right about these five jobs the last couple of months—"

"And very funny little jobs they were," said Poor.

"I take it you mean funny peculiar," said Mary. "Why?"

Katz rubbed his nose and said seriously, "Well, on the one hand, very pro jobs, and on the other, anything but the usual break-in. He's either a midget or a contortionist, for one thing. At three of those places he got through a window—glass just smashed in, no finesse—barely twelve by ten inches. Closet, back porches. The fourth place it was a window on the service porch— I measured it, and it was nine by fourteen inches. I ask you. And the fifth one, it was the dog door—not a foot square —even if the dog hadn't died, it couldn't have done much harm to the burglar. It's peculiar, all right. And once he was in, there were all the pro touches—drawers dumped, pictures unhooked, rugs turned back, all the places the pros know people hide things were looked at. And the loot just what the pro goes for— small appliances, tape recorders, radios, cameras, jewelry if any. At one place he passed up an expensive camera that had the owner's name stencilled on the back, and that damn well is a pro touch. But they were hardly professional break-ins. And how in hell he gets through such impossible spaces—"

"And no smell of the loot, so the midget knows a tame fence," said Poor, finishing his coffee.

"Well, there are a lot of those around," said Katz.

Patrolman Morris came in, looked around, spotted them and came over. "Nobody seems to know where Guernsey is," he said to Mary, "but Sergeant Dick said you were probably here. Though it's just crazy to say, it's something to do with Juvenile. You'd just better hear about it—we've got the word on the street there's a gang rumble building. Maybe tomorrow or Sunday."

"Oh, fine," said Mary grimly. "Just what we need." She looked all of her forty-four years suddenly. She'd been a policewoman for eighteen years, in some hotter spots than Glendale, and knew about gang rumbles.

But the rest of them had found out, necessarily, the last few years. Where it was once unknown, the gang activity had invaded Glendale, as the influx of Mexicans and Cubans increased, mainly in the south end of town just across the line from Atwater and Hollywood. The idle louts of kids, either school dropouts or let loose from the system with a minimum of so-called education—they were mostly in that age group, sixteen to twenty, roaming around making trouble. Usually it was the petty trouble, purse snatching, shoplifting, vandalism, but some of them had the expensive dope habits to support and were probably responsible for quite a few of Katz's burglaries—oftener the heists. And they got into trouble with each other. The three principal gangs in Glendale were the Guerreros, the Eldorados, and Satan's Angels. The first two were exclusively Latin. The Angels conceived of themselves as superior whites, and now and then mounted wholesale battles against the others, separately or together.

Morris said, "The word's out, the Latin *amigos* are feuding over something. You pulled in one of their heroes lately, Bernie Ramirez."

"That we did," said Delia equably. "Or rather Vic and Jeff did. We had a couple of good eyewitnesses to say he's the one knocked down an old lady waiting for a bus, and grabbed her handbag. She died of concussion the next day, so he's up for Murder Two, and he couldn't make bail."

"Well, the idea seems to have got around that somebody turned him in, a snitch from the other gang."

"And the snitches are very useful," said Delia.

"Well, that's the word." Morris shrugged. "It's the hell of a lot more trouble for us riding the squads than the front office, and what in hell good it does to haul the bastards in and bring a charge of disturbing the peace or whatever—they're back on the street the next day."

They agreed morosely. Morris sat down at the counter and reached for a menu, and the waitress came up with their orders.

When Delia got to the modest frame house on Maple Street, she found Gilmore there as well as Mrs. Gilmore and the boy Richard. Gilmore was a big sandy man with blunt features, and there was pure pain in his eyes.

"I just couldn't leave to go to work," he said. "There's nothing I or anybody can do, but I just couldn't. Connie— I know I spoiled her. But she was—so pretty—she was—"

"It doesn't matter now," said his wife dully. "I'm sorry I ever nagged you over it, hon."

They were all together in the shabby living room, just sitting there.

"I'd like to talk to Richard again," said Delia gently.

"Sure. Anything he can tell you, miss. Only none of this makes any sense at all."

"Did you see the car?" she asked the boy. "Enough to tell us anything about it?"

The boy swallowed. "Well, some. It was a big black car, I think that was the one. I don't know what kind it was, but it wasn't what they call a compact. It was kind of old, I think." He paused. "See, I wasn't looking, I mean, I was kinda looking down at the sidewalk, it was raining awful hard and me and Connie were hurrying to get home, see, and—and Connie, she'd just said she sure hoped Mother had a fire in the fireplace—when—it happened. I heard this big bang and I looked up and she fell right down, she never screamed or nothing—and I just saw the car a second, it was already way past, but the only one anywhere near in the street—and—and I think I maybe saw part of a gun sticking out the window—something like a sort of stick, anyhow." He stopped again, and then added miserably, "It was just a big black car."

And that was probably all they'd ever get, barring unexpected luck. "Well, thank you, Richard," said Delia.

"You said—yesterday—about the funeral arrangements," said Gilmore. "The—the body. Could we—"

"She liked to go to Sunday school," said his wife suddenly. "She'd just learned that Psalm by heart, the Twenty-third. She used to say it every night before bed."

"We'll let you know when you can have her," said Delia. Where indeed was any sensible pattern, any reasonable cause and effect, for Connie Gilmore's short life? As a reasonable adult, you knew better than to expect it—but Connie Gilmore had believed there was a benevolent power managing things. In the Lord her Shepherd.

It began to rain again, dispiritedly, as Delia drove back to headquarters. Before she went upstairs, she looked into Dr. Goulding's little office in the basement; he wasn't there. When the homicide rate outgrew the space, the lab had spread out into what had once been a small morgue. They used the morgue at the Glendale Adventist Medical Center on Chevy Chase now, and Goulding, who had acquired a couple of assistants, was seldom in his old office.

She went upstairs and called the morgue, and talked to Dr. Raymond.

"Oh, I was just about to start the autopsy," he said, "but there won't be much in it. It was obviously a shotgun, so there won't be any ballistics evidence for you. I'd have a guess it might have been .410 ammunition. She was killed instantly, poor little devil. The other one— I haven't looked at that at all. Give us time."

"Yes, doctor. You'll send the slugs over to the lab when you do get to it?"

"Teach your grandmother," said Raymond. "Somebody'll be on it."

Delia put the phone down, and Gonzales came in, looking wet and annoyed. He shrugged out of his coat and draped it over the back of his desk chair. He had just said, "Well, the sister gives us this and that, but nothing useful," when a man hesitated in the door and asked, "Is this the detective office?"

"Yes, sir, what can we do for you?" At the moment they were alone in the office except for Boswell brooding over a report and a paper cup of coffee.

"Well, the officer suggested I should come and tell you about it, though I really don't know what you can do. Excuse me, I'm Dr. James Barlow, I'm the pastor of the Bible Presbyterian Church here. We've been having some trouble, and it seems to be getting more serious—we've had to call the police a number of times, but it doesn't seem to do much good."

"Sit down and let's hear about it," said Delia.

He folded himself into the chair beside her desk and looked from her to big muscular Gonzales. "I didn't expect to find a young lady detective, Miss—"

"Riordan. Detective Gonzales."

"Oh," he said. "Yes." He was a tall lanky man in his mid-thirties, with an unruly shock of prematurely gray hair and a rather craggy blunt-featured face that creased into an unexpectedly charming smile. "The worst of it is," he said diffidently, "that I feel it's been partly my fault. To begin with—my wife says that's silly, and of course it was the very last reaction I might have expected, but—well, I had better explain it from the beginning. I took over the church here about ten months ago, when the former pastor, the Reverend Mr. Grafton, died. I had been assistant pastor at our largest church in Los Angeles before that. This isn't a large congregation. I should explain that we're not affiliated with the actual Presbyterian Church, we're an independent denomination. Well, the Reverend Grafton hadn't been well for some time, and had rather neglected his duties, I'm afraid. The attendance was down, especially among the young people. Naturally I've been trying to build up the congregation, stimulate interest in church affairs, and we've instituted some new activities for the children and teenagers. My wife is a professional musician, and we've formed quite a good choir—fortunately we have an excellent organist, Mrs. Ziegler. And I'm glad to say that attendance is up very strongly, we have had to recruit several new Sunday school teachers. But I'm digressing, excuse me. You see, at the outset I wasn't at all familiar with the neighborhood, and I'm afraid I did something a little stupid, though I never expected—"

"Where is your church, Dr. Barlow?" asked Delia.

"Adams Street, just up from Scofield. You see, hoping to encourage young people—and others—from the neighborhood to come, I made a special effort to reach them. One of the deacons, Mr. Acker, and I called at houses down the nearest streets, introduced ourselves and left printed invitations with a list of the service times and so on— I was disappointed that we had no results from that—but the result we did get— Well!" He looked rueful and extremely worried. "I'm afraid it was stupid. I did realize belatedly that a good many of the families around there are —er—of Latin descent."

Gonzales sighed; he and Delia exchanged a glance. In that old section of town, with cheap rentals, there would be a majority of Mexicans and Cubans, some on welfare, some in low-paying jobs, and quite a few of them non-citizens, not proficient in English.

"But I must say I was disconcerted," said Barlow sadly. "The first time was one Sunday when my wife and I arrived at the church, early as usual, and found several children—quite young children—using chalk to—well, they had drawn all sorts of obscene words and sketches on the front of the building. And they shouted at us— I don't know Spanish, but my wife caught a few words and looked in a Spanish dictionary, and it seemed we were being called, er, dirty Protestants—"

"*Sucio Protestantes,*" murmured Gonzales wryly.

"Er, yes. It was surprisingly difficult to wash off the chalk, and of course the church is not in use a good part of the week, and the vandalism went from bad to worse—obscenities drawn all over the sides of the building, and—"

"In Spanish or English?"

"Oh, English. It was—"

"Yeah," said Gonzales. "They pick up the dirty words fast enough."

"And, excuse me," he said to Delia, "there's been filth of all kinds littering the parking lot, once a couple of dead cats, which distressed my wife greatly—we're both very fond of cats—and, well, excrement and so on. I had already called the police a number of times, and last month a very nice young officer, Officer Acosta, went to the trouble of asking questions through the neighborhood. Of course it's quite absurd, I couldn't believe it at first, but he assured me there's a definite belief on the part of at least a few people that we are trying to convert them from their own church, that we're prejudiced against Catholics. And he said something about gang members."

"And that could be the truth all right," said Gonzales thoughtfully. He looked at Delia again. Technically the marauding gang members might fall under Juvenile, but inevitably they overlapped into other categories, and Robbery-Homicide knew this and that about them. Two of the top leaders of the Guerreros lived in that area when they were at home— Tony Aguayo and Carlos Ramirez. Any little controversy would be meat and drink to that pair, any excuse to make trouble, guarding their Latin image as fiercely as they did.

"But now it's become a really serious problem," said Barlow anxiously. "There was an attempt to break into the church, and the last couple of weeks we've had things stolen, damage. A week ago last Sunday, several members of the congregation found their car windows smashed after the service, there was a valuable camera stolen, and a lady's new coat. And at the prayer meeting last Wednesday night five cars were broken into, mine among them, and Mr. Acker's briefcase stolen, and a couple of umbrellas, and my wife's choir scores for next Sunday— she was most annoyed, it meant she had to do them all over again, of course—and other cars were badly damaged, windows broken and the obscenities scratched all over the paint with a sharp nail or some such thing. It's really very distressing, but I don't know what more the police can do about it— I do realize it's no more than petty theft, vandalism—"

"Well, we can try to do something," said Delia. "What times would there be a good many cars in the parking lot?"

"On Sundays, of course— Sunday school at nine-thirty, the regular church service at eleven. There is choir practice every Friday afternoon at three-thirty, we have twenty members now, most gratifying—and prayer meeting on Wednesday night at eight."

Gonzales sighed. "Well, we can have a couple of squads patrol that block regularly during those times, and with luck we might drop on the ringleaders and scare them off."

"I most certainly hope so," said Barlow. "But I've taken a good deal of your time, I'm afraid." He stood up. "Thank you very much."

"It's what we're here for, sir," said Gonzales politely. And when Barlow had gone out he added, "That's just the stupid little kind of situation those damn bullyboys love to use, stir up trouble. And what the hell use it would be to pick them up—the gang members or any of the damn-fool kids they've egged on, say naughty-naughty? They know we can't do much to them. The minor charge, they just get probation." But he grinned. "Funny side to it, of course. Couple of excitable idiots getting all worked up over the sly Protestant minister—my God."

"Not so funny for the church people," said Delia. "What did Alice Bailey's sister have to say?"

"Nothing useful. She went all to pieces—there were just the two of them, parents got killed in an accident last year. She says Alice couldn't have had any enemies, that's just silly, she didn't know many people at all, she worked long hours, was taking that course, hadn't much free time for socializing. She didn't date much, hadn't time. And it was only two fellows, Roy Streeter and Harry Schultz. Streeter lives next door to the sister —did I say her name's Marian Webber?—where Alice met him. He's twenty-four, works for Parks and Recreation. I saw his mother, she says he was home all last night. Schultz lives in Hollywood, works at a gas station. Mrs. Webber says Alice wasn't serious about either of them. And Schultz is twenty-five, so neither of them can be the X Mrs. Tarbell describes, can they?"

"No," said Delia. "And I wonder if she made any of the mug shots."

Gonzales uncovered his typewriter. "Paperwork— I don't know why I bucked to make rank." He rolled in a form, started the follow-up report.

Delia went downstairs to Records. Ada Tarbell had looked thoroughly at all their books, Helen Campbell said, hadn't picked any pictures, but seemed sure if they'd had him on record she'd have spotted him. "Yes," said Delia, "it might be worthwhile to take her downtown."

It was getting on for five o'clock. She took off early, and it would be a waste of time to drive all the way home. She went up to the Shaker Mountain Inn, and before hunting a table used the public phone in the lobby.

"Oh, Delia, he will be so disappointed you're not coming. It has been a better day, and just now he was asking for you."

"I'm sorry, Hildy. You just try to make him understand I'm doing a favor for a brother officer. He'll forgive me for that, if I know Alex. I'll come tomorrow if it's a good day."

"I will tell him. But on the good days, the time goes so slowly for him, you know."

"I know," said Delia gently. "I know, Hildy."

It was still overcast, but not raining; the brother officers and their wives could enjoy the evening out, though Delia couldn't picture O'Connor sitting patiently through a symphony concert. She ordered at random, and came out at a quarter to six to head for Hillcroft Road. It was pitch dark and had turned very cold; she was glad of the heater in the car.

In the last couple of years, she and Laura Varallo had become good friends. Laura was older, of course, but not all that much. Laura was the only one who knew about Neil Fordyce and the wrong turning she'd taken in life, deciding life from now on. But Laura was quite safe; and it was good to have a friend again.

The Varallos were all ready for the evening out. "We were going to The Castaway," said Laura, "but not in this weather. Maybe Pike's."

"It's a waste of money to take Charles," said Varallo. "He'll probably sleep peacefully all through the concert."

"There's cheese and crackers and avocado dip in the refrigerator if you get hungry," Laura told her.

"Yes, yes, we'll be fine." She waved them off and turned to the children. She'd never known many children, but she liked Ginevra and Johnny—nice children, and amenable. She superintended their suppers, put the dishes tidily into the dishwasher, straightened up the kitchen. She got Johnny to bed by seven-thirty, after a few fairy tales, and Ginevra soon after. In the living room, she noticed the headline on the front page of tonight's *News-Press,* lying in Varallo's chair, and picked it up to glance at it. Some enterprising reporter monitoring the police radio had probably got to Marian Webber before Gonzales had. There was a studio portrait of Alice Bailey in the right-hand column, and the headline GLENDALE GIRL MURDERED: MYSTERY ATTACKER.

That did sum it up. Well, see if Ada Tarbell could find him in the records downtown. But it was such a handleless thing—apparently no rhyme or reason to it—it wasn't all that likely that he had any record.

She had brought her book with her this morning, and curled up in Laura's armchair in front of the fire. One of the unexpected benefits living alone had brought her was the joy of reading for pleasure, a thing she'd never had time for before. She was reading voraciously, shopping around among authors old and new, at random. At the moment she was working her way through Elizabeth Goudge. She had just finished the latest, *A City of Bells,* when the Varallos came home at eleven-thirty.

On Saturday morning she called Ada Tarbell and asked if she'd go downtown to look at more pictures. "You bet I will. I'd sure like to see you get that guy."

"Fine. I'll pick you up in twenty minutes."

And on the way downtown, Ada said, "I've been thinking. I don't know why it didn't occur to me before, except you don't expect anybody to shoot a person for no reason. I mean, it'd have to be a nut. I guess everybody's told you Alice was a nice girl, kind of a quiet girl, and she wouldn't know any nuts. Like that. But they're around, aren't they? And a nut might do anything. I just thought about this. Maybe it doesn't mean a thing, but I thought I'd mention it."

"What is it?"

"Well, we get a pretty nice clientele at the cafe—not high society exactly, a lot of local truckers and the fellows work around that end of town—and they're mostly nice and friendly. I don't call to mind any of them getting fresh, but then"—she laughed — "I'm not twenty-three and I never was a beauty queen. Alice was a pretty girl."

"Yes, she was. Did one of the customers get fresh with her?"

"It was a guy made a real pass, she said. Twice. And I never laid eyes on him. See, the usual thing, there'd only be the two of us out front. Mr. Owens'd be in the kitchen, and there's no regular cashier, either Alice or I'd take the money at the register. Only once in a while, when it was slow, maybe only a couple of customers in, one of us'd take a break. I might be back in the ladies' room, having a cigarette, or Alice'd go into the kitchen after coffee. The first time, it was about three weeks or a month back, I think. I'd been back in the ladies' room about ten minutes, and when I came back Alice said this guy had given her kind of a rough time. And the funny thing is, he must've been there before I left the front, but he was sitting in Alice's section and I never even looked at him. I got a vague idea he was reading a paper, holding it up, you know."

"What did she say?"

"That he made a couple of dirty cracks, when he paid her— he was the only one in then—and asked her for a date. He tried to paw her a little, she said, and she told him off. She said another minute and she'd have yelled for Mr. Owens, but the guy just gave her a dirty look and went out. And about two weeks ago, he was in again and I never saw him then either. I was on my coffee break back in the kitchen. Alice said he didn't even sit down and order anything, he just tried to pressure her into a date again and talked dirty. She was alone in front then. It was about four o'clock."

"Did she say what he looked like?"

Ada shook her head. "Only thing she said was, he was old. An old man. And I just wondered—" she sighed. "I suppose somebody forty-five or fifty would've looked old to Alice. But it wouldn't make any sense—if it was the same one. Unless he was a nut."

But things very seldom made any sense in a blind universe, thought Delia.

In the R. and I. office at Parker Center, she told Ada that this might take a while. There were a lot of pictures to look at. "We'll take a break for lunch—the city can afford it."

"That's okay," said Ada. "I just hope his picture's somewhere here."

The policewoman in charge of the mug books had been in Delia's class at the Police Academy nearly ten years ago. They settled Ada with a collection of books to go through, and chatted desultorily.

O'Connor got lonesome in his narrow office; and there was usually Narco business on hand, but in fits and starts, and it wasn't the same as the old days, taking everything that came along. He wandered out to the detective office just before noon and eyed it nostalgically. Katz was typing a report, Poor on the phone; it was Boswell's day off, and nobody else was in but Varallo, who was looking harassed and muttering to himself.

"Anything interesting down?"

"Just more human nature—and more paperwork," said Varallo. "I've spent the whole damn morning on this suicide, and of course there's nothing in it, but if there are any relatives we ought to locate them. At least he seems to have had enough of a bank balance to pay for a funeral. If you want a job, you can help out calling department stores asking if anybody remembers him, knows about relations. Duncan John Winter."

The suicide had been called in at eight-twenty by a Mrs. Myra Colby. It was an old California bungalow on Jackson Street. Mrs. Colby was in the mid-fifties, a tall stout woman in a plain cotton housedress and old-lady oxfords, and she was distressed but not in floods of tears.

She said, "It's an awful thing, Officer, but you can understand it in a way— I guess the worst was when I saw that old newspaper clipping, we never knew about that at all. Mr. Winter wasn't much of a talker, very quiet sort he was. He was a nice old man, we both liked him. A real gentleman, but, well, not a talker. You see, when our son Bob got married last year it left us with a spare bedroom. And Harvey—my husband—he earns a good living, he's head mechanic at the Chevy agency on Central, but these days anybody can do with extra money, and I said we needn't take the first one answered, could pick and choose. So we put an ad in the paper, and Mr. Winter answered it. I could see he was the right sort—well, you'd hardly have known he was in the house. He was a great reader, he'd bring home a stack of books from the library every week. He was retired from some office job, he'd been in the personnel office at some big department store, I forget which one. He's been here for nearly a year, board and room—it's as easy to cook for three as two, and he wasn't at all fussy. Such a nice old man. Quiet. He never said much about himself, his family, we took it he was a bachelor, never married, you see. But he did say once he had a sister back East. Well, we got up this morning and I got breakfast for Harvey and me like always, and Harvey went off to work at seven-thirty. Mr. Winter didn't like to get up so early— I went to call him about eight o'clock, ask if he was ready for breakfast—and there he was." She drew a deep breath. "I saw right off he was gone, and at first I thought he'd just passed away in his sleep, and then I saw the note, and the bottle. And that newspaper clipping under the note—" her eyes filled with tears. "The poor old man. He was a nice man, Officer."

It was the back bedroom. A comfortable room, double bed, a good-sized closet, an armchair, view out over a pleasant back yard. The old man lying dead in the bed had once been a hand-some man, with a regular profile; he looked nearly noble in qui-escent death.

There was a prescription bottle on the bedside table, labeled "Nembutal"—a doctor's name. There was a glass half filled with water. There was a note written in a shaky copperplate on a sheet torn from a cheap tablet. *My dear Mrs. Colby, I am very sorry to cause you any inconvenience or distress, but I have been very tired lately and this seems to be the most sensible thing to do, before I become incapably ill. I hope to join my dear ones in heaven. Duncan J. Winter.*

Under the note was the newspaper clipping, yellow and brittle with age. It had been cut from the top half of the page, and there was no indication of the paper's name; but the story bore a dateline: Spokane, April 3, 1942. It told briefly of the deaths of Mrs. Claire Winter, twenty-six, and her three children, Linda, five; William, three; Brenda, one, in a fire that had completely destroyed the house at such-and-such an address. Mrs. Winter's husband, Duncan, was in the armed services, to be given com-passionate leave. The fire, believed to be of accidental origin, was caused by faulty wiring.

Varallo looked at it all sadly; but of course there was the paperwork to do. There was a bankbook; it showed a balance of under five hundred dollars. Mrs. Colby said he hadn't had a car. There wasn't any address book, any correspondence.

But if there were any relatives— Varallo had come back to the office and after knocking out the report had been calling personnel offices of department stores, with no luck so far.

"Not all that important," O'Connor said now, and Varallo agreed that it wasn't. They knocked off for lunch, and when they got back he made one more try for luck, and hit pay dirt. It was the downtown Bullocks' store, and he talked to a Jerome Langer. "Mr. Winter?" said Langer. "Yes, I knew him. This is *police?* What's it about?" Varallo told him and he was agitated.

"Oh, that's just terrible—just awful. Why, he gave me my first job here—he was such a good man, I'm very sorry to hear about this—quite a religious man too, I believe— I can't say how sorry I am to hear this." But he didn't know about any relatives. Winter had worked at Bullocks', he thought, since shortly after the war, had retired about eight years ago.

"Well, that's that," said Varallo, putting the phone down. It immediately shrilled at him and he picked it up again. "Sergeant Varallo."

"Well, *paisano*," said a bass voice. "Sergeant Lisi, Hollenbeck. We just picked up the guy on your APB—Jerry Rubio. We'll be sending him over *pronto*."

"And thank you very much indeed," said Varallo.

CHAPTER 3

Just before the squad from Hollenbeck delivered Jerry Rubio to the station, they had the word from Communications that that gang rumble had erupted down in Central Park. There were twenty squads dispatched already and probably there'd be more needed. That might mean some business for the front office; wait and see. Meanwhile, they had Rubio.

Varallo and O'Connor talked to him without much finesse, without bothering about an interrogation room; not much tact was needed. Rubio had acquired quite a little pedigree for his age, which was thirty-one: a j.d. record of B. and E., rape, assault: an adult record of pimping, assault, attempted rape. In a sane society, he would still be inside, but he had never served much time, the judges handing out probation. But he was thoroughly familiar with cops and the law.

"I don't know no Rosalie King," he said. "I don't know what you're talkin' about." He was short and stocky, with long dirty-blond hair and a ragged moustache, furtive quick-moving eyes, and a brash voice.

"Come on," said Varallo coldly. "Let's not waste time, Jerry. You were running her, over in Hollywood, and she got out from under, and that made you mad."

"I don't know what you're talkin' about. I don't know no Rosalie—"

"Oh, for Christ's sake," said O'Connor roughly, "you left a couple of dandy prints in her pad, or was it your ghost? And one of them was on that metal vase you grabbed up to hit her with—that was pretty damn stupid, wasn't it? But all you punks are so Goddamn stupid. That puts you right there, doesn't it? We'd just like to know—"

"Oh. Prints," said Rubio. He looked disgusted more than alarmed. "Oh, for God's sake. For *God's* sake. Prints. I never meant to put that bitch out for keeps. Sure I was mad at her, I knocked her around some, teach her a lesson— I never meant to kill the little bitch."

"Yeah, it was stupid," said O'Connor.

"How did you find out where she was?" asked Varallo.

"I don't know why the hell I bothered," said Rubio despondently. "Just another chick—but I was damn sore at her. Running off like that. I figured that other one'd know where she was, that Sally, they were pals. And she did. I got it out of her finally. Don't know why the hell I took the trouble, now." They could deduce that he'd had to knock Sally around a little. "I never meant to kill the damn girl, she must've had a thin skull or something, I only batted her a couple of times."

"Sally who?" asked O'Connor.

"Oh, hell, Sally Brady." He shut up after that, and they had all that was necessary; with the physical evidence it was cut and dried. Varallo got on the phone to the Hollywood precinct; that was one of the regular beats for the hookers. He talked to a Sergeant Abbott, who said they could probably turn up Sally if she had showed on their beat, they'd have a look. The DA's office might want to establish the connection, though it wasn't strictly necessary. They already had the warrant on Rubio, and Varallo took him over to the jail and booked him in. There'd be a final report to write on it.

When he got back, Gonzales and Forbes and a couple of uniformed men were in with a handful of sullen and battered gang members; the Traffic men looked a little disheveled too. "Little punks got themselves in some real trouble this time," said Gonzales with grim satisfaction. "There's a corpse. Tony Aguayo, believe it or not, multiple knife wounds, and there's a witness, if it's worth a good Goddamn." He was hanging onto a bruised bloody hulk of a young fellow, and Steiner had a grip on another one who might have been his brother, on looks; they glowered at each other, ready to start the fight all over.

"They jumped us first, we wasn't doing nothing—dirty bastard Guerreros, they—"

"*Bastardos!* Damn snitches, we hadda reason, it was you *bastardos* put the mark on Bernie—"

"Both of you shut up," said O'Connor forcefully. The Guerrero was Alberto Villa, the Eldorado, Eddy Cardenas. Varallo and Gonzales took Villa into one interrogation room, O'Connor and Forbes took Cardenas into another, to sort it out.

"Listen," said Villa, after he'd automatically tried the one about no speak Inglees and been foiled on that, "listen." He nursed a blackening eye and a knife slash on one arm alternately; he sounded aggrieved. "I seen Cardenas knife Tony. Tony and me was right together. It was Cardenas we was out to get, sure, on account that bastard, anyways one of his boys, snitched on Bernie last month, we knew that—and we had the word Cardenas and some of his boys, they hadda meet set up with a dealer down inna park, we figured jump them there, we just dint expect so many dudes be with him, that's all. But I seen Cardenas stick the knife in Tony, I wasn't a foot away. I swear to that."

It was all a little confused. That was suspect testimony, and it was all up in the air how a judge might look at it. At least both of them were well past eighteen, not minors. Villa was under arrest for assault and disturbing the peace, would probably make bail and be out tomorrow. They took the bare statement from him, and Gonzales ferried him over to jail.

When O'Connor and Forbes emerged with Cardenas, Forbes marched him out and O'Connor said in a growl, "My God, the punks. He never had no knife, don't know what a knife looks like, don't know nothing about nothing, the dirty Guerreros jumped on them first, they were just sitting around the park not doing a thing, all quiet and peaceful. My God." And there hadn't been a knife on him. Try to locate it—unlikely—and find any physical evidence.

The sergeant at the jail called about then and said to O'Connor, "Say, Lieutenant—all these punks are still getting booked in, and half of 'em are carrying the grass, and angel dust. But this one guy, my God, he's a walking pharmacy. He's got about a thousand bucks' street value of the stuff on him, and a wad of cash."

"Ah," said O'Connor. "How nice. The dealer. The innocent bystander. Thanks so much."

He went over with Varallo to take a look at that one. He was a sallow discouraged-looking fellow in the forties. He'd had a driver's license on him, in the name of Samuel Skinner, an address in Boyle Heights, and not much else except the dope:

marijuana, heroin, cocaine, angel dust. It was all professionally packaged in plastic bags.

He wasn't saying anything. "What the hell?" he said despondently, with a shrug. "So you got the merchandise, you got enough to lay a charge. These Goddamned stupid spicks got to start a fight. I just been running into the Goddamnedest bad luck lately. But all right, that's how it is."

Back at the office, O'Connor called the Narco office at LAPD and asked if they knew Skinner, talked to a Sergeant Willis there. "My God, do we know him?" said Willis. "You've got him? On a real charge? I'll be damned. Yeah, he's got a pedigree from here to there, I think he's still on P.A. from his last little while inside. We're pretty sure he's working for Sandor—listen, if you pick up anything to link in that one, for God's sake pass it on—we've never been able to get enough evidence there, the bastard's clean as a whistle, never even a parking ticket, and we know for a fact that about a third of all the dope in the county is handled by that mob. It's also possible that Sandor's tied up with some smugglers bringing it in from Mexico. But he's got such a dandy clean front, owns a poker palace in Gardena, all on the up and up."

"I don't think we can hand you any help there," said O'Connor. "There wasn't much on him but the dope and his driver's license. But thanks very much." Off the phone, he added to Varallo, "Speaking of which, we'd better locate his car—it'll be somewhere down there." They queried the DMV in Sacramento, got the plate number, and put the word out to Traffic to look for it.

It was past the end of shift; they'd all be late getting home.

Ada Tarbell didn't make any of the mug shots in the collection downtown. "I'm real sorry," she said to Delia on the way back to Glendale at three-thirty. "He just wasn't there. I'd have spotted him."

"If you don't mind giving some more time to it, I'd like you to have a session with the Identikit."

"Sure, anything to help you get him. What's that?"

Delia explained. "There are all sorts of different face-shapes, ears, hairlines, mouths, eyes, and so on, and the artist"—actually it didn't take an artist, only a technician—"can go on superimposing them all together, until you're satisfied he's got a composite sketch of the person you're describing. It just takes a little time."

"Say, that's a smart idea," said Ada. "I guess the cops are smart these days. You know, since I told Chrissy there's a lady cop working on the case, she's real interested. Says that's the kind of job she'd like, sort of glamorous and all."

Delia laughed. "You tell Chrissy she'd be bored stiff. It's not glamorous or even exciting."

But, letting Ada off at home, she wondered where else to go on Alice Bailey. And there wasn't anywhere else to go. A few names in her address book—look them up and ask questions, and hear what they'd heard from everyone else, a quiet serious girl, not a socializer. Well, Gil Gonzales was a nice fellow, but only a year's experience as a detective; it might be worth an hour to see the sister herself.

It wasn't. Marian Webber wasn't as pretty as Alice had been, if the same general type. She said the same things she'd said to Gonzales. There was a baby about a year old, and she was just about to produce another one. She asked fretfully about Alice's car. "The other fellow said you had it."

"Yes, you can have it any time." There hadn't been anything suggestive in the car.

"Well, I'll tell my husband."

Little exercise in futility, thought Delia, dawdling along in the beginning rush-hour traffic. No reason to go back to the office at this hour, and she drove straight home. Home. The too-big old house had been home all her life. She could probably get a court order to sell it; but it was paid for, if the taxes were up. Alex's pension took care of the convalescent home. Wait and see.

After she'd had dinner, having called Hildy, she drove over to the convalescent home. It was a big one out on Vermont Avenue, clean and quiet and well run, with its own parking lot. Alex was in the newest wing on the other side of the building. The regular visiting hours were only up to nine o'clock, but the staff was lenient with her.

She smiled at Hildy, behind the counter at the nurses' station halfway along the hall— Hildy calm and motherly looking with her broad bosom and thick blond braid pinned flat. "I'm so glad to see you, Delia. He has been asking."

Alex's room overlooked a little courtyard with trees, invisible now, but she'd been pleased he had the bed nearest the window, something pleasant to look at in the long hours. There had been a couple of different patients sharing the room with him; for the last few months it had been a senile old man who seldom moved or spoke.

She sat by the bed where he was propped up against the pillows, holding his hand. He couldn't talk easily, the paralysis reaching his throat, but she could tell by his eyes that he was understanding her, interested and aware. He had lost a good deal of weight, and his cheeks were sunken, but he was still the shadow of handsome old Alex, with his Roman profile, if the white hair was thinner and the mouth pinched. She told him about Alice Bailey. He'd been a police officer most of his life, and it had been his life. His eyes stayed on her unblinking.

"You can see there aren't any leads at all."

He opened his mouth and tried to speak. "N—" he said. And, carefully, "N—n—a nut. Must. No m—m—"

Delia nodded. "No motive at all. That's what we think. It probably was."

Presently he asked, "S— S—?"

"Steve? No, I haven't heard since the last letter. He'll be writing again soon." She always had to read Steve's letters to him, the brief dull little letters, and sometimes she dared to embroider them.

A little while after that he fell asleep suddenly, his mouth open slightly, and she stood up. The doctor said he might live five or ten years like this, or die tomorrow; nobody could know. It was a very reasonless universe.

She came past Hildy's desk and said good night. "He's asleep."

"Ah. So we hope for as good a day tomorrow."

Outside, the wind had risen and it was even colder.

The night watch sat around until after nine o'clock with no calls, but that was normal. Then they got two calls at once, at nine-twenty. One was to a body, so Rhys and Hunter went out on that and Harvey on the other, a heist.

The address was north on Idlewood Road, above Kenneth. The squad was sitting in front, and Weiss waiting in it. Rhys pulled up behind and he and Hunter went up to the squad. "What's the rundown?" asked Rhys.

Weiss got out. "Well, like I called it in, the woman's dead. In the back yard. Looks as if she might have surprised a burglar. I didn't question the husband much, he's pretty shook up as you can imagine, he just came home and found her. I don't know where he'd been. They're not young people. He's real shook."

"He the one called in? Okay, let's have a look," said Rhys. They followed Weiss down the drive. This was a good residential area, older homes but all well maintained.

"The name's Garvin," said Weiss. This was a fairly big stucco house with a tile roof; there was a long driveway to a detached garage. Back there, where a double floodlight on the garage roof peak cast a glaring light up the drive, into the back yard, they could see that the house was built in two long wings; and between the wings, at the rear of the house, was a cemented patio or porch. There was lawn, a border of shrubs, down from that; it was a deep back yard. The body was lying face down on the lawn, just beyond the porch. They went up and looked at it in silence.

Not a young woman, by the gray hair, and she was fat and rather shapeless, in a long blue cotton housecoat. One velvet bedroom slipper had fallen off a stockinged foot. There was matted blood in the gray hair at the back of her head. Lying a couple of feet away was a long thick piece of wood, a length of two-by-four, with one end sharpened to a point.

"Well, put out a call to the lab," said Rhys to Weiss. "Maybe that was the weapon, but it won't have taken any prints. Get some pictures anyway. We'd better talk to the husband."

"Sure," said Weiss.

The husband let them in to a long narrow living room, tastefully furnished and neat. His name was Edward Garvin, and he said yes, that was his wife, Eleanor. He was a tall thin fellow with scanty gray hair, a little gray moustache; he was well-dressed in a gray suit, white shirt, and tie. They asked enough questions to get a general picture; he was looking a little dazed, as if he hadn't quite taken it in yet, but he was automatically courteous.

"You weren't at home this evening, Mr. Garvin?"

"No, I was— I had some work to do at the library, I—excuse

me, perhaps I should explain that I'm on the faculty at Glendale College. I left home about seven, I was at the library until just before it closed at nine o'clock. I suppose it was a little after nine when I got home. When I drove into the garage and got out, I—well, I saw Eleanor at once, of course, with the lights on— I tried not to lose my head, I thought she'd tripped on the step to the porch, or fainted—but I couldn't find— I couldn't find any pulse—" His hands were shaking as he lit a cigarette. "You hear about all the violent crime, but when it hits you personally—"

"Excuse me, sir, do you have a family? Are you all right to be alone?"

"Oh, yes. Yes. Perfectly. Both the children are married—" He put a hand to his head. "Must call Bob—ask him to call Lisa. That'll be best—"

"Have you had any trouble with prowlers or burglars in the neighborhood?" asked Hunter.

"Yes. Yes, there have been. Eleanor heard from Mrs. Powell down the block that they'd called the police twice, a prowler in the back yard—and there was a burglary at the Talmadges' across the street last month. But we're seldom out in the evening, and there are good locks—"

"Was your wife nervous, Mr. Garvin?"

"How do you mean? Why, no, not especially." He blinked at them. "One thing— I should mention. While I was—waiting for the patrol car, I noticed that stake—there beside her. I think it could be out of the garage. It's just like the one— Eleanor had for staking the dwarf orange tree until it got established. I don't know, but—"

"All right, sir. We don't want to bother you anymore tonight. You've had a shock—are you sure you don't want us to call your son for you?"

"Oh, no. I'll be quite all right. Well, yes, a shock. But I'll be —all right. Thank you."

"There'll be some other detectives to see you tomorrow, go into it when you're feeling steadier."

"Thank you," he said. "Yes. Thank you." His voice was numb, but still polite.

In the back yard, Ahearne had just finished taking photographs, had the two-by-four packaged to take in. The squad was gone. "Well, we can see what it looks like," said Rhys. "She heard the prowler—or burglar—in the back yard. Probably the lights weren't on then. There'll be a switch inside. She put on the lights and stepped out on that porch to have a look, and surprised him right there. He batted her and took off."

Hunter agreed. "Maybe he was already at one of the back windows, even right on the porch. Reason she did hear him— everything'd be shut up on a cold night."

"Maybe." The morgue wagon pulled up out in front, and they couldn't do any more on it now; leave it for the day watch.

They went back to the office and found Harvey typing a report. "We haven't had a cabbie heisted in a while," he said. "What it was. Sort of a funny one—it was a young couple, he said. And they stole the cab. He got called by the dispatcher to pick up a fare at San Fernando and Broadway, and of course he only got a casual look at them when they got in. All he can say is, a young couple, girl in the early twenties, he thinks blonde, dark pants, and a coat, and the man a little older, ordinary clothes. They gave him an address on Mountain, and that's a damn dark street at night. They get up there, the man pulls a gun and gets him out of the cab, took all he had on him—about sixty bucks—and he and the girl drove off in the cab. He was mad as hell, he couldn't get any householder up there to let him in to use the phone, had to walk all the way down to a fire station on Dryden to call in."

"Well, put out an APB on the cab," said Rhys.

"I have. They probably kept it just long enough to get back to their own car."

Rhys sat down at his desk and started to type a report on Eleanor Garvin.

That was waiting for the day watch on Sunday morning. O'Connor, of course, was off—he'd be exercising that idiotic dog of his up in the hills somewhere. It was still cold, but clear and sunny.

Delia heard about yesterday's suicide with a little grimace, and the gang rumble. Gonzales told her he'd briefed the Traffic commander to put on an extra patrol around that church today. They told Varallo about that, and he agreed it wasn't so funny for the congregation. About then, as they were discussing the

night report, a messenger came up from the desk with two autopsy reports: Constance Gilmore and Alice Bailey.

There wasn't much on the Gilmore girl, of course. Just the
bald fact: a shotgun blast. On Alice Bailey, there was a little
more. There had been four slugs in her abdomen and chest, and
she would have died within five minutes or so. She'd been a
healthy female, no evidence of drugs or alcohol, a partly
digested meal present in stomach, probably eaten four or five
hours before death, which had occurred between nine and midnight last Thursday night. She had been a virgin.

And that got them no further. Varallo called the lab. He got
Burt, who said those slugs had been sent over yesterday and
he'd had a look at them. They were .32 caliber, out of a Colt re-
volver that hadn't seen much use, but if they ever pinned down
the gun, he could match them. That at least was something.

"And now we've got this to do the routine on," said Varallo.
Delia had just passed the night report on to Gonzales.

They agreed, on the heist of the cabbie, it was just worth asking Records here and downtown about similar M.O.'s, Gonzales
went to do that, and Varallo and Delia drove up to the house on
Idlewood Road.

Edward Garvin was looking gray and ill, but he welcomed
them in with precise courtesy. "I know you have to ask questions. Please sit down." He offered cigarettes; Varallo held out
his lighter for him.

"We understand you were out all evening, Mr. Garvin," he
said, to get the ball rolling.

"Yes, at the library. I am writing a book on the history of the
English novel, there's quite a lot of research—you won't be interested in that, I suppose. I'm afraid I lost track of time, I was
quite surprised to find it was nearly nine o'clock. I hadn't meant
to be so late."

"What was your wife doing when you left?" asked Delia.

"Why, she was in the den watching television. She'd been out
to a bridge party yesterday afternoon, and she got partly
undressed and put on a housecoat after dinner. Well, the den's
down the hall—" He led them there, to a small room with a
couch and chairs, a big console color television.

"I just wondered what lights were on. Was there a light on in
the living room then?"

"Not when we weren't sitting there. There was this table lamp on in here."

"No lights anywhere else?" He shook his head. "Well, this wouldn't have shown much from outside, Mr. Garvin—that's what we're getting at," said Varallo. "This is the middle of the house, on the side away from the kitchen and garage, and there's only one window."

"A lot of people leave one small light on when they're out," said Delia. "A prowler—or a burglar—could have thought the house was empty."

"I suppose that's so," said Garvin. "You think Eleanor heard something, and went to investigate?" He sighed. "I'll have to say, it's what she would have done. She wasn't at all a fearful woman, or timid. Yes, I suppose she'd have gone to switch on the outside lights—the switch is inside the back door—and gone right out on the porch to look around."

They went to look at the terrain. There was a door from the dining room out to the porch-patio, also one from the end of the big kitchen. "That stake—" said Varallo.

Garvin said mournfully, "The one we had is missing from the garage."

Delia said tersely, "Just what Joe says, Vic—doing what comes naturally. He was roaming around looking for a likely house to break in, decided nobody was home here, and had a look for something to smash a window with. Did you leave the garage door open, Mr. Garvin?"

"Well, yes. Yes, I did. It's rather a nuisance to have to get out and open it, coming home—"

"Yes. So he had it in his hand when she came out and spotted him. It was just damned bad luck he hit hard enough—" Varallo stopped.

"Yes," said Garvin thinly. "And Eleanor's bad luck."

"And then he just took off," said Delia.

"Do you think there's any chance you can find out who—"

"Well, we'll do our best, sir," said Varallo noncommittally.

"Yes. My son's coming—" Garvin's eyes looked a little glazed. "He and his wife live in San Luis Obispo— I called last night—they're driving down this morning. My daughter lives in San Francisco. Bob called her and she reached me after midnight—" He gave a long sigh. "I don't know when—she'd been worried about the baby, he's running a fever— I don't know if she'll come—until later. Later. The—the funeral—"

"You understand there has to be an autopsy," said Delia quietly.

"Yes, I realize that. It's quite all right. I suppose you'll let me know—"

"Yes, sir, we'll be in touch with you."

As he opened the front door for them, a stout middle-aged woman was reaching for the doorbell. She gaped at them excitedly, but her eyes were friendly.

"Oh, Mr. Garvin! We've just heard—the awful news about your wife, and I can't tell you how very, very sorry everyone is —if there's anything any of the neighbors can do for you—"

"Why, thank you, Mrs. Powell," he said gravely. "I don't think there's anything, but thank you. My son and daughter will be here."

"Oh, of course. But such a dreadful thing—all these awful burglaries—" She was still talking volubly as they got into Varallo's car at the curb.

"Poor man," said Delia. "Why can't they leave him alone? I'll tell you, Vic, I'd like to hear something about that burglary across the street."

"I was thinking the same thing."

They found Katz sitting at his desk staring into space. Varallo pulled up the chair from Poor's desk for Delia and perched a hip on the corner of Katz's desk. "Like to pick your brains a little, Joe."

"That won't be difficult," said Katz sadly. "What about?" He listened to the story, looking more interested, and said meditatively, "Talmadge. Idlewood Road. It rings a bell, but I've seen so damned many burglaries the last year they all blend into one big montage. Lessee. If it was that recent it'll still be in the current file." He rummaged in the steel file beside the desk, found a manila folder, and took it out. Inside were three typed report forms and the carbon of a list. He glanced over them. "Yeah. Three weeks back. It was the usual shapeless thing, but here's something—he used a hammer out of the garage to break a back window. Talmadge identified it, it had his name on it. No prints, of course. The garage door was left open—people will do it, won't they? They'd been out to a party. Not a smidgen of physical evidence, but he got a nice haul—fur coat, jewelry, radio, two tape-recorders. That section of town is where the more affluent citizens live—naturally where the majority of burglaries happen. And you can't really say it constitutes a definite M.O., the hammer and your stake, but—"

"Yes," said Varallo. "Just suggestive. And that damned thing wouldn't take prints anyway. This is another one that'll end up in Pending. Hell and damnation."

"Bricks without straw," said Katz mournfully.

Gonzales came in and said believe it or not the R. and I. office downtown had turned up the M.O. and a couple of names. "A young couple picked up for heisting a cabbie eighteen months ago—the cabbie put up a fight and knocked him cold. I just checked with Welfare and Rehab, and they're still on probation. Only count on them. They're a husband and wife, Jean and Howard Perry. I've got an address in Hollywood. Like to look them up?"

Varallo got up resignedly. "Did the cab ever turn up last night?"

"I haven't heard."

A man came barging into the office, a big florid middle-aged man in expensive sports clothes. "I've got to see somebody about a burglary! It's the damnedest thing—burglary, it's a Goddamned *mess*, that's—"

Katz got up and went to meet him, looking tired. Varallo and Gonzales went out hastily.

"Look," said the victim, getting out keys, "I'm sorry if I yelled at you, Sergeant Katz. I was a little excited, I guess." He had given Katz a card; he was Adam J. Vinson of Vinson and Stegner Realty on Glenoaks. "But you never saw such a *mess*, and we're responsible for the place. I showed it last on Thursday, hadn't been here since. The woman who owned it died, left it to a nephew back East, and it's up for sale all furnished, it's full of valuable stuff—"

"Safer to put it in storage."

"But easier to sell it furnished—it makes a show. Naturally there's nothing valuable here except the furniture, all her personal stuff the lawyer took, but there are antiques—but what worries the hell out of me, Sergeant, there's not a sign of a break-in, and there are good dead bolt locks on every damned door—it looks as if he or whoever had a key, and there can't be another key around—but look at this *mess!*"

It was a big house, at the top of a hill above Glendale College. And the burglars usually made a mess, but Katz had never seen anything quite like this. It looked as if the burglar had been drunk. In the big living room, one of a pair of elaborate porcelain lamps had been smashed to pieces, its table knocked over and one leg cracked; a couple of needlepoint pillows from the couch were ripped savagely to pieces, the stuffing scattered all over; all the pictures in the room were hanging at crazy angles, still attached to the wall. Down the hall, more bits of the pillow stuffing were scattered. In the kitchen, every cupboard door was open, and there was a pile of broken china and pots and pans littering the counters and floor.

"I don't *know* what's missing," said Vinson. "If anything. There can't be much missing—there's nothing here but the furniture—"

Katz spotted something. "That dog door."

"Cat door. She had a cat."

Katz instantly thought of the mysterious midget burglar. This was right off that one's beat, miles away, but—he looked at the little circular opening with its protective plastic flap. The damned thing couldn't be nine inches in diameter; there was a lock on the doorknob, but it was a good three feet up and to one side, and nobody's arm would work that way. He looked at the pile of smashed china in the sink and sighed.

"But there can't be another key anywhere around! There just can't be!"

"Well, if you'll look and tell us what's missing—" Katz was getting very tired of the anonymous burglars.

Delia, of course, had got stuck with the follow-up report on Eleanor Garvin. About the only new thing to go in it was Katz's information on the Talmadge burglary. She didn't hurry over it, and she'd just finished it at eleven-forty when Communications called to say that a Traffic unit had spotted the missing cab. It was parked out on east Broadway.

"Thanks very much," said Delia, and called the lab and told Thomsen where to find it. If the heisters had left any prints in it, and if they had records anywhere, that would be a shortcut, but as an experienced cop she didn't expect it. Few cops are optimists.

She got her handbag from the bottom drawer, went down to the ladies' room and tidied her hair, renewed powder and lipstick, and started downstairs to see if Mary wanted to join her for an early lunch.

Sergeant Bill Dick was sitting at the desk reading a paperback; he didn't look up. Down the hall leading off the lobby, toward Communications and the Traffic briefing room, the door was open to what had been the fingerprint section of the lab but was now the Juvenile office. She hesitated outside in the hall; a woman was talking rather loudly in there. Delia could see her back where she was perched on the chair in front of Mary's desk —a thin small woman with dark hair and a fierce voice.

"I tell you, I *know!* I'm not a real psychic, a medium or anything, but when I do have the real vivid dreams they're always *true*— I've had a lot, and they always work out true, they're always *real!* I tell you—"

"Really, this isn't anything we can act on, Mrs. Frantz." Mary was polite, but also amused and annoyed.

"I just *know!* Now look, I love that child, I had her over a year and she's a sweet little girl—she was so scared when I first had her, she'd never had a real mother—not to love her—and she loves me and she trusts me—my little Melanie." The fierce voice suddenly uttered one racking sob. "And four times now I've dreamed she's crying and saying they're hurting her, and I know it's true! I never could understand that judge, giving custody back to the mother—when she'd been arrested for beating Melanie like that—and I told you, the Social Service office in Hollywood wouldn't tell me anything except she'd moved to Glendale—just passing the buck—and the office here won't tell me anything—and now you're as good as saying I'm a silly fool! But I *know!* My darling Melanie, I know she's trying to ask for help—when I have the real strong dreams they're *always* true— I've got to try—"

"Mrs. Frantz, we can't act on imagination. And I'm sorry, we're really quite busy."

The woman stood up so suddenly that she nearly sent the chair over. She said angrily, "You stupid *cops*—you don't believe there's anything *to* the psychic things, don't believe there're guardian angels and—and spirits working—to help—and things besides *facts!* You're just too stupid to know a lot of very smart people are studying all that now—and if you'd listen to some real good psychics, you'd probably solve a lot more crimes than you do! If you'd just get the welfare office to tell me where the Floyd woman *is,* I could go look for myself—"

"We can't do that, Mrs. Frantz," said Mary coldly. "You'll have to excuse me now, I'm afraid."

She came half-running out, brushing past Delia in the hall; her thin dark face was contorted with intense emotion and she was crying, but her eyes were furious.

Delia went into the office. "Well, at least we don't often get a nut like that."

Mary said crossly, "My God, dreams. I ask you. I thought I'd never get rid of the woman, she kept saying the same thing over and over. Lord, yes, I'm ready for lunch—let's get out of here."

Howard and Jean Perry, readily visible at a three-room apartment in Hollywood, were indignant at cops descending on them. "Damn it, we never did nothing like that before," said Perry. "Or since. Down on our luck, it was a damn fool thing to do— I guess we got what we deserved."

"So all right, where were you last night?" asked Gonzales. "Say eight to ten?"

They looked at the cops resentfully. "Ken and Angie'll tell you, rest of the people there. We was at a party—at Ken and Angie's place next door," said Jean Perry. "They're gonna get married, it was celebrating that. They decided to make it legal on account of the baby."

Ken and Angie were home, and confirmed that: gave them the names of four other people who had been there. "Do we waste time finding them?" asked Gonzales.

"No," said Varallo. "Let's go have lunch."

Patrolmen Moore and Abrams, in their respective squads, took turns patrolling that couple of blocks on Adams and down Scofield pretty constantly that morning, and up to about one o'clock. About eleven-thirty Moore spotted a little crowd of late teenage boys half a block down from the church, and cruised past very ostentatiously watching them. On his next pass, they were nowhere to be seen.

At twelve-forty Abrams saw the minister and a woman come out of the side door of the church; there was only one car left in the lot. He swung in there and got out. "Dr. Barlow?"

"Yes?"

"Haven't had any trouble here today, sir?"

Dr. Barlow smiled at him. "No, indeed, I'm glad to say." The woman with him, probably his wife, was good looking, a little bit of a thing about thirty, black hair and a milky complexion. "If you've, er, scared them off, we're very grateful."

"We'll be on the job," said Abrams.

The beautiful dreamer made Delia even less disposed to welcome the visitor after lunch. She had set up a session for Ada Tarbell to try the Identikit, down in the lab at two o'clock; she wanted to monitor that and see what eventuated. Varallo and Gonzales hadn't come back by one-thirty, and Katz was the only one in, brooding over a stack of manila folders on his desk, when the lab sent up some photographs. The photographs Ahearne had taken last night at the Garvin house.

She looked them over without much hope. In the sharp black and white, dark marks showed on the blunt end of the two-by-four. The lab would say whether it was blood. In one of the close-ups she spotted something, a little blur, just beyond Eleanor Garvin's outflung left arm. She found a magnifying glass in Varallo's top drawer and peered at it, and it was a rather peculiar little thing. Part of a candy bar. Still in its paper wrapping, a Hershey milk-chocolate bar, she thought.

She frowned at it, and a quiet voice asked, "Is this the detective office?"

Delia looked up. "Yes, can I help you?"

The woman was middle-aged, but a slim, dark, nice-looking woman with rather lovely dark eyes and a friendly smile. She was smartly dressed in a neat navy suit, cream-colored blouse, navy pumps. "The man downstairs said just to come up."

"Yes, what can we do for you?"

"It's about that girl. The story in the paper on Friday night. Alice Bailey."

"Do you have some information on that? Sit down, Mrs.—"

"Stover. Frances Stover. Miss. Well, I don't know what you think about these things. But you know, I felt such—such *rapport* with that girl—just seeing her picture—" She sat down, looked at Delia silently for a moment and then went on, "I own the Silver Comb Beauty Salon on Glenoaks. I suppose it could be that, she was taking an operator's course, it said— I don't want to waste your time, I know a lot of the police don't believe in the, you know, psychic business."

Oh, my Lord, thought Delia, another one? She'd spoken too soon to Mary.

"No, I'm afraid we don't, Miss Stover," she said rather frostily.

"Well, I just felt I had to come and tell somebody. For whatever it's worth." She seemed quite rational, even unemotional about it. "You see, I felt this *rapport*—her picture reminded me of my sister Leila, we were very close, she died twenty-four years ago of leukemia. We always felt we'd been together often before, in past lives—"

"Miss Stover, I'm afraid we're not interested—"

"Oh, yes, you're the complete skeptic, I can see. I'm sorry. I can only try to explain it to you. For what it's worth. I've always been psychic, and you can develop it, you know, with meditation and practice. I won't bother to tell you the true things I've seen, and of course I'm not good enough to be a professional at it, but I've had a lot of hits. I really have. And I felt such a—a closeness to that poor girl— I've been trying to get something on it. And I think I have. I really do. Have you found out who killed her yet?"

"No, but—"

"You don't know a thing about this, do you? Quite the skeptic —well, it doesn't really matter, I've got to tell you anyway. Just in case you find it helpful. I just asked, in my usual meditation, for some help—so whoever did that terrible thing can be caught and punished. Of course he will be, either on this plane or the next, but— And I was given something about him, and it feels like one of my true hits. It really does. There was this awful feeling of hatred, resentment—he hated that girl, and it was because of something she said to him. He's not really sane, because it wasn't anything much at all, I got that. And his initials are G.B. I saw him driving an old Mercedes sedan, it's either tan or light gray."

Delia said formally, "It's very good of you to come in, but I'm afraid we can't use this type of information."

"Yes," said Frances Stover, "I was afraid you'd take that attitude. I'm sorry. I just felt I had to tell somebody." She got up and started out; at the door she looked back and said with a slight smile, "I hope you catch him. If you do, it'll be interesting to see if I'm right, won't it?"

CHAPTER 4

At about ten-twenty on Sunday night rookie Patrolman Chris Pearson was cruising up on North Central. It was, as usual, a quiet part of town, deserted of traffic at that hour for the most part. He hadn't had any business at all, not even a ticket, since he'd come on shift at four o'clock. He had just gone up Pacific to Glenoaks, past the freeway, and down Glenoaks to Central, and under the ramp of the freeway, and just as he got to the next corner some people ran out into the street and hailed him with a flashlight. It was the corner of Doran and Central.

"We just saw a girl kidnapped! He dragged her into a car—"

"We started over there and yelled at him, but he sort of threw her into the car and took off—we didn't get any kind of look at the car—"

"Now let's take one thing at a time," said Pearson, out of the squad and notebook poised. They were excited and upset, but he got the story straight after a few minutes.

Mr. and Mrs. Frank Abel had been on their way home from a movie when the car quit on them; it was parked at the curb half a block down on Doran. "I've been having radiator trouble," said Abel, "I should have taken the damn thing in last week." That had been half an hour or forty minutes ago. He had walked to the nearest public phone, at the Shaker Mountain Inn on the corner and called the automobile club. The auto club man, in a tow truck, had got here about fifteen minutes ago.

That one was a young fellow named Tad Barnes. "I was just telling them I'd drive them home, have to tow the thing in, when we heard the screams—there by the restaurant on the corner—there's a street light right there, and there's a car pulled up in the parking lot, lights and engine on, and this guy wrestling with a girl on the ground alongside—she was screaming blue murder and trying to fight him—" "My God," Abel broke in, "we both started to run over, we yelled at him to leave her alone, but before we got halfway there he just threw her into the car and drove off—" "It was an old clunker by the sound," said Barnes, "the engine sounded damn rough—hell, I couldn't guess what, not a compact, middle-size heap—" "And the restaurant's closed, no phone anywhere around. We were just about to start looking for the nearest phone when you came along—"

Pearson wasn't too sure what to do here, but he figured it ought to be called in. These people could be imagining things, it could have been a couple having a little argument. But he called it in to the night watch in the front office.

There wasn't anything the night watch could do about it either. It was being a quiet night for once. There was another storm forecast, and maybe that was keeping people inside.

But an hour later the night watch got another call, from Patrolman Weiss.

"Listen," he said exasperatedly, "I don't suppose there's anything in this, but the woman wants to file a missing report. I got this call here about twenty minutes ago, it's Clement Avenue. She says something must have happened to her daughter, she should have been home by ten-thirty and there's not a sign of her. Well, the daughter is twenty-three, she probably stopped to see a friend or have a drink, but the woman's all to pieces—a Mrs. Emery, she's alone here."

Rhys said, "The citizens will borrow trouble. No, nothing to it, probably. Where was the girl coming home from?"

"She's a waitress at that Shaker Mountain Inn on North Central," said Weiss. "It closed at ten, and she was supposed to be coming straight home, but like I say—"

"Wait a minute," said Rhys. "That's on the corner of Doran and Central, isn't it? My God, now I do just wonder—and what the hell we can do about it at this time of night—"

On Monday morning Delia found one of the Identikit sketches on her desk, sent up courtesy of the lab. Ada Tarbell had spent a couple of concentrated hours with Thomsen down in the lab yesterday, and he had come up with what she swore was a good likeness. She couldn't say anything about the man's hair, she'd only seen him with a hat on, but otherwise she said it was just like him. The sketch showed a middle-aged man with a round fat-cheeked face, a small straight mouth, a pug nose, the hat low on his forehead; he had on squarish dark-rimmed glasses. If it was anything like the man who had shot Alice Bailey, someone who knew him ought to recognize it. The lab would be sending copies to all the newspapers in the county for reproduction; with any luck, some helpful citizen would be coming or calling to say, that looks something like so-and-so.

And there was this new thing left by the night watch, the possible abduction. And just before the end of the night-watch shift, a Traffic unit had brought in a slightly shot-up heister; he had tangled with an armed pharmacist. Rhys had just stashed him in the jail hospital; they didn't even know his name. It was Gonzales' day off. Varallo and Forbes went to get that straightened out. Delia drove up to Clement Avenue to see Mrs. Julia Emery, find out whether Cynthia Emery had come home.

She hadn't. Mrs. Emery was barely in control of herself, and said she'd been walking the floor all night. It was a middle-class house in a middle-class neighborhood. She was a thin woman in the forties, with graying dark hair and a long nose.

"She'd never do such a thing, to worry me so like this—she's a good girl. I just know something terrible has happened! She's never done such a thing, she'd never—should have been home by ten-thirty at the latest. Of course, as the officer suggested last night I called her closest friends, Marilyn and Sarah, and of course they didn't know a thing. She wouldn't go to see them at that time of night—"

"Does she have a car, Mrs. Emery? Was she driving?"

"Yes, of course, but it's been in the garage, there's something wrong with the transmission. Dan had been picking her up since, that was on Friday, but he had to work late last night and she said—"

"Dan?"

"Dan Rathbone, she's been dating him for about six months. I never liked him, it's the only thing Cynthia and I disagreed about, I just don't trust him, he's too brash and cocky—he told her he had to work late, but I don't see how he could have, he works at a men's gymnasium place in Burbank. Anyway, she said she'd get a cab home, call from the restaurant—oh, I wish I'd gone to get her myself! I could have, just as easy, but she said it'd be late to be out, easier just to call a cab— But she never got home, and I know something terrible has happened, I just know it—"

Delia tried to calm her down without much success. And of course she didn't know much about the little tale Pearson had heard from the Abels and Tad Barnes. She asked for a description of Cynthia and was given a recent snapshot as well—a pretty girl, five-five, a hundred and twenty, brown hair, blue eyes, appendectomy scar. She'd have had on her waitress's uniform, yellow and white, with a black-and-white checked coat over it, black moccasins.

It wasn't any use to tell Mrs. Emery not to worry.

The restaurant wasn't open until eleven. Mrs. Emery said she'd have called the Yellow Cab Company. Delia went to the local dispatch office, a big garage and parking lot over in Burbank, to check. The badge got her friendly cooperation; the dispatcher had a look at last night's record and said there'd been a cab ordered to the Shaker Mountain Inn at nine forty-five, and their driver Martin O'Brien had been called on it. He wouldn't be on until three, but she got his address— Franklin Street in Montrose.

He was a middle-aged man, fat and slow-witted and literal-minded. "Yeah, I got that call," he said. "I'd just dropped a fare pretty far out on Colorado in Eagle Rock, I wasn't that close. You know there aren't many cabs out around, nights or any other time, there just ain't the business, it's not like New York. I used to drive a cab in New York. There just ain't the business here, practically everybody's got cars."

"Yes," said Delia patiently. "So what happened?"

"I don't know why the hell the cops are interested," said O'Brien, yawning. She had interrupted his breakfast. "Well, I should've made it back there—north in Glendale—in about twenty minutes or twenty-five, but I got held up. I hit every damn light on Colorado, and then when I get to Central, there's been a pile-up there right in the intersection and a couple of squad cars out, the cops won't let me turn. I had to go all the way down to Pacific and all the way around that damn Galleria shopping center, to get back on Central. I guess it was maybe ten-twenty, a few minutes later, I got to that restaurant up there. And there wasn't nobody there, waiting for me. The call said, the parking lot." He shrugged. "Nobody there."

"Did you notice anyone else around?"

He thought, picking his teeth carefully. "There was a tow-truck down the block and a couple of people, I think. I pulled into the restaurant lot, but the fare wasn't there like I say, prob'ly got tired waiting, picked up a ride, how should I know. I pulled out on Central and called in I was empty."

"Did you notice a police car?"

He thought some more. "Oh. Yeah. Just as I pulled out of the lot one went by me on Central. I took the freeway back to Brand—"

And that had been split-second timing, thought Delia. Whichever way you looked at it.

She came back to Glendale to the restaurant, open now, and saw the manager, who was cooperative, concerned. He told her there were five girls on the eleven to four shift, six on the four to eleven. She got the names of the six. The nearest was Inez Valdez on Columbus Avenue.

Inez was vapidly pretty, nineteen, lived in one side of an old duplex with her parents. She was immediately excited. "Cynthia never got home? She was right there waiting for a cab when the rest of us left! My God, what could've happened? See, I ride with Linda, I don't have a car, Linda picks up me and Alicia on her way to work—sure we all knew about Cynthia's car, a guy picked her up the last couple of nights, but last night she called a cab. We come out all together just like always, Mr. Ardappel locked up, he's the night cashier, the cooks had already left half an hour before—and Amy and Doris got in their cars and Mr. Ardappel got in his and drove away, and we got in Linda's car—and Cynthia was right there, by the front door in the parking lot, she said the cab'd be there any minute—well, there wasn't anybody around at all, at that hour. What could've happened? Well, yeah, the lights were turned off, but you could see, there's kind of a glare from the freeway right up there, and a street light on the corner—"

Delia reflected that she'd hear the same story from the other girls. Like Mrs. Emery, she was thinking that something fairly terrible could have happened to Cynthia. But if she'd been raped or even killed, where was she? And would it do any good to talk to Dan Rathbone? By what Rhys had put in the report, they couldn't expect much in the way of description, of the man or the car, from the Abels and Tad Barnes. They couldn't say much, they'd been too far away. But Cynthia had been waiting there alone in that parking lot, and it looked as if she had to be the girl those three witnesses had seen dragged into a car.

She headed back to the office to think about it. As she got to the top of the stairs, Lew Wallace was standing at the coffee machine filling a paper cup. He gave her his crooked smile. "Busy day," he said. "Your two sidekicks hardly back the first time when you got handed a new homicide, and now it looks as if the lieutenant's little dramatic production's about to pay off."

"Oh?" said Delia absently. "That's nice." She went on into the office.

The heister, who wasn't hurt much, had a little record and was still on parole. There was a report to write on it, and a statement to get from the pharmacist; but before they got to that, the new call went down, and Varallo and Forbes went out on that, swearing. It was raining again, a steady thin drizzle.

It was Wing Street, an old narrow residential block southeast in town. The squad car was sitting in front of an old frame house; the little front yard looked unkempt and the house needed a coat of paint. Varallo pulled up behind the squad, they got out, and Patrolman Stoner came to meet them, a plastic cape over his uniform, hunching his shoulders against the rain. They could see a woman in the back of the squad; she seemed to be crying. There was an old Dodge Dart in the driveway.

"Just more of the same," said Stoner sourly. "I don't suppose they got much loot, it doesn't look as if the old lady was loaded. That's the daughter—" he jerked his head at the squad— "Mrs. Kilmer. She just found her."

They went to have a look. The front door was standing open. It was the kind of thing police were seeing more and more of all the time, and it was sad and depressing. The house was old and shabby; the furniture was solid and once good, though not expensive or elaborate, and the chances were there hadn't been anything valuable here at all. But the house had been ransacked thoroughly, contents of drawers yanked out and thrown all over, clothes out of the closet thrown around, pictures torn down— the usual.

The old lady was in the kitchen. It looked as if she'd been

beaten; there wasn't anything that looked like a weapon, and she looked like a frail old woman, small and thin—it might not have taken much of a beating to kill her. She lay on her back on the kitchen floor, and there was blood on her face. She was dressed in an old cotton nightgown with a plain blue corduroy robe over it, and felt bedroom slippers.

"Well," said Varallo tiredly, "call up the lab. Let's see if the daughter's up to answering questions."

"Something a little funny, Vic," said Forbes. "It doesn't look like a break-in."

"What?"

"Well, the front door was open, but—" They looked. There wasn't any sign of forced entry, either there or at the back door. That was locked, and there were good dead-bolt locks on both doors.

Varallo rubbed his nose. "Yes, a little offbeat."

They went out again and used the radio in the squad to call the lab. The woman in the back seat had calmed down a little; they introduced themselves, asked if she could talk to them.

She said angrily, "Oh, we should have *made* her move! I tried to get her to come and live with us, we've got plenty of room, she shouldn't have gone on staying here alone after Daddy died, four years ago—but she was so independent—we should have insisted, should have made her move somewhere else at least!" Mrs. Kilmer looked to be in the middle fifties, a little plump woman with short gray hair and a round plain face. "This used to be a perfectly good neighborhood when I was growing up here, Mother and Daddy bought the house in nineteen thirty-four, but all these foreigners flocking in, a lot of riffraff, and don't tell me I'm prejudiced, you know as well as I do the crime rate's gone up so high just since they've all been coming into town! Oh, my God, to see Mother like that— I was always afraid something would happen, her alone here, and she was careful, she always kept the doors locked, my husband saw to it that there were good locks and we made her promise—but we couldn't convince her to move, she'd lived here so long—" She pulled herself together and blew her nose. "Oh, my God. I'd better go home and call Fred."

"What was your mother's name, Mrs. Kilmer?" asked Varallo.

"Mrs. Ann Milburn. She was seventy-nine—they'd lived here

since nineteen thirty-four, a nice neighborhood then. She taught in the Glendale school system for forty years—she retired fourteen years ago—"

Varallo interrupted her gently. "Later on, we'll want you to take a look around and tell us if anything is missing from the house. The lab men will probably be finished here by the end of the day. Have you got a key?"

"Yes, yes. Yes, I will. I called her every morning to be sure she was all right, and when I couldn't get any answer this morning I came right over—and I knew something had happened when I saw the front door open—the rain all coming in on the carpet— What? No, she didn't know any of the neighbors, not anymore, not these people— What? Well, she usually went to bed about nine-thirty— Oh, my God, to see her like that!" She gave them an address in Pasadena, and Forbes asked her if she felt all right to drive home. If not, they could call her husband. "No, I'm all right," she said shakily. "I'll be all right." She backed the Dart out of the drive and drove off slowly, and the mobile lab truck pulled up behind Varallo's car and Burt and Ray Taggart got out of it.

They watched the lab men start to set up for the photographs, for dusting for latents, and then they split up and went to ask questions at the houses on each side, if anyone had heard any disturbance here last night. At the house to the right, the door was opened by a plump dark youngish woman in ragged slacks and blouse, who didn't look unduly disturbed at the badge. "*Policia? Sí?* Is about the needles, for the school? I see doctor tomorrow."

"Needles?" said Varallo, taken aback.

"For the—" she hunted words—"not to get seek by the bugs."

"Oh. No, it's nothing to do with that, Mrs.—"

"Cabrillo. Anita Cabrillo."

"Mrs. Cabrillo." He explained, asked his question, and her eyes rounded in horror.

"*¡Qué atrocidad!* I do not believe! Such terrible to happen! She good old woman." Behind her he could see a much cluttered, barely furnished living room. There were two rather dirty-looking children, perhaps two and three, and a baby in a playpen. "Hear? Nothing, nothing— Alfredo and me come late home —it is my sister's name day, is party. Her house."

"Were the children with you?"

"No, my Juanita, is eleven and good to take care of *niños*. Oh, *pobrecita* Juanita, she cry out her eyes, know about Señora Milburn, she like old woman much, much—was kind to Juanita and help with the school working—oh, is terrible, terrible—" She said they'd got home about midnight. Of course, Varallo thought, they hadn't any idea what time it had happened, and in any case—the frail old lady—it needn't have made much of a disturbance.

He came back to the car where Forbes was waiting. It was raining a little harder. Forbes said, "The place on the other side, the woman doesn't know a word of English. Vietnamese or something. Damn it, many more of these people drift in, every department in the country'll have to hire interpreters for a dozen languages. And damn it, Vic, it used to be when people came here they were anxious to be the good citizens, learn the language right off. These days they couldn't care less. Just enough to fill out the welfare claim."

"All too many," said Varallo, with a grimace. "Well, see if the lab turns up anything."

After lunch Delia went hunting a place called the Health and Happiness Mens' Club. It was way out on Chandler Boulevard the other side of Burbank. She was now talking to Dan Rathbone in the narrow slice of bare lobby; it appeared that females weren't allowed inside.

"Look," he said, "look, I hope nothing's happened to Cynthia. My God, that's awful, her never getting home. I sure hope she's okay some place."

It was automatic, easy, meaningless. Delia, looking at him, saw what Mrs. Emery meant; he'd never think more of anybody than Dan Rathbone. She also saw why Cynthia had gone for him. He was built like Tarzan, big and muscular and good looking in an obvious way. He was wearing yellow boxing shorts and a thin T-shirt, and all the muscles were very visible, and impressive.

"You'd been meeting her, to drive her home from work."

"Yeah, since Friday. Her car—"

"Yes, we know. You told her you had to work last night."

"Yeah, that's right. You know, I never met a lady cop before." He grinned down at her, inviting the admiration.

"Doing what? What do you do here?" asked Delia coldly.

"Well, I'm one of the gym instructors. We get all these fat old guys coming in, want to get back in shape after they've neglected their bodies for years, the damn fools. We got regular courses of exercise and diet, all that jazz. And regular gym courses— I teach boxing too, I been in the ring a little." He flexed the muscles absently.

"Were you teaching here last night?" asked Delia.

He tried the winning smile again. "Hell, seeing it's an official question, from a real cop, no. I had a poker party on with some pals, I didn't want to leave it and go all that way to pick Cynthia up. She isn't my only girl—she may think so, but she's not. Hell, her mother could go and pick her up, it's not that far. Why should anybody think anything could happen to her, for God's sake?"

"So where were you and who with?"

"All very businesslike, aren't we? Dave Roth, Ted Wheeling —at Bill Keyser's place." He parted with the addresses readily. Roth and Wheeling worked at a garage in Burbank, Keyser at Lockheed.

Delia went back to her car and decided, as long as she was here, she'd see the first two, whether they backed him up; undoubtedly they would. She didn't think much of Dan Rathbone, but also she didn't think he'd had enough real interest in Cynthia to have been the abductor in the parking lot last night.

It was now some seventeen hours since anyone had seen Cynthia Emery.

Ruth Sawyer had called O'Connor about ten-thirty. "Something you might want to move on, Lieutenant. I cut second period to come out and call, I was never any good at algebra anyway. Look, we told you that this senior boy, Mark Ryan, is the big man selling on campus. A lot of the kids know that his supplier is this Dutchy character, and what Wanda and I piece together, there's been quite a lot of infighting—half a dozen of the senior boys would just as soon not pay Mark's mark-up, and have some ambitions toward getting into business too. They've been prodding Mark to introduce them to the supplier."

"Yeah," said O'Connor, "you made a little buy from him the other day, the grass." That evidence was neatly tagged in his desk.

"Well, one of the hopeful pushers has been making eyes at me — Allen Sprague." She laughed. "I guess I haven't lost my touch yet. We've got an English class together first period, and he just told me afterward in the hall that Mark's set up a meet with Dutchy, after last period today. I batted my eyes at him all thrilled—my God, Lieutenant, most of the kids in school know what's going on, there's nothing secret about it. Allen and I usually have lunch together, and I think I can get it out of him where the meet is. If I do, I think we can call it a day and break the cover."

"Well, I don't know."

"Honestly, Lieutenant, by what we've got, a few of the kids may know a couple of other sources, but Ryan's been handling practically all the dope floating around the campus."

"Well, see if you can pinpoint the meet."

"I'll get back to you if I do."

She showed up in his office, unexpectedly, at one-thirty. "I thought you'd want it as soon as possible. Allen came apart without any trouble. They're all meeting at Ryan's place—that's right, where he lives. Allen says the parents both work, are hardly ever at home—which may explain a few things." Even in the teenage uniform, jeans and sloppy sweater, she now looked her usual efficient twenty-one-year-old self—fallen out of character. "There are five or six boys going to get introduced to Dutchy. Four o'clock. I went to the principal's office and got the address for you. And I really think, if you gather them in, that'll dry up the main source."

O'Connor massaged his bulldog jaw, absently reaching to adjust the shoulder holster. "Okay. I guess you two can change your clothes and get back to your legitimate jobs."

"Thank God," said Ruth. "I never set out to be an actress, and it's been awfully *wearing*, being a teenager again. I'd better go up and rescue Wanda."

O'Connor grinned after her, looked at the address and said to himself, "Christ. The *kids*. Babies playing with dynamite." Cloud Avenue, La Crescenta. He went out and found Boswell, and they set it up. Plain and simple. "We can call up the squads to ferry them in later. I don't suppose one extra car parked on the block would be conspicuous."

They went up there in his Ford, getting there at three-fifteen in case the kiddies were early. They had roped Lew Wallace in as an extra hand. It was an expensive big house with a glimpse of a pool at one side. There were only a few cars parked in the street, and in the thin rain not a sign of life around any of the houses. O'Connor parked directly across the street. Boswell and Wallace, both big men, with some difficulty crouched below window-level in the back, and O'Connor disposed his bulk along the front seat. They waited silently, with protesting muscles.

At three-forty a car came up the block, and O'Connor rose up cautiously to peer out. Two cars. Old ones. They both pulled into the drive of the Ryan house, and seven late-teenage boys piled out and went into the house, talking and laughing. They settled back to wait some more, and at five to four another car came cruising along and parked right in front. A man got out of it carrying a briefcase, went up and rang the doorbell.

They gave them three minutes to get settled, and O'Connor said, "Let's go." They got across the street fast, and on the front step got out their guns as O'Connor rang the doorbell.

In thirty seconds the door opened. "Mark Ryan?" said O'Connor.

"Yeah—" he saw the gun then, and froze. He was a hand-some dark boy with an arrogant carriage, an incipient moustache. "What the hell—" Then he saw the badge in O'Connor's other hand. "In, boy," said O'Connor.

They found the rest of them in the living room. There wasn't any trouble; the kids were too inexperienced to make any, and the pro dealer didn't have time. He was a fat little fellow about fifty, and his briefcase was probably stuffed full of the dream powder.

They called up the squads to ferry them in, and the lab to tow in Dutchy's car. It was registered to August Schroeder at an address in Huntington Park, and of course they shouldn't have looked that far without a warrant, but there'd be a warrant, and what the eye didn't see—

"First things first," said O'Connor, surveying the sullen little crowd in the detective office. He put in a request for search warrants on the Ryan house and Schroeder's car. He roped in

Varallo, Forbes, and Katz to help out with the questioning; he was old-fashioned about females in policework, let Delia finish the report she was typing. It was going to be a little job to get this all tied up, the hell of a lot of paperwork.

All of them were carrying something, mostly the grass, the angel dust. For the moment they'd be held for possession. Ryan and Schroeder were something else. Get hold of Ryan's parents when they could. There'd be, he gathered from Ruth and Wanda, sufficient evidence that Ryan had been dealing—and pushing.

Just before the end of shift, Thomsen called up to say, "That car is packed with anything anybody might want. Uppers, downers, barbs, coke—the works. In spades."

"Fine," said O'Connor. Schroeder hadn't uttered a single word, but he'd been giving the kids some very dirty looks.

They had phoned down to R. and I. at LAPD, asking about him, and that information came in just before six o'clock. He had a long pedigree of dealing, and he'd also done some time for rape and child molestation.

They stashed them all in jail, left a note for the night watch to contact the parents, and went home. Tomorrow would be a busy day.

Tuesday was Delia's day off, but she called in the first thing to ask about Cynthia. She hadn't turned up anywhere. There weren't many places in town where somebody could be conveniently held prisoner; of course a body might be anywhere. She thought somberly about Cynthia.

She did the usual things she did on days off, the necessary things. Changed the bed and put a big load of laundry through the washer, the dryer. The housework—just dusting would do it this week, the kitchen and bathroom floors were passable. She had shut off the entire second floor of the old house, moved into Alex's old bedroom at the back, with the three-quarter bath next to it. It made the housekeeping a lot easier.

She had a chat with Laura on the phone while she waited for the laundry to dry, and folded that and put it away. She had her usual appointment at the beauty salon at two o'clock, had her hair washed and set, and stopped on the way home to do the week's marketing.

It was Hildy's day off too, so when she called the convalescent home she talked to the rather prim Mrs. Mentor. It had been another good day for Alex, so after dinner she went to see him, stopping at the library on the way, and sat with him until after nine o'clock.

Back at home, she called the night watch. "Not a smell of the girl," said Rhys. "If you want an educated guess, she's raped and dead. Maybe up in the hills somewhere, maybe still in somebody's car trunk. You didn't turn up any leads on it? No fight with the boyfriend?"

"Nothing," said Delia, "but a stupid cab driver." Split-second timing all right. Whatever had happened to Cynthia, it wouldn't have happened if the Abels' car had been parked nearer the corner—he and Barnes might have got there faster—or if O'Brien hadn't taken his time about getting up there, or if—

She would never understand how anyone could believe there was a reasoning, planning power in the universe. Things happened blind—things good, bad, indifferent.

It was raining harder. She took a hot shower and went to bed with Goudge's *The Dean's Watch,* but for once she had difficulty keeping her mind on a book.

On Tuesday morning, the lab sent up a report on Eleanor Garvin, but there wasn't anything in it. There was blood on the piece of two-by-four, type O. The commonest type, and her type. There wasn't any other physical evidence at all. As Varallo had said, that one they'd probably end up putting in Pending, but there was another cast they could try. He wanted to find out if there'd been any juvenile in trouble in that area lately—that kind of trouble. Or if Katz had any possibles in mind at all for any of his recent burglaries.

The *News-Press* had obligingly run a shot of the Identikit sketch last night; it was to be hoped that Glendale's newest paper, the *Daily News,* would do so today. Of course a lot of people in town habitually saw the L. A. *Times,* the *Herald,* and the newspapers were usually cooperative; that sketch would get a lot of coverage.

But there'd been another heist overnight, at a dairy store in Montrose. More to the point, all those louts picked up on the gang rumble on Saturday were up for arraignment this morning, and so was Jerry Rubio. The DA had decided to call that Murder Two. They would be in court most of the morning.

And Forbes said, "Just as well, with Charles cluttering up the office with kids."

O'Connor, Boswell, and Wallace were busy tying up all the loose ends, and there was a lot of confusion and uproar. They got search warrants for all the lockers at the high school, and routed out a lot of Traffic men to help out on that; there'd be something like two thousand kids in that student body. They found about forty lockers harboring the stashed dope, and brought all those kids in. Most of them were under eighteen, so Guernsey and Mary Champion sat in on the questioning. Going by the rules and regulations, they contacted the parents. The night watch had borne the brunt of the first batch of parents last night, but hadn't managed to contact the Ryans at all. In the middle of the foray on the school, O'Connor asked the principal what was known about them, if anything, and found out that they owned a classy restaurant in Toluca Lake.

Boswell got hold of Ryan about the middle of the afternoon, and shortly afterward the two of them descended on the office.

"Goddamn cops just picking on the kids!" said Ryan loudly. He was a big man in flashy clothes. "What the hell's a little grass? Most of the kids smoke pot, what's the big deal? You Goddamn fuzz got nothing better to do than pick on the kids—"

"Haven't got the brains do anything else," she shrilled. She was little and skinny and dark, with too much makeup and jewelry.

"Mr. Ryan," said O'Connor—he'd herded them into his cubbyhole of an office, away from the crowd in the big office— "your son's been pushing dope, selling to younger kids, getting them hooked. He's turned eighteen, not a minor. And it's a lot more serious than just the grass. The hard stuff, a lot of it."

"So what the hell?" Ryan looked at him contemptuously, and O'Connor knew just what he was seeing: a dumb Irish cop with a big gun and a yen for power.

He didn't move from his desk chair, but his dark eyes were very cold. And it might have been an orphanage, but it had been a very good one. "Mr. Ryan," he said, his voice soft, "you really don't know much about the facts of life. You go down to UCLA Medical Center some day, Mr. Ryan, and have a look at the end results. The human wreckage that doesn't look very human anymore. You talk to some doctors at the jails and prisons, Mr. Ryan, and hear about the people reduced to the most despicable crimes because they've got to have the stuff, it's all there is to their lives—and their deaths. A lot of death, Mr. Ryan. You don't know the statistics on how many young people die of overdoses every year. We do. By God, we do. They used to call the manufacturers of military hardware the merchants of death. That's a little damn obsolete, Mr. Ryan. The biggest merchants of death in the world today are the dope dealers and pushers. And about ninety-seven percent of them are just the common criminals out to make a fast buck, they've got no remote interest in politics or ideologies. But it's a very strange thing, Mr. Ryan, that the dope's being so efficiently pushed and smuggled in by the ton, and the kids sold on the idea that it's harmless, in the few remaining free countries in the world. We know all about that too, Mr. Ryan. In the countries they—the people who want to fill the whole world with slaves—are trying to take over from inside. Even half, a quarter, of one generation already slaves to the hypos and the pills, their brains destroyed, they're not going to care much about losing the rest of their freedom, are they?"

Ryan was just staring at him stupidly. "Politics?" he said.

"Oh, go away, Mr. Ryan," said O'Connor. "You make me sick. You're a big success, you've made a lot of money, because you live in a free country and had the chance. But you are ignorant as all hell about that and a lot of other things. You go and get your son a good mouthpiece, go and do whatever you want, but right now you get the hell out of my office, Mr. Ryan, and don't waste my time."

Surprisingly, they went out in silence.

Varallo and Forbes got back about two o'clock, after the court session. It was too soon to expect a lab report on the Milburn house, but there was one on the stolen cab. No prints in it except those of the regular driver.

It was annoying, but expectable. "We ought to see Mrs. Kilmer about any loot they got," said Forbes. "That door being open—somebody she knew? But anybody who knew her would know there wouldn't be much there."

"Now, Jeff," said Varallo, "the punks don't mind killing for ten or twenty bucks. So, the daughter called her every morning, probably around the same time. And she was still in her nightclothes. She might not have got dressed yet, on the Sunday morning, say—after the daughter called. She wouldn't be nervous about answering the door in daylight."

"Wait for the autopsy report to give us the time," agreed Forbes.

They went over to Pasadena and talked to Mrs. Kilmer. She said that she and her husband had cautioned her mother to keep the doors locked all the time, and she thought she had. But she'd lived there such a long time, it had been a nice quiet neighborhood up to the last few years. No, she hadn't known any of the people on the block for at least ten years, old neighbors dying, moving away. Varallo asked about the Cabrillos next door. "Oh, yes," she said vaguely, "Mother had mentioned the little girl, a nice enough little girl, she tried to help her with her English." She blew her nose. "I— Fred and I went and looked last night, the way you asked me. My Lord, that house is in such a mess—but I'll think about that later." This was a middle-class house on a nondescript street in central Pasadena, but it was extremely neat and clean. They had heard now that her husband was a clerk in the local Social Security office. "Mother didn't have anything that was really valuable. Her engagement ring— I made a list for you—that's gone, and a couple of old garnet rings, and her mother's garnet brooch, her wristwatch—it's an old Bulova—and Daddy's watch and Masonic ring, and a couple of old-fashioned gold bracelets, they were fourteen karat, I know. There wouldn't have been much cash there. She just had the Social Security, her own and half of Daddy's, it was four hundred and eighty a month. Fred and I have been paying her taxes, she didn't want us to—so independent—but we argued her around. This time of the month, she might have had fifty or sixty dollars left. I took her to the market once a week—"

"Well, thanks very much, Mrs. Kilmer," said Forbes. They would get out the description of the jewelry to all the pawnbrokers; with amateur burglars, that often turned up the loot and a lead.

"Oh, my God," she said, and put a hand to her eyes. "We should have insisted she come to live with us—should have made her. Oh, my God, I hope you can find out who did it, see he gets what's coming to him—"

But the courts being what they were, there wasn't anything certain about that if they did pick him up. Varallo said somberly, "So do we, Mrs. Kilmer."

Back in the car, as he switched on the ignition he said suddenly to Forbes, "Say, I meant to ask you, is the baby all right? You were worried—"

"Oh," said Forbes. "Yes, she's fine—the doctor said it was just a little cold. They run a temperature for any little reason, but of course you always worry." He laughed sharply, looking back at the Kilmer house. "And then I guess later on, they worry about you. Life's a funny proposition, isn't it?"

CHAPTER 5

Wednesday was a slow day; nothing much happened at all. O'Connor and his crew were still busy at all the red tape and paperwork on the narco business. There had been a couple of feature stories in the *News-Press* last night about the raid on the high school, a lot of students to be expelled or suspended, and an indignant editorial about the deplorable changes for the worse in a formerly upright community. To that they could say amen.

There was, of course, always the legwork to do; Varallo and Gonzales spent most of the day at that, looking for the heisters on the latest several jobs. They hadn't any very good descriptions; and it might seem a roundabout way to go at it, but it was the only way that sometimes—just sometimes—paid off. You looked in Records for the pro heisters around who had pulled similar jobs, conformed to the descriptions, and went and found them and leaned on them. Once in a while one came apart and admitted, yeah, I did that one. Once in a long while the physical evidence turned up.

Nothing came in on Cynthia Emery, and Mrs. Emery had stopped calling every hour. Now, getting toward the end of shift on Wednesday, Cynthia had been missing some sixty-seven hours, and the outlook on that wasn't good. She might not be found for a long while, or—it had happened before—she might never be found.

The only things that turned up on Wednesday, in late afternoon, were a lab report on the Milburn house and the autopsy report on Eleanor Garvin. The lab men had picked up fourteen fairly good latent prints in Mrs. Milburn's house, which didn't belong to her; they weren't in Glendale's records, and had been sent to the FBI and LAPD. The autopsy report didn't provide any obvious suggestions, but they hadn't expected it to. Eleanor

Garvin had died of a depressed skull fracture caused by several blows to the back of her head—detectives automatically translated the precise medical terms—by a fairly heavy weapon. She would have died within a few minutes. The estimated time of death was between six and ten P.M. last Saturday night—well, they knew it couldn't have been before seven, at least—there was a paragraph about stomach contents, slightly enlarged heart, surgical scars, no evidence of alcohol or drugs. What chiefly interested Varallo was that there had been several blows struck.

"It's a chancy deduction," he said to Delia, "but that doesn't look to me like the amateur burglar hitting out in panic before he ran away."

"On the other hand, Vic, the amateurs—and the juvenile maybe doped up—are just the ones who do use the unnecessary violence."

"Damn it, yes. And no smell of a lead. I want to have a look at the Juvenile records." But it was five-fifty then. Tomorrow another day. It had stopped raining half an hour ago.

When the night watch came on later, Harvey brought along tonight's *News-Press*. There was a human interest story on the front page about Connie Gilmore's funeral, scheduled for tomorrow morning at Forest Lawn. *The police have no clue to the perpetrator of this wanton murder of an innocent child. The* News-Press *is offering a reward of $500 to any person who can give any significant information about the crime.*

"Now that," said Rhys, "is what I call noble. Cheapskate, but noble after a fashion."

"The gift horse," Harvey reminded him. "There are people around would turn in their grandmothers for five Cs, Bob."

About ten minutes after that, Patrolman McLeon came in with a pair of kids about fourteen, and said, "I picked up these two in the parking lot of that church on Adams, the one we've been asked to keep a special eye on. I brought them in because they're both holding—the grass—and they'd already smashed in a back window, they had a wrench and they're both carrying switchblades."

"We dint steal nothing," said one kid resentfully. "We dint even get in."

"What's your name?" asked Rhys.

"Manuel Aguayo. We wasn't—"

"Any relation to Tony?"

The boy raised burning eyes. He was a small thin boy in ragged clothes. He said defiantly, "Tony was my brother—that Goddamn Cardenas, no call knife Tony, them Eldorados think they such big men—"

"But Carlos gonna show 'em something," said the other boy.

"That'd be Carlos Ramirez, I suppose," said Rhys. "You're both Guerrero members?"

"No, you gotta be sixteen."

"Look," said Dick Hunter reasonably, "just what's all this stupid business about that church? You heard the officer who brought you in say we're keeping a special eye on it. Any of you punks who get to fooling around there are going to get dropped on. The church people aren't bothering you."

They were silent, sullen, heads down, and then Manuel said, "They think they're so damn much better'n anybody else. *Anglos bastardos.* They got no call come in our *barrio.*"

"For God's sake," said Rhys, "that church has been there a long time. It never bothered you people before."

The other boy said darkly, "They never cause no trouble before either. But we gonna show 'em something, we gonna—" Manuel kicked him sharply on the ankle and said something quick in Spanish, and he shut up.

Rhys and Hunter shrugged at each other. They hadn't a Juvenile Hall; they confiscated the marijuana, getting called dirty thieves, and sent the kids home in a squad car. They'd pass the word on to the Juvenile office, but it wasn't really anything to follow up.

And half an hour after that, they had a very angry man in, a tough-looking fellow by the name of O'Neill, who'd been heisted and had his cab stolen. "Me thinking I'm so damn tough!" he said. "Me, the big ex-Marine! But I got better sense than to argue with a gun, especially in the hands of an amateur, which I think he is." O'Neill drove a cab for Yellow, and about forty-five minutes ago the dispatcher had sent him to an address on Colorado; the fares were a young couple, and of course he'd only given them a casual glance. Blond girl, pants and a coat; man a little older. They gave him an address on Kenneth Road, and when they got up to Kenneth and Grandview the man pulled a gun. They took all he had on him, about seventy dollars, and made off with the cab. "There's a block of stores right there, all closed, but there's a public phone on the street. I called the dispatcher and she sent Al to pick me up. He's been kidding me all the damn way down here, get took like that. The whole night's take, damn it! And I wouldn't have been on so late, but I was doing overtime while Smiley's out with the flu."

Rhys did a report on it, and that was all the business that came in. They got a little bored sitting around, and monitored the calls for a while. Their business might be slow, but it was a busy enough night for Traffic: three big pile-ups, a couple of people dead, and two more on the freeway—but that belonged to Highway Patrol.

Forbes was off on Thursday. There wasn't anything in the night report but the new cab heist. There was nothing on Cynthia. Gonzales went back to the legwork on the heisters, and Varallo and Delia went down to Juvenile to ask some questions, about any sort of trouble lately anywhere around that area on Idlewood Road.

Guernsey, clutching his empty pipe in habitual gesture, said reflectively, "Idlewood Road. I can't say I call anything to mind off the bat. Traffic picked up a pair of kids on a prowling charge somewhere along there a couple of weeks back, but it didn't amount to anything."

Mary said, "There was that Porter kid, but that was six months back. Wasn't that address on Idlewood?"

"Oh, him," said Guernsey.

"What was that about?" asked Delia.

"Traffic had been getting complaints about a peeping Tom along one block," said Mary. "Eventually they picked up this kid. Robert Porter. He struck us both as a little off mentally— maybe only slightly retarded—and he was sent for psychiatric evaluation. It ended up the usual way, probation to parents—it was the first time he'd been in any trouble. We didn't follow up on it. The parents seemed to be good responsible types. If you're interested, I can look up the file—"

It was an address a block and a half from the Garvin house. "What," asked Delia, "was the result of the psychiatric examination?"

Mary glanced over the file. "Usual four-dollar doubletalk."

She ran an absent hand over her untidy hair. "He had a low-to-middle IQ. He'd never been in any trouble before, and there was no history of violence."

"There's always a first time," said Varallo. "Name?"

"Robert Porter. He'll be sixteen now. Father's an attorney."

Delia said to her cigarette, "You know, Vic, if Mrs. Garvin would have recognized him, he'd have had some reason to do more than run away. She could have put him in trouble again. A block and a half away—neighbors in an area like that don't always know each other, but—"

"Yes," said Varallo. "Yes, it's a thought."

They went back upstairs and talked to Katz, who was brooding over his manila folders again. Delia was irrelevantly struck by the contrast of the two as they conferred, heads together—handsome big tawny-haired Varallo towering over wiry little Katz with his brilliant dark eyes and narrow intellectual face.

"Well, there are a lot of burglars around," said Katz, "at any given time. Lately they're coming out of the woodwork. We've got a lot of burglars listed in records, but if you're asking me about any suspects on particular jobs—" He shut his eyes. "Says somewhere in the Talmud, I think, *A man's mind is wont to tell him more than seven watchmen that sit above in a high tower.* Imagination. No, there's no evidence whatever to say that this particular burglar might have pulled that particular job. You know the routine—you do it too. You look up the burglars in Records, look for them and lean on them, get a search warrant and look for the loot. But most of the jobs are so anonymous, most of them look so damn much alike—" He sighed and sat up. "The only thing I can say, your address falls in that area, and I don't suppose that says anything about your homicide."

"What area?" asked Varallo.

"Well, it's the damnedest thing I ever ran across. The midget." Katz was pleased to have an audience, and went into detail—the break-ins through the impossible spaces— "That damn dog door wasn't ten by twelve inches, and those tiny little back windows only a kid could get through, but he's no kid, believe me. Very pro, once he's inside, knows all the right places to look, and he's taken a very nice haul over the last couple of months, none of which has showed up, so it's been professionally fenced. But another funny thing about it, which I just belatedly realized, is the tight little area in question. It's all north Glendale, affluent part of town, but a very small section of north Glendale. All those jobs were pulled in the area—call it ten square blocks—bounded by Sonora and Highland east to west, and Glenwood and Olmsted north to south. It sounds absolutely crazy, but I'm wondering if he hasn't got access to a car."

"Very funny," said Varallo absently. "Well, thanks for nothing."

He had borrowed the Porter boy's file from the Juvenile office, and they went up to that address to talk to anybody there. It was on the same side of the street as the Garvin house, a block and a half down, a trim white-stucco place with a manicured lawn in front and bordering shrubs. They found Mrs. Porter at home. She was older than they had expected, very smartly dressed, an obviously intelligent woman. She looked alarmed at Varallo's badge, but followed his careful casual questions quickly, and she was readily cooperative.

"You're—checking up?" she said. She had asked them in, and the living room was tastefully furnished, well kept. "Robert's home with a cold if you'd like to see him. But you needn't worry, we've been keeping an eye on him. I admit, he's been a little worry to us—he's the youngest, our other two are grown and married. Robert's always been a little slow, but perfectly normal. We were terribly upset when we found he was doing that, looking in the windows—we hadn't any idea he'd been getting out of his room at night when we thought he was in bed. But he'd never done anything wrong before, and the police and the judge were very understanding. He's on probation—and his father talked to him, we tried to handle it intelligently. The psychiatrist said he's late developing sexually. Of course, he's always been a quiet boy, no very close friends. But since then, believe me, we check on him every night, and he knows we do. He understood what a wrong thing it was to do, and he was afraid of the psychiatrist, afraid he'd be sent back to—" She stopped abruptly and said, "You asked— Saturday night? Last Saturday —you're not thinking about—about Mrs. Garvin? The terrible thing that happened— Oh, no. No, you can't possibly think that *Robert*—"

"Did you know Mrs. Garvin?" asked Delia.

Mrs. Porter's eyes were frightened, but her voice was determinedly normal. "Our older boy—Jim—had Mr. Garvin for his English teacher in college. He liked him very much. We don't know them socially, but Mrs. Garvin always came collecting for the Red Cross and United Way, I knew her by sight."

And, both Varallo and Delia were thinking, she could have known Robert Porter by sight. They asked to talk to the boy, and in silence she led them down a hall to a back bedroom. He was dressed, lying on a made-up bed reading a science-fiction novel. He was an unhealthy-looking boy, a gangling six-footer, with a pale skin and a case of acne. When he heard who they were he said instantly, excitedly, in a high nervous voice, "I don't do those things anymore. I know it was wrong to do, and I don't want to anymore. I'm not supposed to be out after dark alone, I never am, Mother and Dad know that— Saturday night?" His eyes shifted easily and often. "I was right here Saturday night. Watching television."

According to what they knew about it, Eleanor Garvin had probably died nearer to nine o'clock than just after Garvin had left at seven, and of course that was early. They followed Mrs. Porter back to the living room and Varallo said easily, "Can you confirm that he was here, Mrs. Porter?"

"Of course he was here!" she said crossly; she was frightened. "John and I were out in the early evening, but just next door for a drink with Marge and George Cook. It was their wedding anniversary. We were back by nine. Robert knew we'd be back any time. Of course he was here, watching TV."

They sat in the car and kicked it around. "He could be a wild one," said Varallo. "I don't like the look of him much. He's just the kind, and he's got just the right history, to pull something like that. They can't swear he was home, and it's likely that that had been his only chance to get out and roam around in quite a while."

"Um," said Delia. "And you know something else, Vic? I might think that now he wasn't just wanting to peek in windows. He just could have been looking for any female alone, a female of any age, because—if it was him—the fact that he'd hunted up a weapon—it could be he intended assault, not burglary."

"I just had the same thought," said Varallo.

They drove a block and a half up to see if Garvin was home. The door was answered by a shallowly pretty auburn-haired young woman, who looked at Delia interestedly and asked them in. She introduced herself as the daughter, Lisa Osborne. "Daddy and my brother, Bob, are at the funeral home making the arrangements, they called late yesterday to say we could have Mother's body— I can't believe this is happening to us, it's like a bad dream or something, and when I think how they were going to be so happy and comfortable in just a little while— Daddy's going to retire in June, you know, and they bought this lovely mobile home in such a beautiful retirement park just outside Elsinore—one of the senior citizens' community parks, you know, with all the planned activities—a big community recreation lodge, shuffleboard, and bingo and a nine-hole golf course and card rooms, a lovely place, Mother was looking forward to it so much. This house is way too big for them since Bob and I left home, even with all Daddy's books. When Bob called me I fainted dead away, you know—scared Jack to death—it just didn't seem possible— Mother! Mother always so busy and cheerful, I just couldn't imagine her—gone. And it was just lucky—of course I felt I had to come to Daddy right away— that my mother-in-law could come to take care of my little boy. I said to Jack—"

Delia had to interrupt her to ask the question. "Porter?" she said blankly. "I don't know if they knew anyone by that name, I don't think I remember any mention of it. But Mother knew a lot of people, she always liked to be busy, she got around a lot, you know—her own car, of course, and she had her regular bridge club and charities and she—"

"Was she fond of candy?" asked Delia.

Surprised, Lisa was halted in mid-sentence for just a moment. "Why, yes, she was— Daddy's not a great one for sweet things, and since they were alone Mother wouldn't bother fixing dessert, but she always had candy for herself after dinner, I don't know how you knew that. I said to Jack, you'll just have to get along the best you can, however long it is, because I couldn't leave Daddy alone at a time like this, and he said—"

They extricated themselves with a little difficulty, and in the car Varallo said, "It's a moot point—doesn't matter whether Garvin knew the Porters. Evidently she got around the neighborhood, could have known the boy. What was that about candy?"

"You haven't taken a look at the photos of the body. It's a funny little thing, Vic. You can just see it with a magnifying glass. She'd evidently been eating a candy bar, still had it in her hand and dropped it when she was knocked down."

"I would have thought she'd have put it down before she went out—but nothing much in that. You know, I think we've got a strong lead here, but damn it, we'd never have enough evidence for a charge."

She agreed soberly. "Especially on a juvenile. Unless he could be got to confess—and that's tricky with a minor. And a minor who isn't just so very normal."

"That's an understatement. Whether he killed the Garvin woman or not, I'll have a bet that he's going to cause the Porters some more grief, and probably trouble for other people, before he's much older. Are you ready for lunch?"

They got back to the office about two o'clock; Gonzales was still out somewhere, but there was a manila folder on Varallo's desk, and it turned out to be the autopsy report on Ann Milburn. He scanned it rapidly and passed it over. Like Eleanor Garvin, she had died of a depressed skull fracture. The doctor thought it likelier that she'd been knocked down on a hard floor, against some hard surface, than that any weapon had been involved. The estimated time of death was between seven and ten P.M. on Sunday night.

"Well, I never claimed to be infallible," he said. "I'd decided it was probably Sunday morning." He ran a hand over his regular profile. "That open door—it's pitch dark by five now, and I seem to remember it was raining—" His phone rang and he picked it up. "Varallo."

"Say, this is Armando down at the morgue," said a plaintive voice at the other end. "You know we've got just so much space here, and the bodies kind of pile up—from the hospital too. This one tagged King, we informed your office it could be released, but nobody's turned up to claim it, and we'd like to know what to do with it. Is the city going to bury it or what? Are there any relatives?"

"*Dio!*" said Varallo. "We never did look for any—all right, we'll get back to you." He put the phone down. "Same as that suicide"—the autopsy report on Winter had come in yesterday, to be filed away—"and what the hell do we do about it? I suppose she must have had a family somewhere—"

"There was that other girl. The one who told Rubio where she was."

"Sally. Said to be a pal. I wonder if Hollywood ever turned her up." Varallo took up the phone again. "You can write the new report on Garvin." Hollywood had indeed turned up Sally Brady, and he went out to find her.

It was now some eighty-five hours since Cynthia had disappeared.

O'Connor, Boswell, and Wallace were still busy tying up the red tape and getting the paperwork done on the narco job, and still occasionally getting interrupted by the parents. Most of the parents were decent people, shocked and grieved, no idea their kids were into dope, a few had noticed that the kids had seemed a little tired lately, a little irritable, hadn't paid much attention —never thought their good, well-raised kids would get into that kind of trouble, they knew there was a dope problem but never thought their kids— "The damn fools," growled O'Connor as the latest pair trailed tearfully out. "If people only recognized a few simple symptoms—"

"They just overestimate the intelligence of the kids," said Wallace dryly.

The phone rang on O'Connor's desk and he picked it up. "Lieutenant, this is Moore, Traffic. I just got sent down here to a burglary in progress, neighbor called it in. It's Dixon Street. There's a phone on the corner and I thought I'd better—"

"That's none of my business," said O'Connor, irritated.

"Well, it wasn't a burglary. It's an empty house scheduled for demolition, and a bunch of juveniles have evidently been using it as a convenient pad. There's a girl here pretty well strung out, I've got an ambulance on the way, and quite a little collection of the foolish powder, grass, and angel dust. And six kids, four of 'em riding high. I called in Miller as back up, he's standing by. I just thought I'd ask how you want to play it."

"Goddamn *kids!*" said O'Connor explosively. "All right, I'll be there. What's the address?"

He went down to look at it—another tired old block southeast in town. The ambulance had just left, and Moore said the girl looked pretty bad. She wasn't more than eleven or twelve. All the others were boys about the same age. Four of them were in no state to be talked to, but the other two were sober and scared at being dropped on. They knew the girl's name, Agnes Novak, and the names of the other boys; they all went to the same elementary school. O'Connor sent Miller over to the school to get addresses, called another ambulance and sent the four into the hospital. The other two he took back to the office with him. One was thin and one was plump. They were dressed in the ordinary shabby nondescript clothes. He sat them down in two chairs in front of Boswell's desk and leaned back against it, hands in pockets.

"All right." He nodded at the thin one. "Name?"

"Luis Mendez."

He looked at the other one. "Juan Martinez."

"We wasn't doing anything," said Luis. "That ole house gonna be tore down anyways."

"Where'd you get the dope?" asked O'Connor. "Buy it or steal it?"

"It's only the grass, that ain't nothin'," said Luis. "We just got the angel dust today, and that pig steal it before we ever got to try—"

"And you don't know how lucky you were," said O'Connor sardonically. The angel dust was about the most dangerous of the available street drugs, but of course it was popular with the kids because it produced a quick high. "Where'd you get it?"

"Aw," said Luis, "from a guy my brother knows, he just gives it to you for your lunch money, you got any, and it don't matter because you tell the teacher you got no lunch money she makes the cafeteria give it to you free. And it was only the grass—"

"Getting the prospective customers hooked with free samples. What's the guy's name? Come on, come on, give."

"I don't hafta tell."

Juan said, "His name's Eduardo. He's a big guy in the Guerreros."

"Goddamn snitch, you shut up!"

"I don't take no orders from your ole Guerreros," said Juan. He looked at O'Connor stolidly. "My dad says they give people bad ideas about us." Luis tried to hit him, and Boswell got up and yanked him away. "His name's Eduardo, I don't know his other one. He gives the stuff to a lotta kids at school. I— I only tried the grass once, I din't like it so good, but everybody says you're s'posed to— I din't want go with Luis today, but he said the angel dust be different—"

"Well, there may be some hope for you after all. So you don't like the Guerreros, hah?"

"My dad says they're bad. And besides it was the Guerreros killed that girl. I heard—"

Luis began yelling in Spanish at the top of his voice. O'Connor gave Boswell one glance, and took Juan down to his office and shut the door.

"What girl?" he demanded.

Juan said, "Well, see, some of the guys at school, like that Luis, they got big brothers in the Guerreros—an' you hear things—they talk about what the big guys say, see?" He shrugged. "What my dad says about it—*idiotez*, he says, no good."

"What girl? What do you know about it?"

"I dunno. Some girl. It was Joe's brother shot her. I heard Joe and Luis talk about it, and Joe said Enrique shot some girl."

"For God's sake!" said O'Connor. "Joe who?"

"Joe Diaz. His brother's a Guerrero same as Luis's, see? He's always braggin' on stuff they do. And he said Enrique—"

"Oh, for *God's* sake!" said O'Connor.

He was a good deal annoyed that Varallo wasn't back. He said to Delia, "I don't approve of females on this part of the job."

Delia gave him a sweet smile and said, "But nobody else in the office speaks Spanish."

"Hell, all these people can talk good enough English when they want to. Look at those kids."

"And if they claim they can't, it's so convenient to have the interpreter handy," said Delia. "If you're going to locate the address we'd better move, hadn't we? All the school staff will be leaving in half an hour."

O'Connor growled. They made a quick trip over to the school and got an address for Joe Diaz, Griswold Street. It was the usual run-down cheap rented house. The mother genuinely didn't have much English, and Delia talked to her.

"She says he's at the garage working on his car," she reported to O'Connor. "She's afraid of the police, but she's also afraid of Enrique, and she'll remember us in all her prayers if we very kindly will not tell him how we found him."

"My God. I like this even less." That garage was a well-known hangout for the gang, and there might be a little crowd of them there.

Delia got in the car beside him. "There's an old saying that you can catch more flies with honey than vinegar."

The garage was way out on Colorado, nearly into Eagle Rock. When they got there, O'Connor went round the block and parked on the side street. "I don't like this one hell of a lot. If anybody makes a move, you yell. Loud."

"You're always looking for an excuse to show off your marksmanship." Delia got out and walked up the side street to the broad expanse of oil-stained cement in front of the gaping doors of the garage. There were five or six of them there—nineteen, twenty, a couple of big ones—working on two cars with hoods open.

She didn't, of course, look very Latin, with her fair skin and blue eyes, but perhaps the good unaccented Spanish would make up for it. She walked toward them across the cement and asked in a friendly tone, "*¿Donde es Enrique Diaz?*"

"*¿Qué es?*" came the automatic response. One of them straightened from the nearest car and stared at her. He was one of the big ones, wide-shouldered, very much the *macho* image. "I don't know you—who the hell—"

"Your brother said you were here," she went on easily in Spanish. "Something's come up—he thinks the police know about Eduardo passing out the dope at school."

"*¡Vaya! Qué diablo—*" He came up to her in a stride.

"He's in my car right around the side, if you'd—"

He followed her like a lamb, and in thirty seconds they were out of sight of the rest, approaching the car, and O'Connor was out of it, the gun visible. Say what you would about Charles O'Connor, thought Delia, it was always a pleasure to watch him in action. Before Enrique had more than noticed the gun, O'Connor had the cuffs on him and shoved him into the back seat and got in after him. He handed the keys to Delia.

Enrique was showing off a meager vocabulary of obscenities

in two languages. "That's the trouble with you Latins," O'Connor told him. "You always talk too much. Now if you hadn't talked in front of Joe—or if Joe hadn't talked to the other kids—"

"Sonofabitch pig *bastardo! ¡Mugre!*"

Varallo was back, and they sat Enrique at the table in an interrogation room and started out by telling him what they knew, bluffing that they knew a lot more than they did. "Your brother Joe let it out that you shot that girl, Enrique." And at that stage, they didn't know what girl, and they were wondering about Cynthia.

"I don't know nothin' about no girl got shot."

"Well, your brother says you told him you shot her."

"I never shot nobody."

"He told Luis Martinez about it—all the kids at school were talking about it. Besides, we've got those other witnesses—" O'Connor stopped.

"We can spring those later," said Varallo. "You'll be up for Murder One, Enrique. If you've got anything to say for yourself, you'd better speak up. If you tell us all about it, maybe we can get the charge reduced."

"Ah, don't promise the bastard anything," said O'Connor. "That one witness can swear it was him, and with the brother putting it all over the school—"

It had all come at him fast, with no time wasted; he was confused and bewildered. He said, "That's a Goddamn lie! Joe knows it wasn't me, he couldn't'a said—he knows it was Rod— I never had no hand on that gun! You can't put it on me— I was just drivin' the Goddamn car!"

O'Connor patted the shoulder holster pleasedly. "Tell us, buddy boy. Tell us the whole tale."

"I never had a Goddamn thing to do with it!" said Enrique. "And nobody meant to kill that kid, for God's sake! It was a Goddamn accident! All right, I tell you how it went. We was out to get Cardenas, the damn Eldorados snitch on Bernie, and me and Rod were gonna blast him when he come out with his chick, we found out she lives on Windsor—and I was drivin', it was Rod had the Goddamn gun, I guess we was both a little high on grass—"

It was crowded in here, all three of them big men, but Delia just had room, on the little stool in the corner, to be getting it down in shorthand.

"It was a Goddamn crazy thing to do, all of a sudden Rod says he gotta be sure the damn gun works okay, and he fires it out the window and I Goddamn near hit the light pole onna corner, I din't expect it, I floored the pedal and says what the Goddamn hell he thinks he's doin', a thing like that— And besides, Cardenas never showed at his chick's place that day. And then Tony heard about it an'—"

"Tony Aguayo."

"Yeah, Tony said lay off Cardenas, there was an operation set up on Cardenas—so we never— And I never knew about that kid gettin' killed until I was inna drugstore down there an' heard people talkin' about it—it was a just a Goddamn accident! And anyways, I din't have a Goddamn thing do with it—I was just drivin' the car—it was all Rod's fault—"

"Suppose we hear Rod's last name," said Varallo expressionlessly.

"Rodolfo Obregon," said Enrique. "That sonofabitch ain't gonna tie me into this—it was him had the gun, Goddamn it—it was just an accident!"

"But the little girl's just as dead, whatever it was," said Varallo. "Isn't she?"

O'Connor took him over to jail and put in a request for a warrant. It was the end of shift, but Varallo went down to Records and without much trouble found Obregon listed. He was nineteen now, and there was a recent address on Garfield Avenue. He'd been picked up by Traffic for possession and carrying a concealed weapon as recently as last Friday, and probably the only reason he hadn't been gathered in at the gang rumble was that he'd still been in jail, hadn't made bail until Monday.

They left a note for the night watch and went home.

Cynthia had been missing for four days, and Mrs. Emery had stopped calling altogether.

Last night's stolen cab had turned up, out on East Broadway again, and the lab would be going over it. Just after the night watch came on there was a new heist called in, and Harvey went out on that. Rhys and Hunter went out to see if they could pick up this Rodolfo Obregon.

At the address on Garfield they found a large family all at home: mother, three sisters, four brothers of assorted ages, a color TV going full blast, and what was evidently the *paterfamilias* snoring dead drunk on the living room couch. The mother didn't have any English.

"Rodolfo," said Rhys, "here?" They had the badges out.

A sharp-faced boy about ten said, "She don't hear you, cop, she's deaf both ears. Yeah, Rod's here, back in his room. You from the welfare?"

"What? No."

"Oh. The welfare, they said somebody come to get *him*"—he nodded at the sodden figure on the couch—"take to the hospital, the welfare lady said."

At the back of the house, the TV was mercifully less obtrusive. They found Rodolfo lying on a studio couch looking at a hardcore porno magazine. He acknowledged his name, and was stupefied to find himself under arrest.

"And isn't that helpful," said Hunter. He and Rhys had spotted it at the same time, the shotgun leaning against the wall in a corner. It was helpful, of course, because when the evidence was in plain sight they didn't have to get a search warrant. They bagged it as evidence, to drop off at the lab, and booked Rodolfo into jail.

At home, Delia called Hildy. Alex was already asleep, and it wasn't likely he'd wake till morning. She had a leisurely vodka gimlet before dinner, and spent the evening over Goudge again, an unexpectedly charming book, *The Blue Hills*.

But they were all, of course, still thinking about Cynthia.

And nobody had called or come in to say that they had recognized the Identikit sketch.

Varallo was off on Friday. It had drizzled again slightly yesterday, stopped about midnight. Laura started off for the market about ten o'clock, and seeing her off he surveyed his roses gloomily. In the back yard, the side yard, the front, they were a sodden mess, and the weeds flourishing everywhere, and it was too muddy and wet to do anything about it.

Ginevra was contentedly settled down with a coloring book, and Johnny busy with toys on the living room floor. It had turned cold again after the rain, and Gideon Algernon Cadwallader was strategically curled up by the floor register. Varallo wandered around at loose ends, looked at Laura's library books, and finally settled down with one about Victorian murder cases. Busman's holiday. He wondered suddenly if he had remembered to tell Delia about Rosalie. What with Enrique and Rodolfo showing up— Hollywood had turned up Sally Brady, at a cheap room on Harold Way, and she had told him that Rosalie came from a town called Lucas in Kansas.

CHAPTER 6

Varallo had remembered to tell Delia, and she tied up that loose
end on Friday morning. Lucas, Kansas, was evidently a very
small town, and eventually she was talking to a Sheriff Enderby,
who sounded fatherly and kind. He remembered Rosalie King
all right, he said—she ran away from home a good three years
back, it was a nice family too, and they'd never heard from her.
He was surely sorry to hear she was dead, and in such a way.
Her folks would probably want to bring her back for a funeral.
"They live pretty far out in the country, miss— I'll try to get out
there some time today, break the news, and get back to you."

There was a report in from the lab: the latest stolen cab was
clean, no extraneous prints. It was a clear cold day, the rain apparently over for a while. And Cynthia was still missing. There
wasn't anywhere to go on it, but there wasn't much to do on the
various cases on hand either. They could bring Robert Porter in
to talk to, and he was a chancy, wild one: if he was the X on
Eleanor Garvin, he might break and admit it without much
prodding, but a juvenile, and all the tricky rules—it was all too
likely he could never be charged. She wanted to talk to Varallo
about that before they made any move.

She went up to the Shaker Mountain Inn and talked to the
manager. Had there been any little trouble here recently, customers getting fresh with the waitresses; any vandalism or theft
in the parking lot? Nothing like that, he said, no hint of any
trouble. He was very concerned about Cynthia; she was, he said,
a very nice girl.

There had been a story in the *News-Press* on Wednesday
night, LOCAL GIRL MISSING. And tonight the Gilmores, if they
saw the paper, would find out how and why Connie had died,

ripped apart by the shotgun. Just because Rodolfo wanted to be sure the gun worked O.K.

Katz was muttering to himself again and vainly studying a map of Glendale for inspiration because the midget burglar had struck again. It was a carbon copy of the other cases, except that it hadn't been discovered right away. The people had been on a trip since Wednesday; the husband was in insurance, and they'd gone to a company seminar in Santa Barbara, just driven home this morning.

This time the midget had gone in through a bathroom window about twelve by nine, and as usual proceeded to pull the slick professional job. The people, whose name was Bechtel, were still counting their belongings, but by what they could say so far, he had got away with a nice pile of loot: some diamond jewelry, a mink stole, two cameras, a portable TV. The address, of course, was smack in the middle of the small area involved: Graynold Avenue.

John Poor was out on another job, a break-in at a liquor store on Glenoaks. Katz had just lit his tenth cigarette since getting back from the Graynold house when the phone shrilled at him.

"He's been here again!" said Vinson in a wail. "You never saw anything like it—and by God, this time he had to have had a key! And there just can't be another key around—"

That house up above the college. Katz went up there to pass the time, though technically it wasn't a burglary; Vinson admitted that. Vinson was waiting, and opened the door to him before he could ring the bell.

"My God," he said. "My God. It was perfectly all right yesterday, I showed it to some people. I got our cleaning service to come up and straighten up all the mess—and like I told you on the phone, there's nothing actually missing—and just like before, no sign of a break-in. And we both said, that damn cat door couldn't be the answer because even if anybody could reach through and up to the doorknob, damn it, you need a key to unlock the dead bolt! But I blocked the damn thing with plywood anyway, and it hasn't been touched. But look at this mess! The only reason I came up, I left my favorite pipe on the kitchen table when I was showing the people through. I came to get it and—"

This time the drunken burglar—or vandal—had gone upstairs. The toilet paper started, or rather ended, on the stairs: it wound dizzily upward and festooned all four bedrooms and the central hall, what looked like miles of toilet paper, all bright pink—until the source ran out in the two full bathrooms. There was a fireplace in the master bedroom, and a pair of large hurricane lamps had been smashed on the tile hearth, and the fire tools—poker, tongs, shovel, broom—were scattered in the middle of the room. The medicine cupboard doors were both open, all the closet doors and the linen-closet doors. All the lamps in the bedrooms had been thrown onto the floor and their shades severely dented. There had been dust sheets over the stripped beds, and they had been torn off and ripped into shreds, the pieces scattered far and wide. There were large and small gobs of dried mud all over the floors.

"Why?" wailed Vinson. "What fun does anybody get out of making such a mess? And how in hell does the bastard get *in*? Look, the lawyer said she was a secretive old lady, no close friends—there simply can't be a duplicate key anywhere— I swear to God—"

Katz looked at the mess and sighed. It was just another mystery.

Just after the lunch break the kickback came in from LAPD: the latent prints from the Milburn house weren't in their records. Delia hadn't been on that, but she had seen the reports, heard Varallo and Forbes discuss it. Last Sunday night, and Vic had been surprised about that. She passed the report on to Forbes when he came back after lunch. "Damn," said Forbes, looking at it. "So, the amateur's not on file yet. Yes, the daughter and her husband had it dinned into her, keep the doors locked and be careful—and by all accounts she would have been. It is a little funny when you think about it—why did she open the door?"

"I think I'd like to see the place," said Delia.

Forbes shrugged. "Maybe female intuition will turn up a lead."

At the old frame house on Wing Street Mrs. Kilmer's Dart was in the drive, and she let them in. "I just don't seem to have the heart to clean the place up myself, but it'll have to be done.

The funeral's on Monday. We'll be selling the house, of course. I've been packing up her best things for the salvage." She looked at Delia curiously.

"Mrs. Kilmer, it looks as if your mother voluntarily opened the door to whoever killed her. There's no sign of forced entry, and we know it was probably after dark on Sunday night," said Delia. "Can you suggest—"

"Well, that's hard to believe," said Mrs. Kilmer, surprised.

"She wouldn't have lived long after she was knocked down. Who would she have opened the door to, let in voluntarily? Who did she know, who were her friends?"

"Well, for the Lord's sake," said Mrs. Kilmer, "nobody who knew her did that to her! What on earth do you mean? No friend would—"

"No," said Delia vaguely, "but people—overlap. Say someone who knew one of her friends came to the door, said he had a message, or—would she have let him in, even opened the door?"

"Not to a strange man, after dark," said Mrs. Kilmer flatly. "And the screen door was unhooked too. She'd only have done that to let somebody in. Do you think I haven't puzzled over it too? But as to people she knew—what did you say your name was?— Miss Riordan, look, she was an old lady, a lot of her friends were dead or can't visit people anymore. She and Daddy used to go to the Fosters' to play cards, they had other friends, they got around, the library, a movie once in a while—but then Daddy's arthritis got so bad it was hard for him to drive, and by then she couldn't drive at night—the year after Daddy died her eyes got so bad they wouldn't renew her license. She didn't get out much at all. I took her to the market once a week, and if she wanted to go shopping, visit somebody, she'd ask and I'd take her, but it wasn't often. You see, so many of her old friends were in the same situation. When people get old— Mrs. Arnold, they taught at the same school for years, she had a stroke two years ago and her daughter has her in a nursing home way down in Orange county. And her other old friend Eunice Ward, she never really got on her feet again after breaking her hip, they used to talk on the phone a couple of times a week and once in a while I'd take Mother to see her, but it's down in Santa Monica—a little drive. And then Mrs. Dagwood, she lived across the street for years, Mother and Daddy knew them well, but she sold the house and moved to an apartment when her husband died, and she can't drive anymore either—she's a little older than Mother. She's right here in town, they talked on the phone— But the Sampsons are both dead, and the Fosters, and the Thomases. And Frances Bradwell, she was another teacher at the school, went back East to live with her daughter, they just wrote to each other. Mother did a lot of hand work, crocheting and knitting, and she read a lot—she never cared for TV, wouldn't have one. And in nice weather she still worked a little in the garden."

Forbes moved restlessly. They were sitting here in the ransacked living room. "Look," he said, "just an idea. If somebody rang the bell and said he had a telegram for her, or a special delivery letter, do you think she'd have automatically unhooked the screen door to take it?"

"Well, I don't know," said Mrs. Kilmer slowly. "We'd both told her over and over, be careful about opening the door to anybody she didn't know, and never at night— Of course, if he'd said something like that, she might have been flustered, afraid somebody had died, and I suppose she might have—"

Delia said, "Or if he said, I've got a note from Mrs. Dagwood, or Mrs. Ward—"

"Well, maybe," said Mrs. Kilmer doubtfully. "But she'd put the porch light on first, before she opened the inside door, and, Miss Riordan, Mother wasn't a foolish old lady, she was pretty sharp, all her mental faculties, and she could see well enough at that distance. She'd never have opened the screen door to anybody who didn't look perfectly all right, respectable, and she'd be extra cautious about somebody she'd never seen before. I just can't see her doing that. But nobody she knew would have done —*that!* I just don't understand it at all."

Forbes got up and said to Delia, "Well, seen all you want?" She followed him out, and at the curb looked up and down the block. The double row of ramshackle little houses—years and years back a pleasantly quiet middle-class street of owner-occupied homes—now stretched drearily out on either side of the Milburn house, now a near slum, if Glendale could be said to possess any. At one end of the block a little crowd of early-teenage boys were playing football in the street—of course school let out earlier now than it ever used to—and the clear cold light was merciless on the cracked sidewalks, the pothole-scarred asphalt street. A mongrel dog ran along the gutter. Forbes opened the door for her and she got in.

"She couldn't be sure about that," he said, settling himself behind the wheel. "Mrs. Milburn was an old lady, and that kind of excuse—the telegram—it's all too likely she'd unhook the screen door without thinking twice. And respectable be damned. It was a dark rainy night, she wouldn't expect a messenger to be dressed to the nines." He was silent, and then added, "But there's still something funny about it, because it doesn't match."

"Oh, yes," said Delia, catching the thought easily. "It doesn't, does it? Nobody would expect her to have anything of much value in that place—why go even to that little trouble to get her to open the door? Yes, so I wonder if there was a little rumor around the neighborhood that she did have. You know how a story like that gets started, about the old person living alone."

Forbes agreed that that was possible. "I'd like to poke around here a little," said Delia, "and try to find out. But nobody here would open up to a cop, and I can't think of an excuse other-wise— Avon lady or insurance agent, no good. But you know, Jeff, it hangs together in a way, because a good many of the people along here now wouldn't have much education, and it'd have been known that she'd been a teacher, a professional woman. They might have thought she had more money than other people. Than any of them, at least."

"And another thing that occurs to me," said Forbes, "is that little collection of jewelry Mrs. Kilmer described is very damn ordinary—garnets, old-fashioned bracelets, old Bulova watch. Even if an honest pawnbroker took it in, he might not connect it with the items on the hot list."

"Aren't you the optimist," said Delia.

"Well, there are always the heisters to chase down."

On Friday night at about eight o'clock Patrolman Bill Wat-kins was cruising down Foothill Boulevard in La Crescenta, an area that the Glendale police also covered, when he got a call to unknown trouble at an address on Rockdell Street. He wasn't far off, and got up there in eight minutes. It was a nice-looking house set far back from the street with a lawn in front, and there were people on the lawn. There weren't any street lights up here, it was damned dark, and he got out with his flashlight in his hand. There were a couple of other flashlights up there. A man came hurrying up to him.

"Where's the damn ambulance?" another man was shouting. "Called the ambulance before the police—where's—"

"What's the trouble here?" asked Watkins. There were some females crying somewhere, and one of them kept moaning, "Michael— Michael— Michael—"

"I'm Albert Victor," said the man. "We don't know—we didn't hear anything—my daughter's boyfriend was coming to pick her up—he was late, and we wondered—she called, and the Fitzpatricks said he left at a quarter to seven—they started down here, we thought maybe an accident, but when they got here they found him—right up there—and we never heard a thing—that's the Fitzpatricks' car, I mean the one he was driving, right in front—he must have just got here—we just don't know—somebody attacking him just when he got here—"

"Where's the ambulance, for God's sake? I can't find a pulse —oh, God, not Michael, don't let this happen to us—oh, God—"

Watkins went toward the crying, flashlight on, and about ten feet up on the lawn a big young fellow was lying face up and unconscious. It looked as if he'd had a going-over all right, jacket ripped half off him and his face bloody. Watkins bent, and after a minute raised a faint pulse.

"Oh, God, where's the ambulance—" But just then it came, roaring up the narrow street, and the paramedics got out. They were quick, as usual; it seemed to Watkins that in about three minutes they were loading the stretcher into the big red squad.

"I'm going with him, John, I've got to—"

"Yes, yes, I'll follow you—oh, God, don't let this happen—" The ambulance took off, and a car parked farther up the street came to life and started after it, and there were left three people standing in the front yard, one of them a girl crying brokenheartedly.

"Can we make some more sense out of this, Mr. Victor? I have to put in a report."

"Yes, I'm sorry, I—oh, my God, I hope he's going to be all right! My God, but we don't know what happened—"

"What's his name, sir?"

"Michael Fitzpatrick— I told you, my daughter Phyllis' boy-friend. He was supposed to pick her up at seven—"

Watkins swung the flash, and the two females blinked in the sudden glare. Suddenly all three people moved and huddled together and the man put an arm around each of them. "We've just got to pray he'll be all right," he said. He was a man in his forties, thin and dark and good looking. The woman on his right looked about the same age, and the other one, Watkins saw, was just a kid—about seventeen, and probably pretty when her face wasn't all contorted with tears.

"He didn't come," said Victor, "and we thought there might have been an accident. Phyllis called the Fitzpatricks and they came—they live up on Hopeton Road— But we never heard anything here—he must have been attacked, been lying there—looked as if he'd been beaten up, but who'd do such a thing to Mike? It's just senseless—"

Watkins went back to the squad to call in. In his two years of riding a squad, he had run into a lot of senseless things. He'd also seen a lot of injured and dead people, and his look at Michael Fitzpatrick led him to call in the report as assault with intent. That was the end of his responsibility here. Whatever had happened to Michael Fitzpatrick, it was up to the dicks in the front office to find out.

Delia had just come in on Saturday morning when Sheriff Enderby called from Lucas, Kansas. "I got out there late yesterday, to talk to the Kings," he told Delia. "Poor folks were all broken up to hear about Rosalie. Never heard a word from her all these years. Like I figured, they want her sent back for a funeral here. They'll pay for everything. It'd be the Rose Funeral Home in Lucas. Can you take care of that?"

"Surely," said Delia. "I'll set it up, Sheriff." She called the morgue and set that up. Varallo came in with Gonzales, and on their heels a messenger came up from Communications with the kickback from the FBI on the prints from the Milburn house. The Feds didn't know them either.

"Fingerprints are only useful if somebody's got them on file," said Varallo mildly.

"Delia has a theory about Milburn," said Forbes.

"After a fashion," said Delia. She told Varallo what Mrs. Kilmer had said yesterday.

"I still think the telegram idea is simpler," said Forbes.

"I rather like that myself," said Varallo. "And for a reason—um, yes—neither of you seems to have thought of. So she was cautious." He passed a hand down his profile thoughtfully. "To a woman of Mrs. Milburn's age—well, when she was a young woman, people didn't send telegrams as a matter of course, to confirm a lunch date or say happy birthday. It was a serious thing—you only sent telegrams to say FATHER DIED LAST NIGHT, FUNERAL SUNDAY, or ROSE'S BABY BORN YESTERDAY BOY NINE POUNDS. So if Mrs. Milburn answered her door Sunday night and somebody said there was a telegram, she'd have—"

"Been flustered," said Delia. "As Mrs. Kilmer said. Yes, I hadn't thought of it like that."

"She'd expect important news in a telegram—the death of the friend back East, for instance—so it's very possible that she'd have forgotten any caution at all in her interest in seeing it. She'd have unhooked the screen door as soon as she heard the word. Yes, I like it."

"I don't think I do, much," said Delia. "Oh, I see what you mean. But Mrs. Kilmer said she wasn't a fool, had all her faculties. And if you stop to think, as long as we're beating the telegram to death, however she may have felt about telegrams fifty years ago, she'd lived in a city all her life, and she was an educated woman—surely she'd know that Western Union doesn't send messengers anymore? They phone you, and ask if you want a copy, and if you do, they send it by mail."

"Well," said Forbes. "Yes. Would she? It's kind of up in the air."

"If we can go by what Mrs. Kilmer says, and she knew her own mother after all," said Delia reasonably, "I think she was a fairly shrewd old lady, and aware of the crime rate and cautious. I don't think she'd have unhooked the screen door after dark unless she knew who was there—unless it was somebody she recognized and trusted."

"Any candidates?" asked Varallo.

She shook her head. "But I thought—well, people overlap. Just off the top of my mind—this Mrs. Dagwood, say. She prob-

ably has a family—grandchildren? Mrs. Milburn had known her
for over forty years, even if she didn't get around much anymore
she'd have known the family. That Mrs. Ward, ditto. Any of her
old friends. So all right, her friends were all respectable law-
abiding people—that kind doesn't always have the same kind of
grandchildren these days. If Mrs. Dagwood's sixteen-year-old
grandson rang Mrs. Milburn's bell and said, I've got a note for
you from Grandma—she'd know him, and never think twice."

"Now that is off the top of your mind," said Varallo.

"I think it had to be somebody like that, Vic."

"And do you have any explanation why somebody like that
used his supposed connection to get let into her house? Why?
The casual burglar isn't often very smart, and nowadays a lot of
criminals use the dope and aren't thinking straight anyway.
Conceivably, one like that could pick any house to knock over,
and not give a damn whether he killed the householder in the
process. But of all people, anybody who knew anything about
Mrs. Milburn would know she didn't have anything worth stealing."

Delia was silent.

"And there is now this damned thing," said Varallo. "This assault last night. We don't know whether it's going to turn into a
homicide. Suppose you chase down to the hospital and see what
it looks like, and we'll take it from there."

"What's it all about? I haven't seen the night report."

He handed it over. "Probably kids fighting over a girl or
something."

"And another thought I had about Milburn," said Forbes,
"that loot was damned anonymous. Even the honest pawnbroker—"

They were still kicking it around when Delia left.

The emergency hospital was the old Glendale Memorial on
the corner of Los Feliz. There, the badge got her cooperation,
but it was a busy place and she was handed from one person to
another until eventually she found herself up on the ninth floor
explaining all over again to a worried-looking RN at the first
nurses' station in this wing. The RN listened with her eyes over
Delia's shoulder, and interrupted her to say crossly, "I understand that the police are concerned, but surely it can wait. I'm
not going to have you infringing on Dr. Terrill's time when he's

been on duty for twenty hours—he hadn't any business staying on like this, but none of them has any sense when it comes to their own health—" She got up suddenly, her eyes focusing, and Delia swung around.

The man in the corridor was just shrugging into a suit jacket, and indefinably he was stamped as a doctor—by the set of mouth, stoop of shoulder, something less visible. Delia marched up to him and began to ask her question.

"Now it can *wait*," said the nurse angrily. "You're tired to death, doctor, and you could have left six hours ago—the idea of calling you out in the first place—"

"Simmer down, Nancy," he said. He was a man in late middle age, with fine wrinkles around his tired eyes and a wide firm mouth. "You're police? Want to know about the Fitzpatrick boy. All right. Come down here." He led her to a little waiting room halfway down the corridor. There were chairs and a table. He sat down, put his hat on the table and fumbled for a pack of cigarettes.

"We'd like to know how badly he's hurt, doctor, whether he's going to live."

"Oh, he'll live," said Dr. Terrill. His voice was level. "I delivered that boy," he said, "back when I was in general practice. Eighteen years ago. You hear a lot about the worthless kids getting into all kinds of trouble these days—but there are a lot of good ones too, you know. I've known the Fitzpatricks for twenty years. Good people. The best. Raised a good boy. They wanted more, but no luck. Michael's about the best too, you know?" He was watching the smoke from his cigarette curl up lazily. "Very mature for his age. Superior IQ. Steady boy, straight-A student and Honor Roll. Quite the physical-fitness nut—he always kidded me about smoking. Due for a scholarship at Stanford—going to be a lawyer like his father."

"Doctor—"

"I don't know why it happened or who did it, but what I can tell you—he was savagely attacked and beaten, with some kind of weapon or weapons—iron pipe, anything like that, hard smooth surface, anyway. I should judge it must have been more than one man—as I say, Mike's something of an athlete, six-one, a hundred and eighty. There are internal injuries—he was probably jumped on after he was down—" Terrill stopped abruptly and after a moment added in a conversational tone, "The Fitzpatricks are both here, but you can't talk to them. I had to tell them the prognosis and they're both in shock. It may have been two or three men who attacked him, or more. Internal injuries as I said, broken ribs, one puncturing a lung, compound fractures of both legs and one arm. But also his spine is fractured in several places"—he put one hand on the back of his neck in unconscious gesture—"and the damage is quite irreparable. With plenty of time, and a lot of therapy, he may regain the use of the other arm, but he'll be paralyzed from the neck down." He stabbed out the cigarette. "Do you have any idea of what happened yet? Who did it?"

Delia shook her head. "We're just on it."

Dr. Terrill got up. "Well, you go and find out," he said in a suddenly hard voice. "We never have enough of the really top people around in the world, and that boy's one of them. It is just one hell of a pity that when you do catch them, they won't be hanged or electrocuted out of hand. And at that, it'd be more merciful than what that boy's going to live through." He picked up his hat from the table and walked out.

No, she thought, there wasn't any plan in the universe at all. Things happening at random.

When she got back to the office and passed that on, Gonzales had brought in a possible suspect for one of the heists and Forbes was helping out on the questioning. "Oh, God," said Varallo, "what a thing. And it's Saturday, I can't get at anybody at the school. I'd better see the girl, she'll know his friends, whether anybody had a grudge on him. What a hell of a thing." He went out reluctantly.

A routine report came in about an hour later from a squad car: a dead body, but nothing to do with them. It was an old lady in a house on Western Avenue, and the paramedics said it was a natural death; the regular doctor had been contacted and was ready to give a death certificate.

Delia went downstairs at noon to see if Mary could go to lunch with her; they walked down to the little coffee shop. "What did you think of the Porter boy?" asked Mary.

"Both Vic and I think he could be the one who killed the Garvin woman, but there's no evidence to hang it on him."

"No. I can see that. Pity. But if he's off the rails that far, sooner or later he'll get dropped on for something."

Varallo went up to the Victor house in La Crescenta and found all three of the Victors there. The girl was a very pretty blonde, still tearful. Cravenly, he didn't tell them anything about the boy's condition; they'd find out soon enough. The girl told him that Mike's best friends were Jay Meyer, Eddy Beck, Denis Piper. She knew their addresses.

He found the first two at the Meyer home, surprisingly playing chess at a very handsome board in a pleasant big family room at the back of the house. They were shocked and shaken to hear about Mike; again, he didn't tell them how bad it was. Jay was short and stocky, Eddy tall and thin. "We hadn't seen him all week," said Jay. "He'd been down with flu, out of school. My God, we had a date to go bowling tomorrow night." These were obviously superior high-school seniors, more than mature for their age, and by what they knew that was expectable: Mike was the same kind. He realized suddenly that Mike and these other boys would be students at La Crescenta High.

"Had he had any trouble with anyone lately? At school? Anybody have a grudge on him?"

"My God, no," said Eddy. "Mike's a very steady guy, kind of a loner, he never has any trouble with anybody. He's a serious guy, all out for the straight As, he doesn't pal around with much of anybody but us and Den Piper. They've both been down with the flu all week, but I talked to Mike on the phone yesterday afternoon, he sounded just like usual— I was kidding him about missing all the excitement on campus, I guess you know about that. None of us could ever understand those idiots who go in for the dope—that kind, not many brains to start with, and the dope scrambles what's left."

"Well, you see, sir," said Jay, "I guess Mike—and the rest of us—don't have an awful lot in common with a lot of the other seniors, we're interested in different things they don't go for, not to say we're any better or anything. This is awful, about Mike. We'd better go see his mother and father, they'll be all broken up. I hope he's going to be all right."

"Phyllis too," said Eddy. "They've been going steady quite

awhile. She's a nice girl. But so far as either of us know, there's nobody'd have any reason to rough up Mike. Do you think it might have been—well, just somebody like a drunk or a hold-up man, just tried to roll him for his wallet? I mean, Mike!—the mildest guy you'd want to meet—"

"Possibly," said Varallo mendaciously. Actually, it wasn't possible. That short residential street was off the beaten path, and a long way from a main drag. Whoever had beaten and stomped Mike Fitzpatrick nearly to death had been lying in wait for him.

"Can we go to see him?"

"I don't know," said Varallo. "You'd better call the hospital."

"Okay," said Jay. "I sure hope he'll be all right." They were good, steady, serious boys, and good friends to Mike; he'd be needing them.

Varallo found the Piper house with some difficulty, hidden behind a forest of pine trees at the top of a hill, and Mrs. Piper, who was a good-looking diminutive redhead, was inexplicably thrown into a rage by his asking for Denis. "I told him he was an idiot!" she said. "But try to talk to an eighteen-year-old! Supposed to have an IQ of a hundred and seventy, and if that's the best use he can make of it—! Well, I suppose I'll be an idiot too and nurse him all over again if he has a relapse."

"He isn't here?" asked Varallo.

"In bed with the flu all last week," she said crisply, "and a fever of a hundred and two up to Thursday. And when his father and Lee, that's his older brother, proposed to spend the weekend skiing at Big Bear, Den had to go along. I told him he was an idiot, but he was feeling fine then, you know how they bounce back at that age."

"Well. When do you expect him back?"

"Late sometime tomorrow night. By the way, what on earth do the police want with Den? Not that you look like a policeman."

He told her about Mike, and her expression changed to horror.

Late Saturday afternoon, a man came uncertainly into the detective office and looked around. Nobody was there but Delia, Katz over in his corner, Poor typing a report. The man looked vaguely familiar to Delia, and suddenly he spotted her and came over to her desk. It was Orley, the part-owner of the Magnolia Cafe, where Alice Bailey had been shot.

"Hello, Mr. Orley." She smiled at him.

"Didn't know if you'd remember me. You got a minute?"

"Surely."

He sat down in Varallo's desk chair and said, "You haven't found the fellow who did it yet. I still can't get over that— damnedest thing I ever saw. I want to ask you something. It's about that picture. That Identikit picture."

"What about it, Mr. Orley?"

"Well—" He scratched his head. "All the papers ran it— I looked to see. And Ada says it's a good likeness, it's him to the life, and she got a good look at him, she ought to know. You'd think somebody who knows him would have spotted it by now, wouldn't you? But a lot of people read the headlines and not much else. I'd like to ask if I can have two or three copies of it, to put up in the cafe."

"Why, yes. The lab can run off as many as you like. Why?"

"Ada and I've been talking," he said. "She's got an idea that he'd been in the place, maybe more than once. We get a good many regulars, and she's got the idea that if we put up that picture where the customers can't help seeing it, it might jog somebody's memory."

"Well, it's certainly an idea," said Delia. "You may have something there, Mr. Orley. Come on, let's go down to the lab."

Burt obligingly ran off five copies for him, and showed him how the Identikit worked, and he went off pleasedly. Delia didn't really think anything would come of it, but you never knew.

Patrolman Bill Watkins, riding on his lonely night job, had lost track of time. The end of his shift was midnight, and it wasn't until he looked at his watch and found it still said twenty of twelve as it had about fifteen minutes ago that he realized it had stopped. He swore and turned around to head in. He was way up on Boston then, and at that hour it was deserted and empty. He went down to Foothill, and two blocks down he came across a sedan rammed up over the curb at the corner of Lauderdale, engine and lights still on, driver's door open.

"Hell!" he said. But of course he had to stop. It was a Chevy four-door, a fairly recent model. He looked in the glove compartment and found the registration all in order: Evelyn Wortman, an address on Paraiso Way in La Crescenta. He went back to the squad and called it in. Communications said, "What the hell are you doing, still roaming around up there? It's twelve-forty and some poor bastard on night shift needs your squad. All right, sit on it until you get a back-up."

But it was a very funny thing, of course, and he took his flashlight and went looking, along Foothill a little way and then up Lauderdale. Just as Yeager drove up in another squad he found her. She was lying in the gutter about twenty-five feet up Lauderdale, all sprawled out, and when the flash showed her staring open eyes he knew she was dead. He waved the flash at Yeager, who came up in a hurry.

"For God's sake," he said. She wasn't a young woman, she was short and rather fat and gray-haired, and she was wearing a nurse's white uniform, a dark coat thrown out to each side, and her eyes were bulging and her tongue stuck out. "She's been strangled," said Yeager.

"I will be damned," said Watkins. You rode a squad day in day out, the tickets, the accidents, all the humdrum things, and then two nights in a row he'd run into the business for the front-office dicks.

"Well, you go on in," said Yeager. "I'll make the report."

Watkins was just as glad to get out of that. He started back for headquarters, to turn in the squad and go home, but he had forgotten that old maxim that said never two without three.

While Yeager, having called the night watch in the detective office, was knocking on the door of a house on Paraiso Way and talking to an agitated elderly man—"We were just beginning to be worried, she's usually home by eleven-thirty, sometimes she'd be delayed but not often—yes, that's right, Officer, Evelyn Wortman, my daughter. She's a nurse at the Verdugo Haven Convalescent Home on Glendale Avenue, she would have come off duty at eleven o'clock, and she always came straight home— she hasn't had an accident, has she? Has anything happened to her? For God's sake—we've been worried, I was about to call and ask if she'd been delayed—"

While that was going on, Watkins drove down Foothill to La

Crescenta Avenue and headed back for town. He got all the way to where Verdugo Road crossed Doran, about eight blocks from headquarters, when a car nearly sideswiped him and went jinking down past where Verdugo turned into Glendale Avenue. Automatically Watkins switched on his red light and siren and took off after it. At the intersection of Broadway the car swerved and hit the light pole and knocked over the street sign and rammed into the building on the corner, and Watkins called that in, got out to take a look.

The driver was unconscious over the wheel, a young fellow with a beard. There was ID on him, a driver's license in the name of Arthur Wade, address in Burbank. There was a woman's handbag beside him on the front seat, and Watkins looked at that. There was a fat billfold in it containing a driver's license, Social Security card, for a Cynthia Emery. And that rang a bell—a loud bell—and he ran back to the squad.

He didn't get home until after two o'clock, and his wife jumped all over him. "You could have called! I've been pacing the floor, probably you getting shot up and me raising a fatherless child alone—you could have phoned!"

"I'm sorry, hon. We just got sort of busy," said Watkins.

CHAPTER 7

On Sunday morning O'Connor was just getting ready to take Maisie for her weekly run up in the hills above the college. She was an outsize Afghan and needed more exercise than she got. Katharine said, "It's going to start raining again any minute, you'll both get soaked, you'd better skip it—" and the phone rang. Heading for the hall to answer it, O'Connor skidded on a toy automobile and nearly fell flat on his face; he said this and that and Katharine said, "Charles, for heaven's sake—he's quick enough to pick up the decent language—"

Vince uttered a heartfelt roar. "Daddy bwoke my car! Daddy bwoke—"

"Oh, for God's sake." O'Connor picked up the phone. Katy wanted another one, but it seemed to him that one was enough of a handful.

It was Varallo on the other end, to tell him about Wade and Cynthia Emery's handbag. "I knew you'd be interested to hear about it. No, we don't know anything yet. Wade's still unconscious, he's got concussion and he was high on angel dust."

"I will be damned," said O'Connor. "They say when he might come to?"

"Today sometime. The lab's going over the car. And we've got a new homicide, could be run-of-the-mill or something else."

"Well, I might come in later to see what's going on. Don't tell me we're going to start to clean up a few things." Once in a while it happened.

He took Maisie up into the hills above the college and she bounced around excitedly, her long legs flying in all directions, until it started to rain and he towed her back to the car.

A place like a convalescent home was operational around the clock; they didn't have to wait for a conventional hour to call, and Varallo and Delia got to the Verdugo Haven Convalescent Home just after nine o'clock, to talk to the staff. It was a sprawling Spanish-styled building down on South Glendale Avenue, with its own parking lot at one side. Everybody they saw was astonished and grieved to hear about Evelyn Wortman, she'd worked there for years, everybody knew her and liked her, such a nice woman, such a good nurse. The staff here last night wasn't on now, of course, but they got the names of several LVNs on duty in her wing, coming off duty at the same time last night. They went first to see a Mrs. Sagamore at an apartment on Louise Street, and she was more incredulous than grieved.

"Why, she was just coming out the side door when I was starting home— I saw her getting in her car, there wasn't a soul anywhere around— Mrs. Fox drove out of the lot just ahead of me— Well, of course everything was just as usual at work— who on earth would have any reason to murder Evelyn Wortman?"

They went up to La Crescenta to have a look at the terrain. "Who indeed?" said Varallo. "She was fifty-three, no raving beauty by the picture on her license, ordinary woman, evidently an efficient nurse." Delia didn't comment; she was thinking about Arthur Wade in the hospital. Arthur Wade, and Cynthia's handbag on the front seat of his car.

Up at Foothill and Lauderdale, there was nothing to show where Evelyn Wortman's car had been found, but Varallo said, "By what the Traffic man tells us, it looks as if she'd been forced off the road by another car. It could be the driver was just another one drunk or doped up, and when she got out to assess the damage, told him off, he just reached for her—" It started to rain about then, and they got back in the car and went back up the hill to Paraiso Way.

The Wortmans were quite elderly, in the late seventies or older; they were shocked and grieved but also incredulous. "Evelyn's whole life was nursing," quavered the thin old lady. "She hadn't any other interest than her job. Since my arthritis got so bad I'm not much account around the house, Evelyn did everything. She had friends, of course, but she didn't go out much, she hadn't the time—nobody had any reason to want to hurt Evelyn— I just can't seem to take it in—" There were two other daughters there, a Mrs. Baxter and a Mrs. Joyce.

"Just another random thing," said Varallo on the way back to the office. "The way we read it at the scene."

"What it looks like," agreed Delia. "I wonder if that Wade is conscious yet."

He wasn't. Aside from the concussion and the dope he wasn't much hurt. They had just got in, and Delia checked with the hospital, when O'Connor came in stripping off a dripping raincoat. A minute later Burt came in and said, "We just started to look over that Wortman car, and found something interesting. Very pretty. I think you'll like it."

"Oh?"

"Take a look." Burt handed something to Varallo. It was an ordinary little notebook, dime-store variety, about five by seven inches. Varallo opened it to a page of neat small writing in ballpoint pen. Evidently it had been in use as a record of gas mileage, oil changes, lube jobs and the like. "Keep going," said Burt.

The last page contained something different. At the top, a single neat notation of an oil change about a week ago. Below that the rest of the page was covered with large, straggly, disjointed scrawls. "What the hell is this supposed to be?" asked Varallo. "Code or something?"

He could barely make out some of the letters, running crooked across the page. *Foll frm corn lom   Verd nrly hit left s beard   rabbit red   old lic*

And then, the last thing on the page at the bottom, in larger size than the rest, *S S L ⊃ N ʲ.*

"What the hell is this rigmarole? Now wait a minute, I just don't see, but it seems—"

Burt lit a cigarette and stood leaning on the door jamb.

"Let's have a look," said O'Connor.

"Very efficient woman," said Burt to his cigarette. "Quick thinker too. She reached for the only paper available to her while she was driving. Probably kept that in the glove compartment. I understand she was a nurse—she'd have had a ball-point pen in her uniform pocket."

"Now wait just a damn minute here," said O'Connor, poring over the page. Suddenly he grabbed up a County Guide from the top of the file cabinet beside the desk, opened it to the map of Glendale. "Where the hell is that convalescent home?"

"Corner of Glendale and Lomita," said Burt placidly.

"All right—yes—and it'd have been about ten past eleven? Oh, I see," said Varallo. "There wouldn't be so many cars on the road at that hour, even on a Saturday night—and heading for Paraiso Way she'd—"

"Oh, my God," said O'Connor. He'd just heard the gist of the story from Varallo on the phone this morning. "She realized he was following her, she tried to jot something down about it. When she realized the other driver was drunk or whatever— Read it!" He jabbed a finger at the page. *Nearly hit left side—* that was somewhere along Verdugo Road—"

"Was it about then she realized it had been the same car behind her all the way? Because—"

"Because she wrote, *from corner of Lomita*— I will be God-damned!" O'Connor rumpled his curly dark hair distractedly. "There'd be traffic lights operating up to midnight—she might have caught lights along the way— Broadway, Wilson, Lexington, anywhere on up—give her a minute to scribble this down—"

"Sure, they both did," said Burt.

"By that time—maybe as far up as Honolulu or Foothill—she knew it was the same car, trailing her deliberately. It was late and dark and nothing was open at that hour, no handy police station in miles—and she wasn't sure what might happen—" Varallo was hunched over O'Connor's shoulders, over the little notebook flat on the desk. "She didn't know—she couldn't know —whether it was a drunk, would-be rapist, heist man, what—"

"But just in case anything did happen, she tried to put down something about the car—by God, yes—"

"Thinking quick and efficient," said Burt. "Cool female, keeping her head."

"It was a red VW Rabbit—" O'Connor suddenly let out a wordless roar. "Christ almighty!"

"You've got there, have you?" said Burt. "Yeah, she left us the plate number."

"My sweet Jesus!" said O'Connor reverently. "She caught a light, and he was right behind her, and she saw his plate in the rearview mirror, by her own taillights—it was an old license plate, orange on black, instead of the new blue and gold ones—"

"She saw it backward," said Burt enjoyably. "Mirror image. But she got it down for us. A very efficient lady she must have been."

O'Connor grabbed for a pen. "J N C— L S S—"

"Try five," said Burt.

"Oh, my God, yes, of course. My God. JNC-155." He leaped up, and he and Varallo headed for the door as one man, for Communications downstairs.

There was a gadget down there connected to the DMV in Sacramento, which could produce identification of any car in California within five minutes. The policewoman in charge fed the plate-number into it, and at the end of five minutes the teletype began to click and printed out the information. The VW Rabbit wearing that plate was registered to Willard K. Upshaw at an address on Alexander Street in Glendale.

Half an hour after Varallo and O'Connor had left, Edward Garvin came rather uncertainly into the detective office, looked around and recognized Delia and came over to her desk. "I hope I'm not interrupting your work—but naturally I've been concerned to know—well, whether you've discovered anything yet—if you know who—"

"I'm afraid not, Mr. Garvin. A thing like this doesn't give us much evidence to go on, you understand."

"I see," he said. "No, I suppose not." He looked tired and gray; at her gesture he sat down in Varallo's chair. "I suppose not. One hears that so many criminals are using drugs these days—removing the inhibitions so they are all the more disposed to violence— It just seems rather terrible that no one should be punished for— I hoped, with all your well-known efficiency now, you would be able to find out—"

"Unfortunately, we don't solve every crime that comes along, Mr. Garvin. We don't like it either, but there it is. Sometimes there's just no evidence."

"Yes," he said. "I suppose I should have realized that. It's— I miss her, you see."

"Of course you must," said Delia gently.

"We were married thirty-four years," he said abruptly.

"Of course you have your son and daughter," she said conventionally. "I understand you're going to retire next year. Your daughter said something about your moving, to Elsinore—"

"Oh, I won't do that now," he said absently. "No. Well, I'm sorry to have taken your time—and sorry you haven't anything definite to tell me. But I see how difficult it must be for you. Thank you."

"I'm sorry too," said Delia.

He gave her a grave smile and went out.

The address on Alexander Street was a little apartment over a garage behind the front house.

The red VW Rabbit with the right license plate was in the carport built onto the garage. The paint was badly scraped along its right side. The lab would be finding evidence of red VW paint on the left side of Evelyn Wortman's green Chevy.

Willard Upshaw stared at the badges held out to him. Varallo said, "It's about Evelyn Wortman, Mr. Upshaw. Or did you know her name?"

He was a big hulking fellow about thirty, with long stringy brown hair and a beard. He was still in pajamas and an old flannel bathrobe. He said, "How—d'you know—about me?" Obviously he was pretty slow mentally.

"Did you know Miss Wortman?" asked Varallo.

He looked from Varallo to O'Connor. "We'll find out, you know," said O'Connor. "Did you?"

"Yeah," he said. He licked his lips. "Yeah, I knew her."

"What did you have against her?" asked Varallo curiously. "We know you were waiting there, when she started home last night, and followed her all the way, up Verdugo and La Crescenta to Foothill. You got alongside and tried to ram her once, somewhere along Verdugo, didn't you?"

"How—d'you know that?"

"And then," said O'Connor, "up on Foothill you did ram her into the side, at the corner of Lauderdale—and you both got out, and that was her one mistake. She should have stayed locked in the car, but she was probably thinking you were a drunk. And you got hold of her and strangled her. Why? Why the hell? Or did you have any reason?"

Upshaw said, high and excited, "Because it was that nosy old bitch got Mother to make that will! I know it was her! Mother

in that place a long while—and that damn nurse always fussin'
around her—and Mother sayin' how nice she was—look down
her nose at me, an' I heard her ask Mother once how far I got in
school—an' Mother prob'ly told her what the damn doctor said
about part retarded. I shoulda got all that money, Mother's
money, but that damn lawyer got it instead, only give me so
much a month—an' I know it was that damn nurse got Mother
to do like that—"

He kept saying it all over again, on the way in. He was docile
enough for all his size. They made him get dressed, and took
him down to the jail, and sent in the request for the warrant.
"There are some loose ends to tie up on this one," said O'Connor.

"And one of them bothers me a little," said Varallo. "Let's go
look at it." On the way up Verdugo, he pointed it out. "What
was she doing as far down as Lauderdale, Charles? Normally
she'd have turned off Foothill at New York, to go up to Paraiso
Way. I've got a little idea about it." Up there, he drove down
Foothill past Lauderdale, and two blocks on pulled into the
curb. "There you are, *amico*." On the opposite corner was an independent gas station. It had a big red sign on the roof, OPEN
24 HOURS. "There you are. She didn't know if he was drunk or
hopped up or what, but she wasn't going to lead him up to that
dark residential street with the two old people waiting for her.
She knew there'd be somebody here to help, the lights, the
phone. Only he forced her off the road before she could get
here."

"I will be Goddamned," said O'Connor. "A very efficient lady
she was."

They went back to the convalescent home to ask questions.
Mrs. Miriam Upshaw had been a patient there for eleven
months; she'd been partially bedridden after several severe heart
attacks, and she had died two weeks ago, of a final one. Did
they know her lawyer's name? Yes, he had come in to pay the
final bills, arrange for the funeral; he was one Darren Underwood, an office here in town.

They found him at his home address on Cumberland Road, a
sharp-faced elderly man with a bald head and shrewd eyes. He
told them that Mrs. Upshaw hadn't had any other relatives;
she'd been a widow. The son was slightly retarded; he could

hold uncomplicated jobs, and the doctors thought it was better for him to be on his own as much as possible. He had a job now as a parking-lot attendant at an office building. But Underwood had advised Mrs. Upshaw to leave her estate in trust, the only sensible arrangement. There was about a hundred thousand in stock.

"Did anyone at the nursing home have any influence on her about that, do you know?" asked Varallo.

Underwood stared. "Good God, of course not. She made that will four years ago after her husband died."

About two o'clock, with everybody out except Forbes, the hospital called to report that Arthur Wade was conscious. Delia insisted on going along to see him.

They knew more about Wade now; the pedigree on him had come up from LAPD this morning. He was twenty-two, and he had been charged with rape first as a juvenile, twice later as an adult; there were additional charges of assault, drug abuse. He had got probation, finally served eight months in Susanville. He was still on parole, and his parole officer said he had a job at a gas station in Burbank, but the owner said he hadn't seen him in a week.

At the hospital, he looked up at them blankly as Forbes held out the badge. "What did you do with Cynthia, Wade?" asked Forbes. "The girl you kidnapped from the parking lot a week ago tonight?"

"I'm sick," he said weakly. "I can't talk to you."

"You'll talk whether you feel like it or not. What did you do to her, Wade? Where is she?"

He began to cry, easily like a child, incongruously because the tears ran down into his shaggy adult beard. "I didn't mean to do nothing like that," he said. "I don't know why I did it—they said if I did something again I'd go back to jail—but I got— I got a deck of H off a guy I know—that day—and I guess I wasn't thinkin' straight—"

"All right, so what happened?" asked Forbes, sounding tired.

"I was just drivin' around—that night— I come past this parking lot and saw that girl there all alone— I just drove up and asked did she want to go for a ride—and she started to run and scream—and I guess that just set me off— I got hold of her and put her in the car— I guess I knocked her out or maybe she fainted."

"Where is she?" asked Forbes. "What did you do with her?"

Wade said plaintively, "I'm sorry. I'm awful sorry. I think— I think I left her—up in that Stough Park, somewheres around that theater up there."

"Oh, Christ," said Forbes.

He and Gonzales took six Traffic men and went up there in the drizzling rain to look. The open-air Starlight Theater was closed in winter, and the sizable park was all natural wilderness, with a good many trees and shrubs and tall brush. They spread out and hunted as best they could, all of them getting wetter and wetter, but it was an hour and a half and starting to get dark before one of the Traffic men gave a shout and they converged on him.

She was on her back under a big wild lilac bush, only her feet sticking out. She was stark naked and her waitress's uniform, her coat and underclothes, were wadded up beside her. The body wasn't very pretty to look at, but it had been cold weather, it was well preserved, and the doctors would be able to say whether she had been raped, how she had died.

Delia had the job of going to see Mrs. Emery to tell her. Mrs. Emery just said dully, "I knew something terrible had happened to her. I knew she must be dead. I gave up hope long ago."

It was annoying that it happened to be Sunday. They'd like to find out what doctors were familiar with Willard Upshaw, his school record and so on—all that would have to be sorted out for the DA's office. O'Connor was in his office wrestling with the phone and Varallo was just starting to type a report when a young fellow came walking in fast, and passing over Katz and Poor with no interest, headed for Varallo.

"By Mother's description, I guess you're the one talked to her yesterday. I'm Denis Piper."

Varallo swung around to him. He was a slender young fellow with his mother's red hair and a triangular face which might hold charm in lighter moments; right now he was looking serious, his expression taut and worried. "I thought you weren't getting home until tonight," said Varallo.

"Yeah. This is just the hell of a thing about Mike—— Mother knew I'd want to hear, and she called the lodge last night. And Dad knew how I felt when I told him—well, we drove back this morning. Hadn't I better know your name?" Varallo told him. "I talked to Jay and Eddy, and the more I think, I might know what's behind it, and I figured you ought to hear about it." He drew a deep breath.

"Oh?" Varallo lit a cigarette. "So tell on."

"I suppose you know I was at home with the flu all week, and so was Mike. Neither of us was in school. All that ruction on campus—police coming down, we both missed that, heard all about it from Jay and Eddy. But that wasn't until Friday when both of us were sitting up and taking notice again—when we heard about Mark Ryan. And that really did surprise me because I'd have said he was pretty straight. I never liked the guy much, just not my type, but I know he never used the stuff himself—well, come to that, Eddy or Jay or Mike or me wouldn't have heard anything about where the dope was coming from, where to buy it, because everybody'd know we'd report anything definite to the principal—"

"Hang on a minute," said Varallo, and got up and went down to look in O'Connor's cubbyhole. "Something you'll be interested in, Charles." O'Connor followed him back and perched one hip on his desk, nodding at the introduction. "Just go over that again for the lieutenant, Piper."

Obligingly Denis said it again, and went on, "I talked to Mike on the phone on Friday afternoon, he was feeling okay then and going out with Phyllis that night, his mother thought it was too soon, but he said they'd make it an early night. Anyway, we were kicking the dope business around, and I said I was surprised about Ryan, and Mike said it didn't surprise him. He said just that day—last Monday, he came to school even if he was feeling lousy, and in fact he went home before third period, he missed the ruction that next day. But he said about ten o'clock he went to the rest room and walked in on Ryan handing over the pot to some bratty little freshman. He was pretty surprised then, and he gave Ryan hell about it, but he was feeling too sick to do anything about it, he just went home. He—"

O'Connor said in a soft voice, "But Ryan thought he probably would do something?"

"That's what I mean," said Denis. "You see—"

"Oh, yes," said O'Connor. "So when we descended on the scene, big businessman Ryan took it for granted that it was Mike who blew the whistle on him. Christ. Oh, Christ, Vic, this is all our fault. The innocent bystander, Mike. And of course Ryan and the rest of them got sprung on, let's see, Tuesday or Wednesday—they're due to be arraigned day after tomorrow—but they couldn't get at Mike until he went out on Friday night. And how did they know?"

Denis said, "Girls talk a lot, you know. Phyllis is a nice girl. But that baby-faced Allen Sprague has a few nice girls going for him. If one of them called Phyllis and asked if she had a date that night—"

"Oh, Christ, yes," said O'Connor. "It's a long time since I've thought like a teenager. I think we go and talk to big businessman Ryan, Vic."

"I thought you'd want to," said Denis. He added quietly, "But it won't do Mike any good, will it?"

The parents hardly ever home, Ruth Sawyer had said. It did explain this and that. At the handsome big house with the pool, they found Mark Ryan, Allen Sprague, and two more of the boys from last week's raid watching football on TV. "What the hell do you want?" demanded Mark when he faced them at the door.

"You," said O'Connor. "Again. I'm not going to say much to you right now, or I might not be able to keep my hands off you. Just go back and sit down and be quiet. We've got a little looking around to do." They had brought Lew Wallace along, and left him to keep an eye on them while they looked. They still had the search warrant on the house, which wouldn't do them any good because it only specified controlled drugs; but they didn't have to look long or far.

In the big double garage there was a workbench, looking unused, and miscellaneous tools lying around. Standing up in one corner were several short lengths of iron pipe. O'Connor squatted and peered at them. "The arrogant bastards," he said. "They didn't even bother to clean them off." Even with the naked eye, they could see the dark marks of blood, a few hairs adhering to it here and there. There were, hopefully, also some usable fingerprints. "And thank the good God, they're all over eighteen," said O'Connor piously.

They maneuvered the pipes separately into plastic evidence bags and took them out to the car. They went back inside and called a squad to ferry the four of them in. And maybe the other three hadn't been the ones who had lain in wait with Ryan, or maybe they were; none of these kids was as tough as they thought they were, and there was no honor or honesty in them; they'd name names, trying to squirm out of responsibility.

"What the hell do you think you're doing? What's this all—"

"It's about assault with intent to kill, if you want the legal term." O'Connor's dark eyes were very cold. "Due to be arraigned on Tuesday, are you? You'll be arraigned on another charge later on, you bastard."

"You can't—" He stepped backward as he saw the cuffs.

"Don't tell me what I can't do," said O'Connor, and snapped them shut with a little clang.

On the way back, he said seriously to Varallo, "It's funny, but sometimes when you clean up one thing a few other things get straightened out too. Like getting olives out of a bottle."

The night watch hadn't had a call yet, and were idly sitting around talking about football teams, when at nine-forty they had another cab heist reported. "This is getting to be damned monotonous," said Rhys when a beefy-shouldered man walked in and started to tell the tale. But he gave them something new and something funny.

He'd been sent by the dispatcher to pick up a fare at Colorado and Chevy Chase, and of course it was the same pair, blond girl, nondescript man. They gave him an address on Cumberland, and once up in that quiet residential area, the man held the gun on him, took about fifty bucks and off they drove in the cab. He had got a householder up there to call the police for him, and the squad had brought him down to headquarters.

"But listen," he said. "All the while I was driving up there, they were having one hell of an argument. I couldn't hear very much of it, they'd drop their voices. But I got the gist, and it sounded like the girl was mad at him because they were kind of broke. Could be that's the reason they're on the heist, no? Anyway, she was calling him names and she said something about living hand to mouth, and he was trying to blame bad luck. And she called him a lying bastard. But one thing she said sounded damn funny, and she said it twice, so it sticks in my mind. They'd been talking low for a minute, when all of a sudden she flares up at him and she says, 'I tell you, I wish to God I was back in equality right now.' And a couple of minutes later she said it again—wish I was back in equality. Funny."

Funny was hardly the word. "Are you sure of that?" asked Rhys. "Could she have said, oh, equity—like Actors' Equity? Or—well, what else?"

"No, no, I'm sure she said equality. I've got no idea what she meant."

Neither had they. They took a statement from him and sent him home in a squad. "What the hell could she have meant?" said Harvey.

"Something to do with women's lib?" suggested Hunter.

"That doesn't seem to fit the phrase," said Rhys doubtfully. "'I wish I was back in equality.' In the quality? Like, in the quality modeling trade, or something like that?"

There was a heist called in a minute later. Rhys and Hunter went out on it, and on the way Rhys took a detour down to the Communications room and put the question to the six policewomen sitting on the board. Did it ring any sort of bells with them?

They looked at him blankly and said it didn't. And the senseless little phrase went on running through Rhys's mind over and over, annoyingly.

Hearing about Cynthia, and now this morning hearing about Mark Ryan and his henchmen, Delia felt remotely thankful that tomorrow was her day off, that she'd get away from the job at least for a day, from the inevitable knowledge of so much death and madness and pain and violence.

But meanwhile there was more of it to show up today. They wouldn't see much of Varallo or O'Connor; they were busy tying up loose ends, talking to those boys over at the jail. Gonzales was off, and while there were always the heisters to look for, it was still raining. Forbes said he wanted to question Wade again, try to get a more coherent statement from him. They were arguing about the Milburn thing again when the phone rang on Varallo's desk and Delia reached for it.

"Detective Riordan."

"Oh, Miss Riordan," said James Barlow. "I'm sorry to tell you that the church has been broken into and robbed. And vandalized. I've just discovered it." His voice was strained and anxious. "I don't know whether the police will want to look for fingerprints, or—but all the communion cups have been stolen, and my extra robes, and—"

"I'll be over," said Delia. "I'm so sorry, Dr. Barlow." Alex had absolutely no use for churches or ministers or priests; they were all hypocritical vultures, he said, and anyone who paid any attention to them were all damned superstitious idiots. But nobody could help liking Dr. Barlow, and all this ridiculous business about his church was worrying him.

She went over and told Katz that she had a burglary for him. "You too, Brutus?" said Katz sadly.

"In a church." On the way over, she told him about Dr. Barlow and the excitable Latins, and Katz said, "At least you give me a laugh. As Solomon puts it, *The way of a fool is right in his own eyes.* These quarrelsome Christians."

"Silly and stupid, yes, but not at all funny for Barlow and his congregation, Joe."

She hadn't seen Dr. Barlow's church before. It sat on a corner, and it was an old church of gray stucco, not very large. It had a peaked roof and a small bell tower, its own parking lot at one side. There was a black and white sign in front. SUNDAY SCHOOL 9:30—SUNDAY WORSHIP 11 A.M. PRAYER MEETING 9 P.M. WEDNESDAY. And, she remembered, choir practice at 3:30 on Friday afternoon.

Barlow was waiting in the parking lot; he looked a little wild, his gray hair ruffled, as he acknowledged the introduction to Katz.

"This is damnable," he said. "Myrna—my wife—everyone will be so distressed. Damnable!" He looked physically ill. "I usually work on the church accounts at the end of the month. I came down this morning to get that bill from the plumber, I had left it in the pocket of my robe, and I found—"

"Hah," said Katz. "This is where they broke in."

"I saw it as soon as I came up." It was the side door next to the parking lot.

"Used a chisel or a pry rod," said Katz. "That's a good heavy door."

"Yes. And when I went in and saw—" Barlow was looking very angry.

The door led to a small room evidently used as a catchall. There were tables with religious magazines and pamphlets, a row of coat hangers on hooks. From there they went into the main body of the church. After a minute of looking around, Delia said, "My heavens."

"Yes," said Barlow grimly. "Yes."

There were high-backed bench pews, and most of them had been attacked and savagely gouged, pieces chiseled out and scattered. All the hymn books had been ripped apart and the remnants scattered on the floor. The Bible on the pulpit had been torn to pieces and the pieces left on top of the lectern. The rather worn old carpets in the aisles had been slashed in a hundred places. There were piles of human excrement in the aisles, in front of the altar. There were obscenities chalked all over the walls.

Barlow said, "Such hatred, such vindictive destruction, I don't understand how anyone can harbor such feelings. That is, I can understand it intellectually, but emotionally—no, no. Hatred is such a stupid thing—a cancer, it only attacks the parent body." His wide shoulders looked stiff. He said, "God help them if I ever lay hands on them."

"I thought you were supposed to turn the other cheek," said Katz sardonically.

Dr. Barlow's usual smile was charming; now it was terrifying. "That's always the mistake so many people make about Jesus Christ, Mr. Katz. Especially some very good pious citizens who go to church on Sundays. He wasn't a sweet saccharine social worker with a mealy-mouthed message of superstitious repentance. He was full of righteous anger at the ungodly, and He didn't hesitate to scourge them with whips. Which is exactly what I'd like to do to the ungodly who committed this outrage." He hunched his shoulders. "It would be a positive pleasure," he said wistfully. "I boxed for my college, and I was never beaten in the ring—but the gentlemanly rules I'd forget if I got these bastards within reach."

Katz laughed. "And it's about the only thing they understand, brute force."

"My God, yes. And violence begetting violence—we've been warned about that too, but we're fallible human creatures."

"Look," said Katz to Delia, "what you said about this—the thefts in the parking lot, the vandalism—it was kids. Early teenage kids? Well, this doesn't look like that, you know. That's a solid door, it took a man's strength to break it in. Can you give me a list of what's missing, Dr. Barlow?"

"The communion cups," said Barlow. "They're silver-plated, three dozen of them. I have no idea what they'd be worth. Two of my extra robes, from the vestry. It could have happened any time after the service yesterday, the patrol cars have only been keeping a special watch when there are cars in the parking lot."

"Well, you'd better give me a description of the cups," said Katz. "I think there's a Yiddish proverb says *money answereth all things,* and I don't suppose they walked off with the silver for anything but religious reasons—if that's the word—but they may decide to make a little profit on the side from a pawnbroker. Silver quotations were up again today."

Technically it was a burglary, but it had started out as Robbery-Homicide business, and Katz conned her into writing the report on it.

She rolled the forms and carbon in automatically. She thought about Cynthia—and the efficient brisk nurse Evelyn Wortman—and Mike Fitzpatrick. And Connie.

If there could be a planning power anywhere, so much of the plan seemed to be bent toward producing evil, not the other way round as the superstitious idiots believed.

Before she started the report she called Laura and arranged to meet her for lunch tomorrow.

CHAPTER 8

Varallo and O'Connor spent all Monday on the red tape, on Upshaw, on the four high-school boys. Sprague and the other two came apart right away, and admitted the attack on Mike Fitzpatrick, naming Ryan as the instigator. Ryan wasn't saying anything, and his father would probably get him a fast-talking lawyer. If they had killed Mike Fitzpatrick instead of crippling him for life, they'd all be up for Murder One; as it was, the charge would be assault with intent to kill, and Ryan might get a five-to-ten, the others less, and they'd all be out in three years or so.

Forbes had gone to question Arthur Wade again; he was now out of the hospital and lodged in jail. But Wade had shut up and was now claiming he'd been delirious yesterday, his rights violated, and he didn't know a thing about Cynthia Emery.

At least nothing new went down; and Delia hadn't actually been very busy, but she was tired to death when she got home on Monday night. When she had called Hildy—it had been one of the bad days for Alex, and she didn't have to go out again, into the rain—she had a drink before dinner, and settled down with a library book.

Tuesday morning was clear and very cold. She changed the bed, and put the laundry in the washing machine, then in the dryer; dusted the big empty living room, mopped the kitchen floor. She decided to wear her new smart navy two-piece dress, the red coat and shoes. But at eleven-thirty, as she was putting on makeup, fastening the gold brooch on the lapel of the coat, she looked at the ring as she picked it up to slide it on, and stopped. Alex's old ring—she had worn it for years, it was part of her: the man's heavy bloodstone ring with the O'Riordan crest cut in the stone. Quite suddenly she remembered that there was a jewel box that had belonged to her mother. Somewhere—

Alex's old room upstairs. A little scene came into her mind vividly, and she hadn't thought of it for all these years, maybe never since it had happened. She had come home from school, and it was Alex's day off, and he was sitting on his bed with the box there beside him, and she had asked about it— "Just some things of your mother's, never mind—" and he had put it away in a drawer and wouldn't answer any questions. He never would talk about her mother at all; she'd stopped asking questions. The only thing Delia knew about her was that her name had been Cordelia Chalfont, and she'd been an orphan without any relatives.

She didn't know why she felt the sudden irrational impulse to pry into the past, but she went upstairs—for the first time in months. She thought vaguely that it would be only sensible to sell the old over-large house; she thought about a conveniently small, bright little apartment somewhere, closer to the job. But the awful chore of sorting out everything, finding a new place, the upset of moving, daunted her as she thought about it.

After a search, she found the shabby simulated-leather jewel case in the bottom drawer of the old dresser in the front bedroom. She'd only seen it that once before. She lifted the lid, and saw that there wasn't much in it. There was an enlargement of a snapshot in the bottom compartment, and she took it out curiously. It was an old black-and-white snapshot, it was a little fuzzy, and it showed a pretty smiling young woman sitting on a couch with a cat on her lap; a black cat with a white chest. Cordelia Chalfont. You couldn't tell, since it wasn't a color shot, whether her hair had been light or dark brown; the color of her eyes. And suddenly Delia thought, she was younger than I am now when she died, and felt a queer little shock at the realization. There was another paper in the bottom of the box, and she picked it up, and suddenly began to laugh. It told her something about Cordelia: that she'd been a very stubborn girl. It was their marriage certificate, and it was signed by a Father John James McCarthy at St. Ignatius' Catholic church in Hollywood, the date nearly thirty-three years back.

Delia sat on the bed with the box on her lap and laughed until her side ached. Alex! He must have been furious—and he must have loved Cordelia quite a lot, to agree to that.

She looked at the other things in the box. There was a small solitaire diamond ring—her engagement ring? And a larger ring, plain yellow gold with a modest-sized ruby; and another gold ring with three good-sized sapphires set in a row. She tried that on, and it fit her right ring finger snugly. There was a little pendant necklace, an open heart with a sapphire suspended in it. She took that and the ring and the picture downstairs. She thought she might get a frame for the picture. Cordelia had been a pretty girl; Delia didn't think she was very much like her, except for a hint, maybe, in the eyes, the mouth— Girls took after fathers mostly, she thought vaguely, though she wasn't much like Alex either. And there was that old maxim for suitors, look at the mother before you marry the daughter.

She thought suddenly, irrelevantly, of the Garvin daughter, the chatterbox Lisa, wondered if she had taken after her mother; not him, at least. She washed the ring and pendant carefully, rinsing them in cold water, and the sapphires sparkled beautifully, rejuvenated. She wondered where they had come from, where Cordelia had got them.

She met Laura for lunch at Pike's Verdugo Oaks, and enjoyed the feminine talk, the couple of hours with a friend; Laura had parked the children with an amiable neighbor down the block. Delia went on to have her hair done, and did the week's marketing on the way home, and after she'd put it away went to call Mrs. Mentor. Alex was already asleep.

Sometime in the middle of the night she woke with a violent start, out of a vivid dream, abrupt and confused. She couldn't remember anything of the dream, except that there were a lot of books in it: shelves and shelves of books. Her heart was pounding absurdly, and she got up for a drink of water, and slept soundly the rest of the night.

By Wednesday morning the red tape was getting tied up, Varallo and O'Connor seeing the end of it. O'Connor had just got off the phone from half an hour's conference with the DA's office, at ten o'clock, when the autopsy report on Cynthia Emery came in. Delia had been looking it over after Varallo had seen it, and passed it on to O'Connor as he emerged from his cubbyhole.

"Well, it's just what we could have guessed," said Varallo. "Forcible rape and strangulation."

"And the warrant already says Murder One," said O'Connor. "Unless the damn head doctors claim he was mentally unhinged by all the dope, he can't slide out from under—deny that confession from now till doomsday—he told us where the body was."

"Yes," said Varallo. "The poor damned girl was just in the wrong place at the wrong time."

Forbes and Gonzales had been questioning a possible suspect on a heist in one of the interrogation rooms, and came out just then and let the fellow go. "All up in the air as usual," said Gonzales, through a yawn. "No evidence, no alibi, nothing to say yes or no."

"And you being back with us," said Forbes, "have you seen the latest on the cab heisters? Well, if you have any inspiration on it, to say whether it suggests a lead—"

They heard about that and ruminated. "She wished she was back in equality," said Varallo. "Damn it, it doesn't make any sense."

"It sounds as if it ought to mean something," said Delia doubtfully, "but I can't quite—"

"They picked up the cab again, by the way. As usual, no prints."

Varallo rubbed his nose. "Where?"

"East Broadway."

"Same as before. They're holed up somewhere around that end of town. The only other deduction I can offer is that at least one of them is familiar with the town. They know the residential areas, dark at night."

"Well, a little looking around would—"

A man came in and looked around the office. Varallo got up. "This the detective office?"

"Yes, sir, can we help you?"

He produced a business card in automatic gesture. "I just thought I'd better report this. My name's Sparrow, Ed Sparrow." He was a small man in sharply tailored sports clothes. "I'm with Reed and Taylor Management, we own property around, manage condos and apartments for the owners, you know the kind of thing. One of our clients owns a whole block of cheap rentals here, kind of area where you get the welfare people and aliens, and one place there we've had to get an eviction notice on. I came over this morning to hand it over personally, otherwise

they'd claim they never got it, and"—Sparrow passed a hand
over his mouth—"when the woman took it, I heard this kid
screaming blue murder in there. She was yelling, 'Please don't
hurt me anymore, Tommy'—over and over—and, well, it didn't
sound as if she was just getting spanked. If you know what I
mean. Sounded as if she already was hurt, maybe bad. It kind of
shook me. My wife was reading an article just the other day
about child abuse being so common now. It's hard to understand a thing like that. Anyway, in case this is anything like that,
I thought I'd better report it."

"We're glad you did, sir. What's the name and address?"

"Larson, it's Cerritos Avenue."

On one like that, they wanted to move fast. Varallo and Delia
collected Mary Champion and drove down there in Varallo's
car. It was another narrow old street, and the house was a ramshackle frame place painted saffron yellow with brown trim;
there was a crooked little apple tree dying in front. There wasn't
any doorbell, and Varallo hammered loudly on the front door.
After a long wait, the door opened halfway.

The woman facing them might have been any age from
twenty to forty. She was rail-thin, slatternly in ragged pants, a
man's shirt, thong sandals; her hair had been bleached a long
while ago and was growing out to an original mud-brown.

"Mrs. Larson?" asked Varallo.

"I'm Mrs. Floyd. Marian Floyd. Tommy just left, he isn't
here."

"Have you any children, Mrs. Floyd?" asked Mary briskly.
"We'd like to see them."

She said warily, "You from the welfare? Well, I— I— I got
one, a girl, she's asleep right now, you can't see her. She hasn't
been feeling good, she's asleep."

"We'd just like to see that she's all right," said Mary. "What's
her name?"

She gave way before them weakly, backing into the living
room. "Melanie. She's okay, she's just asleep."

The tiny room held a couch with the stuffing coming out, a
couple of ancient chairs, the inevitable TV. There was a narrow
hall off that room, and to the left Delia could see part of the
kitchen, with dirty dishes scattered all over the counter and a
movement of black scurrying things on the floor—roaches. The

other way, past a bathroom probably in no better state, was a single bedroom with a sagging double bed and a child's cot. They went over to look.

The child lying there might be five, and small for her age. She was rather recently dead; the blood on her face, in her hair, hadn't darkened yet. It was dirty tangled blond hair, long uncombed or washed, and under the blood her face was dirty with long-engrained grime. She had on a single garment, a faded cotton nightgown. Varallo reached to pull it up, and Delia drew in a deep breath. The small body was a mass of old and new bruises, welts, what looked like raw burns. "My God," said Varallo quietly. He turned and took the woman by the arm. "You're coming in to answer some questions. Is there a phone here?"

"Inna living room. I never hit her, Tommy did. He don't like Melanie because she ain't his kid. I didn't have nothing to do with it."

Varallo called the lab, called the morgue wagon. "Where's Tommy?"

"He took off after that guy was here—about havin' to get out of this place. I don't know."

"Has he got a car? What kind?"

"Yeah. Dodge, I guess."

"My God," said Mary, noticing the kitchen floor for the first time. The lab truck came. They took Marian Floyd back to the office. Hearing about this one, O'Connor came to sit in on the questioning.

"All right," said Varallo sharply; he stood towering above her where she huddled in a chair. "You know your little girl is dead. What happened to her? Tell us about it. What did Tommy do to her?"

"I don't know, he sort of spanked Melanie some yesterday because she wouldn't shut up—when he was watchin' TV. I was in the other room, I heard her yell, but she was always yellin'."

"Did you ever spank Melanie, Mrs. Floyd?" asked Mary.

"Well, I get nervous, she gets on my nerves, yeah, I spank her sometimes."

"Why was Tommy spanking her this morning?"

"I guess she got on his nerves some way."

"Did you ever have to take Melanie to a doctor?"

She said, "I want a cigarette." Varallo gave her one and lit it. "Oh, that was a while back, it was Randy did that. We hadda fight about it. It was before I ever met Tommy. Randy took her to a doctor, but it was just a busted arm. I told that nurse there wasn't nothin' wrong, she'd just fell down some steps." Suddenly her dull eyes looked sly and she giggled. "Randy—they didn't believe what he said because he was a li'l bit drunk."

"Are you getting welfare money, Mrs. Floyd?" asked Delia.

"Yeah, I couldn't get a job when we moved here, and Tommy got laid off that construction job."

Delia gave Mary a glance and turned away to her own desk, got on the phone to the local Social Services office. She could hear the monotonous questions and answers going on behind her. O'Connor had been down to Communications and they had a make on Larson's car, an old Dodge sedan; there was now an APB out on it, and him.

She got handed around, and finally talked to a Mrs. Ott who seemed to have some records available. Yes, Marian Floyd was on the assistance list, the food stamp program— "Weren't they investigated when they applied?" asked Delia. A lot of those bruises and welts on Melanie's body weren't recent, and anyone calling at the house should have noticed something, you would think.

"Yes, of course," said Mrs. Ott.

"Who saw them? I'd like to talk to her."

"Well, just a moment, I'll have to look up the record—" After an interval she came back and said, "It was Miss Viborg."

"Is she there now?"

"I think she's out to lunch."

None of them had realized that it was past lunch time. "Will you please go and see?" said Delia. She hung on the phone patiently, and in about five minutes a different voice came on and announced itself as Ida Viborg.

Delia told her bluntly why she was asking questions, and Miss Viborg was horrified. "When did they apply for welfare?"

"My heavens—oh, dear, what a terrible—well, I'll have to look at the files—" She went away, came back, and said it had been six months ago. Mrs. Floyd had been on welfare in Ventura County, had to file a new appeal when she came back here.

"Back?" said Delia.

"Yes, the woman told me she used to live in Hollywood before that. Certainly we investigated her, we don't just hand out money to anyone who asks, after all—"

Delia said dryly, "Sometimes it looks that way to the taxpayers. Did you go to the house?"

"Yes," said Miss Viborg. She gave a loud sniff, righteous. "What can you expect of these people? A lot of people on public assistance are inadequate, weak people to start with, and you don't expect to find them in immaculate houses in a nice part of town. No, the place wasn't very clean, but I see a lot like that."

"Did you see the child?"

"I think she was playing in the back yard when I was there," said Miss Viborg vaguely. "I didn't notice."

"Did you call the Ventura office to check on them there?"

"Yes, naturally, that is, to ask about Mrs. Floyd. I didn't know there was a man living with her. I wanted some history on her, of course. Really, this is quite horrifying, but after all we're not responsible, we haven't the time or the facilities to do more than verify that there is a legitimate need—"

"I should think when people apply for aid to dependent children there would be some investigation—"

"It's not called that anymore," said Miss Viborg crossly, "and Mrs. Floyd applied for straight support. How should I know she was living with some man? We're not here to judge people's morals—"

"More's the pity," said Delia. She next got on the phone to the Social Services office in Hollywood, got handed around some more, and they were annoyed with her because they had to look up old files; she hadn't any dates to give them. A clerk finally got back to her and said, "It was four years back, the only record we've got. I remember the case now, she went off our rolls when she was arrested for something and put in jail. I see there's a note here that we had to send Xeroxes of her file to Juvenile Hall for some reason."

Delia repressed some unladylike language, thanked her, and called the Hollywood precinct. At least, talking to another police officer, she would be hearing some sane sense. She got a Sergeant Hayworth in Juvenile there, and he said, "Well, you know how paperwork is the curse of the twentieth century. All the files are about to crowd us out of here, but I'll have a look for the record and get back to you. Floyd, four years back. No idea of the charge? Well, it'll be cross-filed."

She put the phone down and exercised her fingers, which were cramped from holding onto it. Mary said, "Vic took her over to jail. They just picked up Larson at a bar on Brand."

Varallo got back just before Traffic brought Larson in. He was a good match for the woman: a dirty, unshaven lout with a vocabulary that seemed to consist largely of obscenities. He was also half drunk, and the rules and regulations being so careful about citizens' rights, they couldn't question him in that condition. Varallo took him over to jail and booked him in. They had requested the warrants for both of them, and Varallo had asked LAPD if he had a pedigree with them; he wasn't known to Glendale records.

The package came up from Communications about half an hour after that. Larson had a record going back to when he was sixteen; he was thirty now. It ran the gamut: possession, attempted rape, assault, pimping, child molestation. He had served little parcels of time, had been off parole for six months.

There wasn't much to say about one like this. Varallo got on the phone to the morgue, and talked to Dr. Goulding.

"Oh, my God, yes," said Goulding. "I was here when they brought her in. My God, Varallo, what that child must have gone through—and over a long period of time, too. I haven't got to the autopsy yet, of course, but there are old and new bruises and burns all over her, and what look like whip marks— and I have a strong suspicion that she's been sexually abused as well."

"Oh, God."

"It makes you wonder how these animals get that way. I'll do the autopsy, but to go on with I can say that she probably died of a skull fracture. She may have been struck with some weapon, or just slammed against the wall or a piece of furniture —it doesn't take much to kill a small child, you know."

"I know," said Varallo grimly. Mary looked a little pale, hearing about that.

At five o'clock Sergeant Hayworth called Delia back. "I got the record for you. This woman, Marian Floyd, was reported by the arresting officers for child abuse—"

"What was she being arrested for?"

"Oh, not her. The husband. Rodney Floyd. I got hold of Don Byrd, I saw he'd signed the report, and he remembered it. Floyd was tagged for a bank job, and a couple of our boys went along with the Feds to pick him up. He's still in Leavenworth, this was four years back. The woman was beating a baby when they walked in, Byrd said the poor little thing was all black and blue, not the first time it's been beaten—little girl about a year old. They reported it and she got a year probation on the charge. Naturally they took the kid away from her."

"Naturally," said Delia. "I should hope so. So why did she have the child with her again? If it's the same child? I take it, it was—she was the right age."

He was startled. "She did? Well, these damn judges—what's it all about, anyway?" He heard, and did some cussing. "Sweet Jesus. I should think Juvenile Hall would have found a foster home—"

"I suppose they did. Then. She didn't spend any time in at all? No, the first time she'd been charged with anything—"

"That's right, at least with us. Probation, like I said—these Goddamn courts—and that's all our files say. My God, what a—"

"Yes, and she'd be entitled—entitled!—to more welfare if she has a child to support, that would be why she wanted custody again. But what soft-headed judge granted it—"

It was too late to do any more tracing back on this tonight, but tomorrow they would do a lot more. Tomorrow they could question a sobered-up Larson. And police officers were like doctors: not supposed to get emotionally involved with victims or patients. Once in a while you couldn't help it. With one like Melanie. Melanie, whose five or so short years of life must have been nothing but pain and torture.

Feeling cold, with the anger cold too at the pit of her stomach, Delia got her handbag and walked down to the ladies' room. Mary was there putting on her coat. Their eyes met in the mirror, and Mary said, "Well. Mrs. Frantz's Melanie. Mrs. Frantz is quite a prophet in her sleep, isn't she?"

"Don't be ridiculous," said Delia. "The woman's over-emotional and imaginative. That must have been the foster home Juvenile Hall found, yes. Melanie Floyd, she said. She was fond of the child, and she knew the mother had been charged with abusing her—she was angry when Mrs. Floyd regained custody, and who can blame her? So her subconscious mind produced the dreams—that's where dreams come from."

Mary got out her keys and snapped her bag shut. "There's just one little thing inadequate about that explanation. You only heard the last of that tirade. Before then, she'd told me that Melanie was in a house painted dark yellow with brown trim, with an apple tree in front. And she heard Melanie screaming, 'Please don't hurt me anymore, Tommy.'" She gave Delia a funny little smile. "See you in the morning." She went out.

Delia stared at the mirror. But things didn't work that way, she thought. That kind of thing couldn't happen. Her mind shut firmly against the impossibility, but a little crack remained obstinately open.

Apple trees were very uncommon in southern California; they didn't do well in this climate.

In the lobby downstairs she ran into Forbes and Gonzales at the door. "Any luck with the heisters?" she asked idly.

"Something more interesting," said Forbes. "We've cleaned up the Milburn thing."

Delia stopped and stared at him. "Well, I'm running late, and it's going to be a full day tomorrow, but I think I've got to hear about that."

About one o'clock, after they'd had lunch, Forbes and Gonzales had been set to start out on the legwork again, after possible heisters, when a pawnbroker called in. He said it was possible he had some of the items on the hot list.

It was a pawnshop on South Brand, and the proprietor's name was Aronoff, but the only accent he had belonged to Brooklyn. "It's all ordinary stuff," he said, "the kind of grandmother's jewelry anybody might have, but I was just looking over the hot list again and it struck me these items are listed all together. In one bunch, and it's exactly the same little bunch of stuff I took in last night. Four old gold rings set with garnets, old-mine-cut diamond in yellow gold, about a quarter-carat stone, wedding ring, old Bulova wristwatch, two bangle bracelets, old garnet pin, Masonic ring, man's old pocket watch." He had it all out on top of the glass case for them to see.

"The daughter can identify it, if it is," said Forbes. "Do you have a record of who pawned it, Mr. Aronoff?"

"Sure. He's brought stuff in a few times before. His name's Navarro, Joe Navarro. The address is Wing Street."

"Well, well," said Forbes. "We'll give you a receipt for this, Mr. Aronoff, see if our witness can identify it for us."

"And I'm out thirty bucks. My own damn fault," said Aronoff philosophically.

They took it over to Pasadena to show Mrs. Kilmer, and she identified it instantly as her mother's missing jewelry. Forbes explained that they had to keep it as evidence, that she'd get it back eventually. The address on Wing Street was at the other end of the block from the Milburn house, and Mrs. Navarro mercifully spoke good English. She was surprised and indignant to find police on her doorstep. "We've never been in any police trouble, we're honest people. My husband? What do the police want with Joe? Well, of course he's not here, he's at work like any honest man on a workday! He works up at Forest Lawn—he's one of the maintenance crew there."

Forbes and Gonzales drove up there, to the beautiful green park a stranger would never take for a cemetery, and at the office found the man in charge of the maintenance crew. He said, "Navarro? He's probably got up to the top of Cathedral Drive about now."

Up on Cathedral Drive they came on a man a hundred feet off the road, riding a big lawnmower, and hailed him. It was Navarro. He was about forty, a stocky man with an open countenance, the weathered complexion of the outdoor worker. He too was surprised at police wanting to talk to him.

Forbes said, "We understand you sometimes pawn things at Aronoff's pawnshop over on Brand, Mr. Navarro."

"Well, yeah, once in a while. With six kids"—he flashed a rueful smile—"sometimes the money don't go to the end of the month, know what I mean. Once in a while we got to hock the radio or something, get by. I always got the stuff back up to now. Why are the police interested?" And then the smile faded and he said, "Oh-oh. Don't tell me there was something wrong about that stuff? I shoulda known. My God, I shoulda known. I was surprised as hell when he give me thirty bucks, I didn't think it was anything much good or it wouldn't have been laying around like that—"

"Like what?" asked Gonzales. "Where'd you find it?"

"I didn't find it, Bert did. Bert's our oldest one. See, I happened to go into the kids' room after dinner yesterday and Bert was lookin' at that stuff, he had it in a little box. I asked him about it and he said him and Harry, that's a pal of his lives across the street, they found it in the alley back of Chevy Chase on the way home from school. Well, I looked it over and I said we might get maybe five bucks for the watches, and Bert said okay, I could have it. So I took it to Aronoff's and like to fell over when he give me thirty bucks. I shoulda known there was something wrong about it—my God, don't say it was hot?"

"It surely was," said Forbes. "It's the loot from Mrs. Milburn's house, Navarro—you know, the old lady at the other end of the block who—"

Navarro said, "Oh, my God, no! No, it couldn't be—how could it be?" Suddenly he lost all his healthy outdoor color; he looked gray. He said incredulously, "Bert? But Bert's just a kid —he's only thirteen!"

They found Bert Navarro and Harry Pascoe from across the street just home from school, and they took them down to Juvenile where Ben Guernsey could see their rights weren't violated. They were both well-grown boys for their age. And they were scared stiff. Both of them had been brought up with some rudimentary morals, and their consciences had been bothering them. They talked without much prodding.

"We never thought anything like *that* happen!" said Bert. "I— I—wanted some money—for a bicycle—an' Harry wanted a new football an' things— I thought I could tell my folks I'd saved it up from my paper-route money—" He was looking down at the floor. "Sure, we knew it wasn't right—do a thing like that—but that ole lady, she didn't know anybody on the block, she wouldn't reckanize—"

"How did you get her to let you in?" asked Forbes.

"An' everybody said she musta got money hid in the house, she was a teacher, an' teachers get paid a lot—"

"How did you get in?" asked Forbes louder.

Bert burst into tears. "I didn't—b'lieve—they said she was *dead*—we wasn't goin' to *hurt* her any—"

Harry was all ready to cry. "She musta been an awful—awful brittle lady—she was mad when I picked up her purse—she yelled, we was in the kitchen, and we just give her a little shove and she fell down—we didn't mean to *hurt* her—"

"An' there was only twelve dollars in her purse—an' we found that jewelry, but the man at the pawnshop, he wouldn't do a deal, he said send your dad, kid—"

"*How did you get her to let you in?*" asked Forbes.

And when they heard about that, it sent them back to Wing Street. To the house next door to the Milburn house. And Juanita Cabrillo, after one look and question, started to cry bitterly, with her mother asking anxious questions in Spanish, uncomprehending, frightened. "Oh—oh—oh! I wanted to *die,* when that happen— I knew it wasn't right to do—but Bert said —oh—oh—oh! I knew we shouldn't—but Bert said—she got lots of money, it'd be easy—oh—oh— I rang her doorbell—and I said our phone didn't work and Mama had to call the doctor —and she—and she opened the door right away—oh—oh!"

Opened her door to the kids. To the nice little girl from next door, and a couple of innocent-looking boys. It had been a lot simpler than the telegram, after all. And just how Juanita had thought she was going to explain her part in it might emerge— maybe she would have claimed that the boys made her do it and she'd never seen them before.

But what did you do with an eleven-year-old and two thirteen-year-olds who had quite inadvertently ended up killing an old lady? You couldn't do much; even when the law was a lot less lenient than it was now, it hadn't electrocuted minors for accidents. They'd go through the motions of justice on this one, and the kids would end up on probation, released to custody of parents.

And they couldn't help wondering what Mrs. Kilmer would think about it.

On Wednesday afternoon about four o'clock, Katz was sitting brooding over his reports on the midget burglar when Vinson came in. He came over and sat down beside the desk and looked at Katz, and suddenly began to laugh.

"What's the joke, Mr. Vinson?" asked Katz.

Vinson wiped his eyes. He took a five-by-seven manila envelope out of his pocket. "I thought you'd like to know the answer to the mystery, Sergeant Katz. I was just so damn mad about all that Godawful mess—twice, I had to get the cleaners out—and I couldn't figure how the hell the guy was getting in— I knew there couldn't be an extra key anywhere, no way! Well, I'm a camera bug and I thought I'd try a little scientific detective work, see? I borrowed six more cameras and I set up the traps in about eight places through the house. Trip wires under the rugs, fast infra-red film so there wouldn't be any flash to warn him his picture was getting taken—cameras spotted around behind things with just the lenses uncovered—it was the hell of a job, but I was so damn mad I figured it'd be worth it if—" He was giggling again. "That was on Monday, and nothing happened that night, but when I checked this morning—oh, my God, you should see the mess up there again! But I guess it was worth it—" He shoved over the manila envelope. "I just finished making the prints, I thought you'd like to see—"

"You got a picture, identified him?" Interested, Katz tipped out four glossy black-and-white prints onto his desk.

Vinson's little camera traps had produced some pretty good pictures of the vandals; by one picture, it seemed there were three of them altogether. They were all masked, which was appropriate for villains. This time, they had—in one eloquent shot —come across a four-roll package of toilet paper in a bathroom cupboard, and were having a ball with it.

"*Raccoons!*" said Vinson, giggling. "I'd heard there were supposed to be some up in the hills back of the college—they're inquisitive critters, you know, and smart as the devil— I figure they got in that cat door the first time. When I took a look at the negatives this morning, I went up there and hunted around, and there's a little hole under the eaves, on the side where that big tree overhangs the roof. Oh, my God—the shot of that big one chasing toilet paper down the hall—" He sat back and howled.

Katz began to howl too, and John Poor, trudging in looking weary, stared at them as if they were lunatics.

At noon on Thursday, Delia put the phone down for the first time in nearly four hours, and looked at Mary across the desk. She was down in the Juvenile office, and Mary had been on another phone, Varallo on one upstairs. Forbes and O'Connor had been over at the jail questioning Larson and Marian Floyd; she didn't know what they'd got. On the phones, here, they had been following the murky trail backward, prodding at courthouse and welfare offices and Juvenile Hall and records out of the 77th Street precinct, records from Ventura County— Marian Floyd had moved around.

She had been charged with child abuse that first time, and Melanie had spent the next year in Mrs. Florence Frantz's home as a foster child. Then Marian Floyd, off probation from that charge, had petitioned to regain custody, and got it from a judge of the juvenile court who had subsequently been indicted on a charge of enticing minors to immoral acts.

At that time, she had apparently been living alone, but in Ventura County there had been a man with her, taken for her husband, using her name. They had verified that her real husband—Melanie's father? maybe only Marian could say—was still in Federal prison. The man in Ventura could have been any casual boyfriend.

In Ventura, she'd been reported to the police by the mailman as beating Melanie with a hammer, and the police had gone to investigate, but found no evidence—so their records said—of actual abuse, and that hadn't been followed up. She had then moved back to Hollywood and got on their welfare rolls again. They didn't yet know when she'd picked up Larson. There wasn't much to choose between them, but it must have been Larson who had finally killed Melanie. Or had it? By what Sparrow had said— "Please don't hurt me anymore, Tommy"—and forty minutes later she was dead.

Eighteen months ago a neighbor in Hollywood had called the welfare office and reported Marian using "a big piece of wood" to beat the little girl. A Social Services investigator had visited her and reportedly told her that she shouldn't do that anymore. That hadn't been reported to the police.

"Lunch?" said Delia tersely, and Mary said, "Okay." They walked down to the little coffee shop.

"I'm not very hungry," said Mary to the menu. "Ought to take off about ten pounds anyway."

Delia told the waitress to bring her a milk shake. She wasn't very hungry either.

They had just got back to the office and Delia was about to call the psychiatrist who had once, on the first charge of child abuse, examined Marian Floyd, when the phone rang and Varallo upstairs said, "I just had a call from Dr. Barlow. He's now had a letter threatening to bomb the church."

CHAPTER 9

"I found it fastened to the side door with Scotch Tape when I came with the new hymn books just now," said Dr. Barlow. "We found a housecleaning service to clean up the church, and I've been down to the church in Los Angeles this morning to pick up the new hymnals, and when I got here—"

It was a small ruled page torn out of a cheap tablet. In straggly half-literate printing it said, THER GOEN PUT BOM IN CHIRCH A FREN.

"Well"— Varallo handed it to Delia—"so far all this has been nothing but the petty nuisance— I'm sorry, Dr. Barlow, I know it hasn't been petty to you, but that's what the legal charge would be. And all of it pulled by the teenage kids. I doubt very much that any of the people behind all this would know how to make a bomb, be able to get hold of the materials."

"Joe said the break-in was probably done by the grown-up males," said Delia. "We'd better be safe than sorry, Vic."

"Yes," said Varallo, "which I was about to say too. But it seems incredible that feeling should run so high, just over—"

"If the Guerreros are mixing in," said Delia crisply, "they couldn't care less what the excuse is to make trouble. Destruction for destruction's sake, and Satan finding work for idle hands."

"These damned louts, God knows that's true. Have you had the door repaired, sir?"

"Oh, yes. You can see—" The side door had been sanded smooth and stained, and there was a new shiny lock on it. "It was expensive, but the locksmith said it should be absolutely burglarproof now, and the front door too."

"Have you been into the church?" Varallo nodded at the note in Delia's hand, and Barlow gave him his engaging grin.

"Well, no. When I saw that—"

Varallo laughed. "Well, we haven't got a regular bomb squad like LAPD, but—better safe than sorry. I can't see any of these people manufacturing a real bomb, but—well, let me call the lab and see what they think."

He found the nearest public phone a block away and talked to Gene Thomsen. "Well, for God's sake," said Thomsen, "explosives in the hands of amateurs—a damn sight more dangerous than if a professional terrorist was on the job—my God. I tell you what, I don't like this one hell of a lot, Varallo, but I guess we'd better have a look."

Varallo went back to the church parking lot. Delia was saying, "And you know, it's not a threat. It's more in the nature of a friendly warning—"

"Well, yes, in a sense—"

"It sounds to me as if someone had overheard some wild talk, one of these hotheads saying they ought to set a bomb in the church, something like that—it needn't be anything more serious."

"I suppose not," said Barlow. "I certainly hope not."

Burt and Thomsen came up; they had on asbestos overalls and brought along a geiger counter and a metal detector. It didn't take them long to search the little church, the couple of Sunday school classrooms, the small lobby, the vestry behind the altar— "I feel like a damn fool, all these precautions," said Burt, stripping off the overalls. "But—"

"Better safe than sorry," said Varallo.

"True," said Burt. "Anyway, the place is clean—no sign of a bomb or anything resembling one."

"Thank you very much," said Barlow humbly. "I certainly hope this doesn't mean any more trouble."

"Well, with the new locks you should be safe enough," said Varallo. "I wouldn't worry too much about it, sir."

He and Delia drove back to the office. They were both thinking more about Melanie than the tempest in a teapot over Dr. Barlow's church. "Have you got any sort of statement out of Larson yet?" asked Delia.

"Not one damn thing. He just sits and snarls. But we don't need one damn thing from him. The lab found a wrench in his car with blood on it— Melanie's type, not his—and it's got a couple of his prints on it. He'd realized she was dead and with some vague idea of getting away with it he was going to leave Floyd and clear out, only he didn't have sense enough to stay sober. She's now claiming it was never her did any of the abusing, it was always the boyfriends, and she was so scared of Tommy she couldn't do anything about it."

"Speaking of boyfriends," said Delia, "we came across Randy. He's Randy Medina—signed Melanie into emergency at Cedars-Sinai about a year ago—she had a broken arm, and he told them Floyd had hit her with a broom, but she denied it and they didn't follow it up. He's got a little pedigree of D. and D., petty theft. What gets me, Vic, is that nobody followed it up! There must have been time after time like that, a good many people who suspected or knew that child was being mistreated, and nothing done—nothing! That judge—did he even know that she'd been charged with abusing her own child? If he did, he couldn't have cared less— That mailman tried, and I don't know how good or bad the Ventura police are, but you'd think there would have been some evidence to see. And all these damned welfare people overlooking the filth and squalor because a lot of people on welfare are like that—my God, you'd have thought they'd at least have found out she was once charged with— Damn it, Vic, it's just that that poor little mite never had a chance!" She was silent, and as he turned into the parking lot behind the station she said, "She was just about Ginevra's age."

"I know, I know," said Varallo. "We all sometimes wonder what we're doing here on this damn thankless job."

"You have said it," said Delia. They went in and up to the detective office. There was another follow-up report to write on Melanie, what they had learned this morning. It was Forbes' day off. They found Gonzales sitting staring into space stroking his hairline moustache absently.

"There are plenty of things to do if you'd like to earn your salary," said Varallo.

"Well, I was just thinking of something," said Gonzales. "Try it on for size. About that pair heisting cabs, what the girl said."

"She wished she was back in equality," said Delia. "Yes. You had an idea about it?"

"Well, damn it," said Gonzales, "could she have meant a place? It seems kind of logical. You say, I wish I was in Hawaii right now, or, I'd like to go to Phoenix to see Mother. Like that."

"It's a funny sort of name for a place," said Delia.

"There are a lot of funny names for places," said Gonzales. "There's a town in Tennessee named Soddy Daisy. My sister had a flat tire there once and was so taken with it she bought all the postcards in town to prove it."

"Soddy Daisy?" said Varallo. "I don't believe it."

"I can show you one of the postcards."

"Well, equality," said Delia. "I suppose we can look." She found an atlas in O'Connor's cubbyhole—he was over at the jail prodding at Larson—and started out with Alabama, running a finger down the list of towns that began with E. She found some queer ones all right—there was a town named Evening Shade in Arkansas, and one named Enigma in Georgia; and just below a town named Energy in Illinois she found it. Equality, Illinois. Just to be thorough she went on through Wyoming, but that was the only Equality in the United States.

"Well, I will be damned," said Varallo, interested. "So the girl wishes she was back in Equality, Illinois. It may be interesting, but it's no use at all in hunting for them."

"I wonder," said Delia, lighting a cigarette thoughtfully. "It's a tiny little place, Vic. It says population just over seven hundred. Individuals would be known to everybody living there. And a lot of people come to California these days, I grant you, and from all over. But the other side of that coin is that a lot of people in other places have friends and relatives in California."

"And how would you propose finding out if anybody in Equality has an aunt in Yucaipa?" asked Varallo.

"Police," said Delia placidly, "are usually cooperative with other police." She dialed Information to get the area code, called Information there and asked for the number of the police station in Equality. She got, within one minute, Chief Jerry Bright, who sounded as if he resembled his name, and was surprised and interested to talk to a female officer way out in California. He asked what he could do for them. "Well, it may sound a little mysterious," said Delia, "but do you happen to know if anyone living in your town, or who once lived there, has a friend or relative in California?"

"Well, I know pretty well everybody in Equality the last twenty years. Have to think a minute."

Delia said, "A blond girl about twenty-three or so. We think she used to live in Equality."

"I can think of four–five blond girls moved out of town the last few years. The Thatcher twins went up to work in Chicago, and Betty Moon married a fellow from Harrisburg. And Susan and Jim French went to Pulaski when they got married, she was old Addy Stengel's granddaughter, nice girl— Jim got a job with the John Deere people in Pulaski, I think."

"All right," said Delia. "Do any of those people know anyone in California?"

"Well, now," said Chief Bright, "Muriel Thatcher's mother had an aunt living in a place called Napa Valley, she's the twins' mother. And now I call it to mind, Jim French has a sister out there, she married a fellow named Tate from New Haven, he got sent to California when he was in the service and they stayed."

"Do you know where they live?"

"Have to think. It's a place named Rock something—nope, I got it, the other way around, it's Eagle Rock."

"Thank you very much," said Delia. "Do you remember Tate's first name?"

"Now there you got me," said Chief Bright. "I think it was some ordinary name, Bob, Jim, Sam, something like that. Why are you interested in all this, anyway?"

"You may be hearing," said Delia. "Thanks so very much, Chief." She put the phone down. "Something to be said for small towns. Let's have a look at the phone book."

There, they found Robert S. Tate listed on Sumner Avenue in Eagle Rock. "Now just look at that," said Gonzales fondly. "In walking distance of East Broadway. It does tie in. Susan and Jim French. I had a real inspiration, didn't I?"

Gonzales and Varallo went over there and found Mrs. Tate at home, an ordinary nice-looking young housewife, a little impatient at being interrupted in her housework. "Jim?" she said. They hadn't produced the badges; she looked at their conservative suits and white shirts and said, "Is it the insurance on the car?"

"Well—" said Gonzales.

"Thank goodness! At long last. The time you people take—
Of all the bad luck Sue and Jim have had, him losing that job,
and they no sooner land here than that drunk runs into his car
parked on the street and totals it, and they've been counting on
the insurance to get back home—"

"Are they staying with you, Mrs. Tate?"

"Oh, no, we haven't got room, only the two bedrooms and
we've got two children. They're at the Evergreen Motel on East
Broadway."

It was an old motel, respectable, clean, quiet. Mr. and Mrs.
French were occupying unit fourteen. Varallo knocked on the
door and a man opened it. He was middle-sized, about twenty-
five, brown-haired, nondescript. Beyond him in the cramped
motel bedroom a blond girl was rummaging in a suitcase on the
floor.

They showed him the badges. "So we finally chase you
down," said Varallo. "You are the pair who've been heisting
cabs all over town, aren't you?"

"Oh, hell," said Jim French. He just looked more despondent
than he had a moment ago, but the girl, looking up startled,
burst into tears.

"I knew we'd get arrested! I said it was a stupid thing to
do—" She was a very pretty girl, and she looked at Varallo and
Gonzales with pleading hopeless eyes. "We were *desperate!* No
money at all, and I tried and tried to get a job and so did Jim,
but they were all miles away, and no car after that awful drunk
ruined the Ford, and we owed back rent here—we were *desperate,* we couldn't ask Bob and Myra— I said we shouldn't ever
have left Illinois and if we ever got back home—oh, I knew
we'd get arrested—"

"Let's have the gun," said Varallo. "Where'd you get it?"

Jim French said hopelessly, "I had it, I didn't have to get it. I
used to use it for rabbit shooting back home." He handed it
over, and it was a little .22 Colt, and it wasn't loaded.

Just after Varallo and Gonzales went out, Delia finally rolled
the forms into her typewriter to start the report, and a woman
came in and looked around the office. Wallace was typing a report, Katz and John Poor were in; but the woman's gaze came

to Delia and she walked over to her desk. "The man downstairs said to come right up. I want to talk to somebody about a murder." She was in late middle age, a shapeless drab woman in ordinary plain clothes, with gray hair in a little bun and metal-framed glasses.

"You can talk to me," said Delia. "I'm a detective."

"Oh, I didn't know there were women detectives, but I'm just as glad, because another woman would understand about it better."

"Suppose you tell me your name. And what it's all about."

"I'm Mrs. Alicia Gleason. It's about the murder of my aunt. Mrs. Louise Tallman."

They did, of course, get the mentally unhinged citizens coming in now and then. Delia said, "I'm afraid we haven't any record of anyone of that name getting murdered, Mrs. Gleason. Don't you think—"

"No, you wouldn't have. It happened last Saturday. I thought everything would be all right, but I was brought up a good Christian and my conscience just won't let me rest, that's all. I murdered her, and I've got to confess and be done with it." She collapsed into Varallo's chair and wept a few bitter slow tears. "There were policemen there, but Dr. Spooner said he'd send a certificate—he didn't know it was murder, of course. I'd just come to the end of my rope— I know we've got a duty to take care of our own people, but she made it so awfully hard, always complaining, never satisfied, and it was all a lot of hard work— terribly hard, she was in a wheelchair and I had everything to do, bathing her and all the housework and meals. I lived with my daughter since I lost my husband, till Aunt Louise got bedridden last year, and we thought it'd be easier for me to move into her house on Western Avenue. But I'd just come to the end of my rope." She looked at Delia drearily. "If she'd been nice about it, even thanked me once—but she just had a nasty temper—the doctor said she wasn't in any pain, no reason for her to be so grouchy except that was just the way she was. I never knew how her husband stood it, he must have had the patience of a saint, and of course he was only fifty-two when he died. And when I saw that sign, the temptation was just too much for me."

"What sign? How did you murder her, Mrs. Gleason?" This

wasn't making much sense; the woman was probably unhinged, though she sounded rational enough.

"The sign on that new gadget of Billy's. My grandson. I was over at my daughter's the night before— I couldn't leave Aunt Louise for long, but after all I wanted to see the children sometimes—and Billy was showing it to me. You know how the children have all these electronic things to play with now, and Billy's always recording things on his tape recorder, and he'd saved up his allowance to buy this thing."

"What thing?"

"They call it a tape eraser. And he was showing me how it worked, and I saw the sign on it. It said, do not switch on or off within twenty feet of anyone wearing a pacemaker. And I thought of Aunt Louise right away. Because she had one. And that morning— I mean the next morning—she was so downright nasty to me, she said I was a silly damned old fool who couldn't even make coffee right, and she threw all her breakfast dishes on the floor, just to make a mess for me to clean up—and I just couldn't stand it any longer. I knew my daughter and the children would be gone most of the day—she always takes the children to the library on Saturday mornings, and they were going to a movie in the afternoon, and my daughter has her bridge club Saturdays, and John—her husband—he has an extra job weekends, to keep up with inflation. I just drove up there—it's Arbor Drive—and of course I've got a key, it was about ten o'clock, and I got this eraser thing and brought it back, and Aunt Louise was sort of dozing over her book. I plugged in the thing across the room, and pointed it right at her and switched it off and on about a dozen times— I thought that ought to do it. She'd had that pacemaker about four years. And then I took the eraser thing back and put it in Billy's room— and sure enough"— Mrs. Gleason drew a long quivering breath —"about two o'clock that afternoon she died. And I called Dr. Spooner and he said she could have gone any time, her age and with her heart, and he told me to call an ambulance and the police and he'd make out the death certificate."

Somewhat astonished at this rigmarole, Delia said, "Well, it could have been just coincidence, Mrs. Gleason—"

"But the sign said it was dangerous, it'd stop the pacemaker working."

Delia asked, "Where's Dr. Spooner's office?"

"Right here in town. It's Dr. William Spooner, on Central Avenue."

Delia went down to O'Connor's office to use the phone there. She got past an officious-sounding office nurse to talk to the doctor personally. He listened and burst into a hearty incredulous laugh. "My God, that woman's got an imagination!"

"But would it be possible, a thing like that interfering with a pacemaker?"

"I suppose it's remotely possible," said Dr. Spooner, "but I doubt if it would have a fatal result—and besides, there's no earthly way to tell now even if we dug her up and looked. She was buried last Wednesday. All anybody could possibly say would be that the thing had failed—if it had—and there could be a dozen reasons. She was a foul-tempered old fiend, and she was getting on to eighty-five— Mrs. Gleason more than did her duty by her. You tell her she's imagining things—that I said so —she couldn't have had anything to do with the death, and she's to go home to her daughter and stop being foolish. A nice old soul like Alicia Gleason, calling herself a murderess!"

It took Delia quite a while to convince Mrs. Gleason that she wasn't going to be arrested, that nobody believed she had committed murder. Mrs. Gleason had just trailed miserably out when Varallo and Gonzales came back to tell her about Sue and Jim French. But five minutes later a new homicide call went down, they went out on that, and Delia could finally get to the follow-up report on Melanie.

The new one was on Hahn Avenue, a short old street just north of the freeway, a neighborhood of older homes but well-kept, with groomed front yards. The squad was in front of a house midway down the block, a small stucco house painted beige, and there were a few neighbors out, mostly women; this would be a working-class neighborhood. On the front steps of the little house the body of an old man was sprawled, as if he had toppled off the front porch and fallen, face down. They looked at him, and at the little crowd there on the sidewalk. "Who called in?" Varallo asked the Traffic man.

"I did. I'm Mrs. Colson, I live next door." A middle-aged woman with a warm voice; her expression was half horrified, half excited. "I saw him— Mr. Bankhart—not two hours ago, walking home up the street, he looked all right then. The poor man must have had a stroke, a heart attack. It was when I stepped out to get the mail just a bit ago I saw him lying there—"

The woman beside her, older but about the same type, said, "He'd been getting pretty shaky lately, I guess he still managed to do for himself, but he was slowing down—"

"What's his name?"

"Andrew Bankhart," said the first woman. "He must have been seventy-eight or seventy-nine. They'd lived here longer than anyone on the block—he lost his wife last year, she was such a nice woman, she had a heart attack and dropped dead right in the bedroom—"

"Well, it's a blessing the poor old man went quick too, Mrs. Colson—at his age, he couldn't have lived alone much longer, and no family—that is, after all the trouble they'd had—"

Gonzales beckoned Varallo up the walk. "He was shot, Vic. Neat little hole behind the right ear, not much blood. The slug's still in, there's no exit wound."

"The hell you say."

"No sign of a gun."

Varallo used the radio in the squad to call up a lab truck. The front door of the house stood open, and he hooked open the screen door with a careful finger, and they went in to look around. The furniture was old-fashioned, but it was all neat and comfortable looking. The kitchen was in order; of the two bedrooms, only the front one looked occupied, the bed neatly made up.

They heard the lab truck pull up outside, and went out again. The little huddle of neighbors had diminished; only Mrs. Colson and the other woman kept watch. There had been no discernible bloodstains in the house, and no visible gun.

"You mentioned that Mr. Bankhart had had trouble of some kind? Recently?"

"Well, yes, poor man—not *recently,* I suppose— It was a terrible grief to them, and they were such good people, he had his own watch-repair shop for years, downtown, I understand he had quite a reputation at his job—such honest, respectable people. They'd probably have kept it to themselves, they were terribly ashamed of it, but it was all in the papers, at least the first time— You see, they were married nearly twenty years before they had any children, and then they had a boy— I don't know," and Mrs. Colson shrugged, "if maybe they spoiled him, or if he'd have turned out that way anyway. He—"

The other neighbor wanted a share in the gossip too. "A real brat that one was. He'd be about fourteen when Ben and I moved here, goodness, Andy Bankhart'll be getting on for thirty-five now—they had a lot of trouble with him, this dope and he stole things at school, and he got into trouble with girls —*you* know—"

"And about fifteen, sixteen years ago he was arrested for robbing and raping a lot of women, and he got sent to prison. Yes, right here in town—"

"I used to go in and see Amelia Bankhart, after she got so lame and couldn't get out, cheer her up a bit. And what she told me—you know, they don't keep that kind locked up as long as they should, and he got out that first time in only about five years. And she said he'd get in trouble again and they'd put him in jail, and then he'd get out and come begging them for money, and they felt they had to give it to him or he'd go and steal it somewhere. Only he did anyway—"

"I remember the name," said O'Connor. "I think I was still riding a squad. It is kind of suggestive, isn't it? Harmless old fellow living alone, probably not much but Social Security, no other relations except the black-sheep son. No gun in the house, no sign of any ransacking—if he did keep money at home the black sheep could probably guess where—"

"Yes, there's only one little *if*," said Varallo.

"Namely, is the black sheep presently incarcerated anywhere? Well, it's getting on to end of shift, but we can start to find out."

The only record Glendale had on Andrew Bankhart, Junior, was that first count, sixteen years back. He'd got a ten-to-twenty, and been released on parole five years later. That was the last Glendale knew of him. But that kind never stayed out of trouble long. They phoned down to R. and I. at LAPD, and there were computers down there, they were quick off the mark. LAPD had a package on Andy Bankhart. He'd been charged with assault, attempted rape, heisting. His latest conviction had been three years ago for a heist job, and he'd got a three-to-ten, been sent to Folsom, which was hard-core security.

"He could be out on parole by now," said Varallo.

"All too likely," agreed O'Connor. At a quarter of six he was talking to the Welfare and Rehab office at Parker Center.

Bankhart was currently on parole, and that was all Welfare and Rehab could say; it was a big department handling hundreds of cases. The P.A. officer attached to Bankhart was Horace Wheelock.

"Well, somebody else can go on with the routine tomorrow," said Varallo. "Thank God it's my day off."

Gonzales, feeling proud of his inspiration, had left a note for the night watch, about Equality, Illinois, and the night watch were intrigued. "Now that is a very funny one indeed," said Rhys. "Who'd ever think any town could be named Equality, for God's sake? I mean, the racehorses and show dogs come by some outlandish names"—he should know, his mother bred champion Cairn terriers—"but a town!"

Harvey had found the atlas and looked it up. He went on leafing through it, looking, and suddenly chortled. "Here's a town called Tiger in Georgia. And, my God, there's a Santa Claus in Indiana—and how about Hiawatha in Iowa?"

"Here, let me have a look at that," said Hunter. Looking for the funny names in the atlas, they were a little annoyed when a call came in on a heist. Rhys and Harvey took it.

And just once in a while the offbeat things showed up on the usually monotonous job. It was an all-night pharmacy on the ground floor of a professional building on North Brand, and when they got there a white-smocked pharmacist met them at the door and said, "That's him."

"Who?"

"The heister." The Traffic man was standing over him, and the heister was sitting in a chair crying. "He put the gun on me and said to hand over, and I was just about to when all of a sudden he sat down and started to cry. I don't know what's wrong with him—he's not doped up that I can see."

The heister stopped crying and looked up at them. He was a weedy-looking fellow about twenty-five, with stringy blond hair and a weak attempt at a beard. "It's just," he said, hiccupping, "it's just all of a sudden I saw—the same thing round and round —and it's no damn way to live—you get hold of the loot so you spend it on the coke and then you're broke and so you do another heist and then you're broke again, and it's no damn good, it's a hell of a way to live. And I guess I'd like to see a minister. I don't care what kind."

Unfortunately there wasn't a resident chaplain at the jail. They would find a minister for him tomorrow.

About five o'clock on Thursday afternoon some people named Elmore, who had been up at Big Bear skiing all week, arrived home to find they'd been burgled, and resignedly Katz and Poor had gone to look at it. The house was on Ardmore, and Katz swore when he saw the window that had been smashed —a lavatory window about a foot square.

"But the *damnedest* thing," said Elmore, "the *damnedest* thing—they took pictures. They left pictures. My wife found them after I called—"

"Pictures?" For one wild moment Katz thought of the raccoons.

"My Polaroid camera's missing, and they must have—they were just lying on the living room floor—"

There were two pictures. One of them showed a solemn-looking dark boy about ten years old, nothing very distinctive about him though anybody who knew him would recognize him. The other one showed another boy about the same age, with bright red hair and a mischievous grin; and he was wearing a blue T-shirt with something printed across the front: *Mark Keppel E. S.*

Katz clapped a hand to his forehead. "Mark Keppel Elementary School—right smack in the middle of that little area—and there won't be a soul there to answer questions until tomorrow morning—my God!" he said. "Just like the damned raccoons! Just like—"

"*Raccoons?*" said Elmore. "What the hell have raccoons got to do with it? They got my tape recorder, and the clock-radio, and all my wife's jewelry—*raccoons?*"

Katz and Poor were waiting at the elementary school on Friday morning when the staff started to arrive. The principal looked at the Polaroid shots and said, "There are a lot of boys that age here— I've seen these two, but offhand I couldn't say—we'd better ask Mrs. Morrison in the registrar's office—"

Mrs. Morrison took one look and said, "Douglas Carmody and Matt Palmer. Fifth grade, Miss Pomeroy's class."

They got hold of the boys and took them back to the Juvenile office, and Mary Champion said to Katz, "You don't mean to say—"

Douglas Carmody was the red-haired one, and it was a fairly safe bet that he'd be the ringleader of any enterprise he embarked on. He said in a surprised voice, "We thought that camera was busted! I heard of those cameras do pictures right away, but when they came out there wasn't any picture, just a blank space, and we thought it was busted! The pictures came out after, I guess—oh, gee, now you know all about it. Gee, my folks are gonna be awful mad at me, and I guess Matt's folks'll be even madder at him."

"What in the world set you two off on the burglaries?" asked Mary. They were both nice-looking boys and obviously well brought up, the way they spoke.

"Burglary," said Matt thoughtfully. "It didn't feel exactly like *burglary*—"

"It was just kind of exciting," said Douglas regretfully. "But I guess we got to tell about it now."

"My mother's never goin' to speak to me again," said Matt.

"It was Matt's uncle had the idea," said Douglas. "Oh, sure, we knew it was *wrong*, kinda, but it was—it was sort of fun too."

"So what did you do with what you stole?" asked Katz.

"Gee, it didn't seem exactly like *stealing*—it was Matt's Uncle Kurt knew where to sell the stuff, he gave us five or ten bucks a week, each, right along," said Douglas brightly.

Katz said, "Oh, heaven give me strength! All that loot—"

Matt's uncle turned out to be Kurt Blenheim, his mother's stepbrother, who had quite a little pedigree with LAPD as a professional burglar. The Palmers were respectable people, and when he'd come around just after he got out of Susanville a couple of months ago, they had warned him not to come near them again; but it had been the first time Matt had ever seen him, and Blenheim was evidently a persuasive talker. And meeting the boy, Blenheim had got the bright idea to turn into a Fagin. He had waylaid Matt at school and, inevitably, Douglas had got in on it, initially more enthusiastic than Matt. It had just been excitement to the boys. They had picked the houses to break in by talking to other kids at school, finding out whose folks would be out late at the movies or parties, about neighbors going away for weekends, kids going to stay with grandma while Mom and Dad went to a show—getting out of their bedroom windows, riding their bicycles down the dark streets—bicycles with the wire baskets for carrying things.

"Matt's uncle told us just where to look for stuff, and the kind of stuff to get. We had a great place to stash it," said Douglas, wistfully reviewing the past. "A big box way under the bleachers at the end of the schoolyard—and Matt'd phone him when we were goin' out, and he'd meet us there early mornin'—"

They had the parents in by that time, of course, all of them furious and talking a mile a minute; by the grace of God, good types and good friends, and putting all their wrath on Blenheim. He was still on parole; at eleven-thirty they finally reached his parole officer, who told them he had a job driving a laundry truck and was living in Tujunga.

Katz said to Poor, "You and Lew can go pick him up—this is one report I *want* to write!"

Forbes had got hold of Horace Wheelock at nine-thirty on Friday morning, and asked about Bankhart. "What's Glendale's interest?" asked Wheelock, and Forbes told him. "My God. Well, I wouldn't be unbearably surprised if he ended up on a homicide rap. If you've seen his record—"

"The incipient violence as the head doctors put it. He's been on P.A. how long?"

"He isn't," said Wheelock, "any longer. I took him off yesterday. He's skipped. He was supposed to have a session with me once a week—believe me, on one like Bankhart we check up—but his employer called me on Wednesday to say he hadn't been to work for four days, and I went up to the little pad I'd found for him, the landlady hadn't seen him since Tuesday. There's a 'want' out on him for parole violation."

"It all fits together nice and neat, in other words. He got tired of the supervision and decided to run, and on the way thought he'd hit Papa for whatever he was good for. And Papa wouldn't play."

"Very possible," said Wheelock. "There's an APB out on him, and the heap he was driving."

"Thanks for saving us the trouble," said Forbes. He put the phone down and immediately it shrilled at him.

"Say, I thought I'd give you the word before we got around to a report," said Thomsen. "The morgue sent a slug over last night, out of your latest corpse, and I've been working on it. I just pinned it down, and it's an offbeat gun. It's a Beretta Minx, chambered for .22 shorts, a seven-shot automatic. A little thing you don't come across very often. It's an old gun, quite distinctive rifling marks."

"Well, thanks very much," said Forbes. "I wonder where the hell a pro like Bankhart came by one like that. He's not the type to go in for a silly little equalizer of that kind."

"Now that's your problem," said Thomsen. "We're just here to look into the microscopes."

In the middle of the afternoon Delia drove over to the Glendale Adventist Medical Center to pick up the autopsy report on Melanie. Ordinarily Goulding or one of the other doctors would have dropped it in at Communications, but Goulding was temporarily minus assistants, one down with flu and another on his regular day off, and he was up to his eyes in bodies from a five-car pile-up on the Glendale freeway the night before.

She left the hospital at a little after three-thirty, turned out of the parking lot and up Chevy Chase. She had just got to the corner of Windsor and Adams, two blocks away, when a terrific explosion went off somewhere fairly close—it seemed to shake the sky. Startled, she hit the brake; she thought, that sounded exactly like a bomb.

A bomb.

No. Not really likely—those new locks—

She was about seven blocks from the little gray church on Adams. She made a reckless U-turn in the middle of the block, and raced down toward that intersection as fast as she dared. From three blocks away she could see the flames, a black pall of smoke towering up—another block, and she saw that it was the church.

Automatically, trained for years to keep her head and act coolly in emergency, she looked around, braked the car and got out in a hurry. Fire-alarm box on this curb; she broke the glass with one sharp blow, setting off the alarm. She plunged back into the car and went down there as near as she dared, swung the car into a red-painted zone to get it out of the way—

Both side walls of the church had been blown violently into rubble, and on this side the rubble had collapsed onto the parking lot, probably burying all the smashed cars—

Choir practice 3:30 Fridays—stupidly, it kept repeating itself in her mind— *Choir practice 3:30 Fridays*—

She looked down at her watch. It was four minutes of four, and that had gone up about twelve or thirteen minutes ago.

The engine came roaring up, and the men got right on it, coupling hoses and directing the streams of water to the great blaze towering up to the gray sky. Another engine came in a block down, and men ran up from it to the back of the church. *Choir practice 3:30 Fridays*—and it was five minutes past four, and she was a practical trained law officer but the foolish tears were sliding down her cheeks and it was the same old thought— why always, why always on the side of evil and pain?

"Oh, my God! My God!" It was a voice behind her, and she turned. She didn't really know the man at all, but she could have thrown her arms around him— Dr. James Barlow, his gray hair wild, his pretty little wife beside him, staring in terrified fascination at the furiously burning church. "Oh, my God!" he said.

And suddenly, in the midst of all the confusion—a third fire engine racing up the next street—there were cars, a surprising number of cars, driving up the block, stopping where they were blocked by the fire engine, and there were people getting out of the cars and running up here, shouts and excited exclamations—

"Mrs. Ziegler! We were so late ourselves— I was afraid everyone would have been—why, Virginia— Kathy, my dear! Mr. Acker— Mrs. Lewis— Wendy! Scott— Carl—why, God be thanked, God be thanked, you're all here and safe—there was nobody inside at all! All here and safe—may God be thanked!"

CHAPTER 10

They didn't get the fire knocked down and under control until after dark, and the lab men couldn't get to it, to have a thorough look, until Saturday. If there was anything left to find, to give any lead to the manufacturers of the bomb—if it had been a bomb—they'd like to know about it, but the destruction had been fairly wholesale, and there probably wouldn't be much to find. And overnight it began to rain again; by midnight it was pouring steadily.

The lab men went poking around in the rain and called in a couple of experts from the LAPD bomb squad. Their conclusions weren't very satisfactory; they collected all the possible relevant scraps from the rubble and put them under the microscope in the Glendale lab, and one of the LAPD men said, "Looks as if it could have been a simple pipe bomb, but that's just guessing. But where most of this came from—the thing was probably set against the back of the building, where it wouldn't have been noticed. These bits and pieces"—he prodded at the collection of metal scraps presently under a microscope—"all that's left of the alarm clock."

"And," said the other expert sadly, "like all amateurs they made it an overkill, by the damage done. You have any idea who to look for on it?"

Varallo and O'Connor had been standing around watching them. "Well, for God's sake," said O'Connor, "none of these punks are big time—yet. Simple enough to put together a devilish little device like that, but where they'd come by the materials—"

"It's a big city, Charles," said Varallo. "And the hell of a lot of urban renewal going on, in all directions. Building sites being leveled up in the hills— If that gang was involved, and that's what it looks like, Carlos Ramirez is older and has a damn sight better brain than Tony Aguayo ever had. You know there's been a vague little rumor that the Guerreros are getting all buddy-buddy with another Latino gang in Hollywood—maybe exchanging ideas, and a few other things."

"Yes, Goddamn it," said O'Connor, scowling. "These damn punks, anything to make trouble, they don't need an excuse—"

"Satan finding work for idle hands," said one of the LAPD men. "You'll never connect anybody to it by what you've got here, even when you think you know."

"Goddamn it, we could have guessed that without your help," said O'Connor bitterly. "There's only one bunch it could be, and I don't think, for God's sake, they were inspired by any religious fervor against the Presbyterians. Oh, for *God's* sake—these punks—"

It went on raining all Saturday. The APB didn't turn up Andy Bankhart. Forbes and Gonzales went back to Hahn Street to ask whether anybody had seen his car around there on Thursday, but nobody had; none of the neighbors had seen Bankhart, Senior, since that morning, when a woman farther up the block had seen him walk by going toward Kenilworth Avenue. She said he sometimes went to sit in Fremont Park up there, but she didn't suppose he was going there then, such a cold day—he had probably been going to the market on the corner of Glenoaks. The next time he'd been seen was by Mrs. Colson, walking toward home about two-thirty. She had thought he looked tired, was walking more slowly than usual.

It looked as if Junior, using rudimentary caution, had left his car a block or so away, walked down to see the old man. "And you know," said Gonzales, "I had another thought about it, Jeff. It could be that the old man had given him money before, because his wife asked him to, but now she's gone he wasn't about to hand over any more."

"That could fit too," agreed Forbes. "So they had an argument, and Andy shot him, and took what he could find. The lab didn't come across a wallet or any money in the house. But I still think that's a funny sort of gun for him to have picked up—given any choice, one like Bankhart goes for something bigger. But that's what it looks like. Well, when we do pick him up he may still have it on him."

"He could be six states away by now," said Gonzales. They had alerted NCIC that Bankhart was on the run from parole and a possible homicide charge, and with any luck he should be picked up sooner or later. Of course, it was unlikely he was still driving the same car.

Delia was alone in the office at a little before four on Saturday when a call came up from Communications: a body, on Geneva Street. She went out to see what it was, and found Patrolman Whalen sitting in the squad in front of an old apartment building.

"Look, it's just routine, I think," he told her. "The guy looks about a hundred years old, he probably just died in his sleep, but he didn't have a regular doctor, hadn't been to one in years as far as this niece knows. She just came in and found him, she's sort of broken up. His name was Brian Gault."

"Just routine," said Delia. It was the way the law read: if the deceased hadn't seen a doctor within ten days, there had to be an autopsy. "All right, it's the end of your shift—just put in a call for the morgue wagon and you can go." She went up to the apartment on the second floor to take a look.

It was an old tired apartment, not very clean or neat, and there was a woman sitting on the couch in the living room crying. Delia went into the bedroom and looked at the old man dead in bed. He must once have been a handsome man, with strong aquiline features, but he looked very old, and he had been dead for a while, probably at least twenty-four hours.

The woman in the living room said her name was Jean Baker. She was at least in her sixties, dowdily dressed. "I talked to him yesterday on the phone," she said, wiping her eyes. "He hadn't any other relations, you know. I was awfully fond of Uncle Brian. He was such an interesting man, didn't seem old at all, but he was eighty-five—" She said he had given her a key to the apartment, and when he didn't answer the door she'd used it, found him.

Delia explained the formalities to her, and she nodded. "Of course Brian Gault wasn't his real name, if that makes a difference."

"Not his real name?"

"No, his real name was Howard Solberg, he just made up the

other one for the stage. See all his pictures?" For the first time
Delia noticed that two big walls of the living room were covered
with old photographs. "They're very interesting, he loved showing them to people—" Jean Baker had her over there, eager and
proud. "He was a pretty well-known movie actor for a long
time, you know—oh, not really famous, a supporting actor they
call it, but he'd been in hundreds of movies and acted with a lot
of famous people. I'm a bit too young to remember the earliest
ones, but he told me who they all were—look, that's Gloria
Swanson—and Patsy Ruth Miller, that's Uncle Brian right beside her in the railroad uniform—he was awfully good looking,
wasn't he? And there he is with Irene Rich and Ronald Colman
in *Lady Windermere's Fan*—and with William Powell in *One-
Way Passage*— And then all the early talkies— Wallace Beery
in *Grand Hotel*—that's Cary Grant and Rosalind Russell—and
Barbara Stanwyck in *Double Indemnity*— He had them all arranged by years to show how long he'd been in the movies. Now
this is the last part he ever did, it was a movie called *Desperate
Characters,* that was about 1972—he had to have the operation
for cancer after that, and then he had the stroke a couple of
years ago. He was eighty-five, you know. Oh, yes, he'd been
married—three times—but he was divorced from all of them.
But he had a wonderful career, he just loved to talk about it—
all those famous people—"

They were just names to Delia. She thought with a little in-
ward chuckle, she'd been feeling so old and staid—thirty and a
half—but she was much too young to remember any of those famous people. Well, everything was relative.

Varallo swore at the rain as he drove home. He knew he
should have done some work in the yard on Friday, he'd just
been too damned lazy. As wet as this winter was turning out, it
would probably be raining again on his day off next week, and
the weeds were coming up fast and furious among all the roses.

Laura had put the garage light on for him. He shut the big
door, came into the kitchen and kissed her—his lovely Laura
with her bright brown hair and the warm smile in her eyes—and
the children came up, Johnny shouting.

"Daddy come and read the bean-stalk story!"

"Now, Johnny, that's after dinner," said Laura briskly.

Ginevra was holding up her arms to him, her dimple showing and a new blue ribbon in her blond curls, and he thought about Melanie, and hugged her too hard so that she squealed.

On Sunday morning it was still raining, and O'Connor probably cussing because he couldn't take the dog out for a run. All the lights were on in the big office against the dark gray day outside. There had been another heist last night, and a hit-run, and the two heists from Friday night still had to be worked on. Everybody but Gonzales and Delia was out, and Gonzales was on the point of leaving, when a husky young blond fellow came in about ten o'clock. His gaze passed over Delia uninterestedly; he walked over to Gonzales and said, "Say, my name's Bill Vollmer, and I came in to say that I know who that guy is in the picture."

"What picture?" asked Gonzales.

"The one that's up in that coffee shop down on Brand. See, all this damn flu going around, I've been down nearly two weeks with the damn bug, and not being married I've got nobody to do for me—it's been kind of rough. But by yesterday I was feeling better, I'll be okay to go back to work tomorrow. Well, anyway, I fixed breakfast at home yesterday, but this morning I went down to that coffee shop—"

"The Magnolia Cafe?"

"That's the one, it's handy to the job and I usually go there for lunch. And while I was having breakfast, I saw that picture. This guy wanted for shooting that waitress. And I know him— I'm positive it's him. See, I work at Phil Judson's garage a block up Brand from that place, and this guy got hired as a mechanic a couple of months ago. He's not just a hell of a good mechanic, kind of ham-handed, and Phil's going to let him go, but he seems to be an ordinary enough guy, I wouldn't think he'd go shooting anybody. But I swear that's him, in the picture. His name's Gary Boardman— I don't know where he lives."

Gonzales thanked him for coming in, told him they might want a statement; he left an address. Gonzales drove down to that garage to get the emergency number from the door, came back and called Judson, who was annoyed at being disturbed on a rainy Sunday but went down to get Boardman's address for them. It was Harvard Avenue. Gonzales went out to see if he could pick him up, and when he came back with him said he'd just got there in time, Boardman had just been getting into his car. They sat him down in Varallo's desk chair and started to talk to him.

"About Alice Bailey, Boardman," said Gonzales. "Why did you want to shoot her?"

"I don't know what you're talkin' about." Boardman was about fifty, bald as an egg, with a paunch and little porcine bad-tempered eyes.

"Oh, yes, you do. We have a witness who can identify you positively as the one who shot her. We'd just like to know why."

"You didn't know her, did you?" asked Delia.

"I don't know anythin' about it."

It went on that way for quite a while, the usual monotonous routine, until Gonzales asked him, "Have you still got the gun? The .32 Colt? We've already asked for a search warrant for your apartment and car, and if we find the gun the lab can tell us it was the gun that killed her."

He was looking nervous by then, and he thought that one over for a while, and then he said sullenly, "Oh, Goddamn it— I should've got rid of that damn thing."

"Why did you shoot the girl, Boardman?"

"Because the damn little bitch insulted me!" he yelled suddenly. "I was just so Goddamn mad at that bitch— I just asked her for a date a couple times, you'd think any girl wouldn't mind a guy showin' interest— Women! Women! Never know where you stand with women! My wife walked out with that Goddamn gigolo—well, hell, it's fifteen years back, forget it—and then Wilma and I had a thing going, but for Christ's sake we mighta as well been married, nag nag nag— I oughta lose weight and quit smoking, and then she walks out on me. I just asked that damn girl for a date, go to a show or something, and she insults me! She laughed and said she don't date old men—she called me Grandpa! She called me Grandpa!" He was still feeling indignant about it.

"Oh, for God's sake," said Gonzales. "All right, will you sign a statement?"

Delia typed it up and he put a straggly signature on it. Gonzales took him over to jail.

The warrants came in after lunch, and with no immediate report to write Delia went with Gonzales to search Boardman's apartment. It looked as if he had lived hand to mouth there; there wasn't much furniture, the kitchen was dirty and in a state of confusion. They found the gun in the top drawer of the dresser in the bedroom, and Gonzales slid it into an evidence bag.

As they came out Delia's eyes fastened on the old gray Mercedes parked at the curb. Casually she asked, "Is that his car?"

"Yep, he was just getting into it when I landed here. An antique, isn't it? Worth something as a classic in a few years."

Gonzales had gone out after heisters, Varallo and Boswell were questioning a suspect in one of the interrogation rooms, and she was alone in the office again when Dr. James Barlow came in just after four o'clock. "I don't want to take up your time," he said, "but I thought perhaps you would be interested. I could see how concerned you were on Friday, Miss Riordan." His smile was warm on her. He looked tired, his suit was rumpled as usual and his bush of prematurely gray hair untidy, but there was a triumphant light in his eyes as he looked at her. He took a piece of paper from his breast pocket.

"I wondered—will you be rebuilding the church?"

"Oh, I really don't know." He didn't seem very concerned. "We didn't own the property, you see—only rented it. I believe some obscure denomination had just moved out when our board —I haven't had a chance to discuss it with the Los Angeles directors. For the moment, I have rented a store building in the Atwater area, where we can meet until some decision is made. We may simply join with the nearest congregation, that would be in Hollywood. But—about Friday—" He gave Delia his warm charming smile. He didn't ask what they'd found out about the bomb, or if they knew who had put it there.

"Yes?"

He sat down in the chair beside her desk. "Ordinarily, one doesn't try to explain a miracle—one must only thank God that they happen. But it seemed to me so strange—all of us, every single one of us, so late starting for choir practice!—so that no one at all was in the church when that happened. We have been discussing it, comparing notes, after the service this morning. And surely the guardian angels were with all of us. Yet it seems all the stranger now, when it is explained." He ruffled his thick hair, and suddenly his eyes twinkled. "I don't explain it," he said, "but it delights my soul. I thought you might be as interested as I am." And his expression said for him that he had seen her tears that day, and she felt herself flushing.

"Ordinarily, there would have been twenty-three people in the church when that explosion occurred, and very likely we'd all have been killed. But—seemingly just by coincidence—everyone was prevented from being there on time. And the reasons —the reasons!" He shook with sudden laughter. "Really, one can almost hear the rustle of the guardian angels' wings! First there's my wife and myself. She directs the choir, of course, and I always enjoy attending choir practice. I had taken the car in for an oil change, and they said it would be ready at two-thirty, but something had come up to delay the mechanic, and it was after three when I finally got it. By the time I had driven back to the house for Myrna— And then there is Kathy Leach. She had had a bad headache that morning, had decided not to come, but she was to do a solo and at the last minute she decided she must come—but by then it was somewhat later than she'd normally have left. Mr. Acker"—he was looking at the paper— "couldn't get his car started. He flooded the engine, and didn't manage to get it started until ten or fifteen minutes after he'd expected to be on his way. Once it did start, he said, it was running just as smoothly as usual. And Linda Brewster, as she put it, got stuck on the phone. She and her mother were coming together as usual, but this very chatty friend had called her, and talked on and on, and Mrs. Brewster kept tapping Linda on the shoulder to remind her it was time to leave, and finally Linda broke in on her friend and excused herself, and they got started —fifteen minutes late. Then there was Virginia Glass. She's a student at Glendale College, and she had plenty of time to stop at the college library before she left at two-thirty, to get a book she needed for some research—but she couldn't find it, though the files indicated that it was in. The librarian finally found it— it had been put in quite the wrong place on another shelf." Barlow was enjoying his recital. "And Mrs. Worth—her mother was coming to stay with the baby, but she was late getting there because a neighbor had dropped by to ask for a recipe. Dick Lynch, who's also a Glendale College student, was home by two, but he stumbled on a TV special, a documentary on archaeology, and wanted to see it all—it ended at three-thirty. Mrs. Lewis—she went to pick up her little boy at school, and he was late coming out, the teacher had kept him after class. She was delayed about fifteen minutes. And William Owens—he too got home from college at two o'clock, but his parents both work, he was alone in the house, and just as he was leaving a phone-company repairman asked to come in to check the line, there was trouble somewhere in the neighborhood. Joan Simons had misplaced her wallet with her driver's license in it, and hunted all over before she remembered she had got it out to pay the paper boy the night before, left it in the entry hall."

Delia was listening quietly, smoking. "It's all so very interesting, isn't it?" said Barlow, chuckling. "Mrs. Hope—her Avon lady had delivered an order to her, and she couldn't find her checkbook. She finally discovered it under a magazine on the desk—but not for about fifteen minutes. Mr. Canning—he owns a pharmacy—and he was delayed because he discovered that his assistant had neglected to put in an order for drug supplies, and it was important that it be filled immediately, so he stayed to phone it in to the wholesale firm. And Wendy Blake fell asleep on the couch after lunch—her husband's been ill with the flu, and she'd been up with him part of the night. She only woke up at three-fifteen, and rushed about getting ready to leave—fifteen minutes late. And Mrs. Penner—she was just getting into her car when the United Parcel truck came with something she'd ordered for her husband's birthday, and she was anxious to see it so she delayed to open the parcel. And Mrs. Babcock—oh, Mrs. Babcock!" chortled Barlow happily. "She was expecting company for dinner, and had the table all set, but just as she was leaving the house the cat jumped up on the table and upset her centerpiece of flowers, and she had to stay to clean it up. Scott Seaton—he manages a Shell station—was about to leave when he had a long-distance phone call from his brother-in-law to tell him that his sister's baby had arrived safely. A little girl. Mr. Kruger owns a furniture store, and one of the wholesale salesmen came in late and kept him talking—he was quite annoyed about it at the time, he said. Mrs. Wycherly had promised to finish making a dress for her daughter to wear on a date that night, and it took her longer than she had expected, but as she was so nearly finished— John Armstrong was working on the accounts in his appliance store and lost track of time. And Mrs. Blackwell hadn't realized that the power was off and the clock stopped, until she looked at her wristwatch. Mrs. Ziegler—our organist—couldn't find the score for the music—she had taken it home to do some transposing—until she suddenly remembered that she had got out an old briefcase of her husband's to put it in, in case it rained. And finally, Walter Brooks—he's a retired tailor, a really fine bass voice—as he was leaving he accidentally dropped his glasses and broke them, and had to hunt for his extra pair." Barlow began to laugh again; it was a beautiful warm tender laugh. "Twenty-three people, and nineteen different reasons—in the same hour—kept them from being where they should have been. Coincidence! Oh, I like it—I like it very much."

"It does seem—strange," said Delia.

"And reassuring," he nodded. "Very reassuring, to know that watch is being kept. I don't really think, you know, that all of us are such important people, to deserve special attention—on the part of the guardian angels." He twinkled at her. "But perhaps all of us have still some job to do here. That must be the answer." He folded up the paper and put it away. "But I *like* it. Because as well as being reassuring, it's all quite hilarious—and I've always suspected that God has a sardonic sense of humor."

The APB hadn't yet turned up Andy Bankhart. The autopsy report came in and that was rather ironic: Bankhart Senior had been riddled with cancer and probably wouldn't have lived six months, said Goulding.

There would be hearings getting scheduled, in Juvenile court —the court calendars always full—for the ten-year-old burglars, for Bert Navarro and Harry Pascoe and Juanita Cabrillo. Mark Ryan and his cohorts would be arraigned on the more serious charge, and a lot of good that was going to do Mike Fitzpatrick.

On Monday morning at ten-thirty a big bank job went down, five very professional heisters hitting the Crocker Bank on North Brand. That brought out the FBI men, but most of the Glendale detectives turned out on it to help with the questioning. All that emerged was a couple of fairly good descriptions, and the Feds thought those two could be a pair of pros who had pulled a similar job in Philly a year ago and gone underground. Nobody would know how much they'd got away with until the auditors were finished checking, but it was an academic question: it was gone. Of course, in the long run it didn't pose any ongoing new business for Glendale; the paperwork on it would be the Feds' headache.

And O'Connor said, "Damn it, I may be getting old and just resistant to change, boys, but I don't know that I'm just so damned crazy about what's happening to this town." He stood, hands in pockets, the bulge of the shoulder holster very obvious, looking out the tall window above Varallo's desk. All he could see from here was the jumble of new apartments and condos up these largely residential streets, but in his mind's eye, they knew, he was seeing the forest of new high-rise office buildings up on North Brand, the huge new shopping complex to be Galleria Two joined to Galleria One eight blocks south of here; and he was thinking of the influx of aliens, all changing the face and feel of the city. He sighed, and turned. "I just hope we can stay on top of it." The crime rate was soaring higher every month; and Glendale was a cream-puff town compared to the murky byways of Hollywood, the rest of the vast sprawl that was Los Angeles.

It stopped raining again on Tuesday, and Varallo had just emerged from an interrogation room with Forbes and the possible suspect, who had surprisingly turned out to have an alibi, when Patrolman Tracy came in with a little paper parcel in his hand. "Something a little funny— I thought I'd better bring it right in," he said. "I got sent down to that little park on Kenilworth, Fremont Park. This P. and R. man had called in. He'd just landed there to mow the grass or something, and he found a gun on one of the benches in the picnic area. And a billfold."

"Well, that's something different all right," said Forbes.

"I didn't know if you'd want any lab work on it, but I tried to be careful. I had the morning's *Times* in the squad, so I wrapped them separately— I hope that's okay."

"Don't expect we'll need to go that far—well, for God's sake! Here, Vic, take a look at this—"

The little gun was an automatic, with a barrel about four inches long, and its grip was labeled in good-sized raised letters BERETTA. "I will be damned," said Varallo.

They unwrapped the other sheet and discovered a worn old black leather billfold. In it there was fourteen dollars, an obsolete driver's license for Andrew Bankhart, a Social Security card, and an old snapshot of a nice-looking elderly woman with snow-white hair.

"But—" said Forbes, "but—"

"I know," said Varallo. He looked at Tracy. "Is the P. and R. man still there?"

"Was when I left fifteen minutes ago."

They dropped the gun off with Thomsen and drove up to that little park. There wasn't much to it, just a square of grass with a walk running around it, a couple of tennis courts, a long open-roofed shelter with tables and benches. The park employee had finished cutting the grass, was pruning shrubs.

"Can you show us where you found the gun?" asked Varallo.

"Sure." He was a phlegmatic square man with a dark Indian-looking face. He led them to the roofed shelter, pointed out one of the tables in the middle of it. "It was right there, on top of the billfold."

"I will be—when was the last time you were here?"

He thought. "Two weeks ago. There's not much to do in winter. And with all this rain, you ask me, I'll bet nobody else has been here since before that. The kids play here—other little parks like this—in nice weather. Summer, you get people coming to play tennis. People on picnics sometimes. But in winter, especially when it's been so cold, who sits in parks?"

They looked at each other. "Somebody said he used to sit in the park," said Forbes.

"He was seen walking this way earlier that day."

"I think I'd like to hear Goulding on this," said Forbes.

They went over to the medical center and found Dr. Goulding taking a coffee break in the cafeteria. They got a couple of cups and sat down with him. He listened to them and said, "This is the old fellow I did, let's see, Saturday. All the cancer. That's a funny one."

"He was shot in the head," said Forbes. "We took it for granted, in the house. I know even a direct head wound sometimes doesn't kill instantly, we thought he'd made it to the front door and fallen down on the porch. Good God, doctor, that park is two long blocks away from the house!"

Goulding sniffed and patted his bald head absently. "Head wounds are funny. You can look up all the classic cases for yourselves. People with brain tumors squeezing the whole brain, still functioning normally and thinking straight up to the end. The head's a funny piece of equipment anyway. Most complicated computer ever invented. And we still don't know as much as we should about it. I've read about a good many cases like this."

"But two blocks—"

"Largely, I suppose," said Goulding thoughtfully, "it must have been pure habit. You can follow the old fellow up to a point. Could be—if he lived alone, nobody close to him—"

"Which was the case," said Forbes.

"All right. He wanted to be found right off, not lie in the house for days. So he walked over to the park and shot himself there. Thoughtfully leaving his billfold out so whoever found him would know who he was right off. He probably lost consciousness for a while. Then he came to, forgetting what he'd done—confused and cold and uncomfortable, and his only thought was that he'd better go home. So he went. Yes, it's perfectly possible that he could walk that far. How was he found? Well, there you are. He made it to the front porch, and then fell down and died."

"Well, I am damned," said Varallo.

By a test slug, the little Beretta was the gun that had killed Bankhart. He hadn't left a note, but he hadn't needed to.

Now all Andy Bankhart was wanted for was parole violation.

Just as Varallo had expected, it began to rain again on Friday and he couldn't do anything about his roses. It was still raining on Saturday. It was about four o'clock, and he and Delia were alone in the office except for Katz typing a report in his corner, and Varallo was hunting through the file cabinet for something. "Damn it, the paperwork. There is stuff here that could be cleaned out." He straightened with a manila folder in one hand. "This Garvin thing—we might as well put it in Pending."

"I don't think so," said Delia. "I wanted to talk to you about that one. You know, Vic— I think he did it."

"*Garvin?* What the hell put that in your head?" He was astonished.

She was looking down at the sapphire ring she'd been wearing lately. She said, "A couple of things. And that autopsy report—we didn't really give much thought to it at the time, but I looked at it again. And certainly, it said between six and ten, but it also said that she'd died about an hour after she'd had a meal. They'd have dinner about six, I suppose. And she was eating a candy bar, she still had it in her hand when she was knocked down."

Varallo passed a hand over his jaw. "But—why? Well, yes, the old joke—just because she was his wife. But—"

"I think that's why he came in that day. To find out if we had a suspect. I think," said Delia soberly, "that he's—an honorable man. There's something I'd like to try on him." She told him what it was, and he was dubious.

"Well, all right. I'm not crazy about the idea, and neither of us is going to do it on city time."

"I just think it could produce a reaction," said Delia.

They got to the Garvin house on Idlewood Road at a little after seven. He let them in with his grave courtesy, and said, "You've got some news for me? Please come down here—" It was a warm, pleasant little study, with a flat-topped desk, and all the walls were lined with bookshelves. He sat down in the desk chair and Varallo and Delia took two straight chairs across the room.

Delia smiled at him brightly and said, "You'll be glad to know that we've arrested someone for your wife's murder, Mr. Garvin. We've got him tied up nicely with some good evidence, and he'll be charged with first degree homicide."

The courteous little smile seemed painted on his mouth. "I thought you told me there wasn't any evidence."

"Oh, the scientific lab can do some miracles these days," said Varallo. "He's denied it, of course, but the evidence looks pretty good. I don't see how he can get out of it."

"I see. Is he—er—a young man?"

"What? Oh, twenty-two," said Delia. "He hasn't got any previous record, which is rather surprising. He claims that he was desperate for money, his wife's expecting a baby, and he'd decided to commit a burglary, that's what he was doing here that night—" It was, of course, pure and direct melodrama, but she had a feeling that Garvin was an old-fashioned man.

He got up and stood with his back turned to them, facing one of the walls of books. He was silent for a long time, and then he said in a quiet voice, without turning, "I see. Then I think I had better tell you that this young man didn't kill my wife. I killed her. I killed Eleanor. I am—very sorry—it has come to this. I had hoped that it would simply be put down to a violent prowler, a burglar— I knew there had been cases of that kind in the neighborhood, prowlers reported and so on—and with no obvious clues, you would never arrest anyone. But I can't let an innocent man pay for my crime."

"Why, Mr. Garvin?" asked Varallo. "Why in God's name?"

"I think I know why," said Delia very gently. "Lisa is like her, isn't she, Mr. Garvin?"

He turned to look at her, and gave a queer little laugh, and turned to face the books again. He put out one of his fine long-fingered hands and stroked the books. "Perspicacious," he said. "Oh, yes—very much. The old cliché—but clichés are apt to be right, aren't they?—the attraction of opposites. She was such a vivacious, pretty girl. We were married for over thirty-three years, and I don't suppose we ever had a thought in common all that time. It was—you see, it was all right for me—up to now. I had my work, my friends at the college, my books— I was away most of the day, and I could spend the little time necessary to satisfy her interests—one has to make compromises in marriage —the parties, the guests, the round of—socializing. You see, she never understood—dear me, that's another cliché, isn't it— she never understood, for instance, what pleasure anyone could get out of reading a book. I don't think she had opened a book since she left school. You see—and I suppose many a man before me has done the same—it was easier to give in to her, and find my real life, my real pleasure, in my work. It was only evenings and weekends I was here—and even Eleanor couldn't have a party every night."

"But you're going to be retiring," said Delia.

"It is, unfortunately, mandatory at my age," he said. "And she had found that place—" He was silent for another long while, and still facing the books he said in sudden quiet fury,

"My God, these places! The senior citizens' community parks! The communal recreation lodge and the bright-eyed social director with the degree in psychology! The planned activities—the senior citizens must be encouraged to keep cheerful and active and busy! The golf course, the shuffleboard, bingo, the bridge clubs. It would be exactly the kind of life Eleanor would love, and there was no understanding in her that for me it would be a living hell. Wasn't there a review once—the review of a play, I mean—a good way of killing time for those who prefer it dead. Yes. I don't know why it should be so hard for most people to understand that some of us *like* to be alone, to read and think and study, that we find pleasure in it, and don't love our fellowmen so well as to desire their company every waking moment, just for the sake of company."

"The Bandarlog," murmured Delia. He gave her a swift, penetrating, rather terrible smile.

"The simian concept, of course, yes. I'd always been given to understand that I was very odd—reading books all the time even when it wasn't necessary to my work—and writing a book. I should have liked to finish that, you know—I'm sorry. Perhaps not an original theme, but I think I had a few pertinent things to say. It's a pity. But you see, the mobile home wouldn't have had room for all my books. There wasn't a decent library within fifty miles. And that terrifying social director!—really, Mr. Garvin must be made to come out of his shell and join in all our fun-activities! The bingo, the bridge—all the hearty extrovert types telling ancient jokes and calling me Ed— I had made a peace for myself, here. With the compromises. Do you see? But all my peace would be destroyed. And the only possible way I could get out of that—living hell—would be if Eleanor wasn't here, to bully me into it."

He waited, and went on, "It wasn't hatred, you know—grant me that. I hadn't felt anything at all about her for a long time. It was just—that she had to go. So I would be left in peace. If you want to know the—er—mechanics of it, she was watching TV in the den, and I had gone out the back door ostensibly to leave for the library. I simply opened the door of the porch into the dining room, after getting that stake from the garage, and called her to come out. I said it looked as if someone had tried to tamper with the lock on the garage door. The lights weren't on at the time, only the ceiling light in the garage. She was quite concerned about the crime rate—she came right out, and I caught her across the back of the neck as she passed me, at the edge of the porch. I am—not a man of action. I was very sorry —for the necessity. I struck her four or five times—to be sure. When I was sure—that there was no pulse— I simply got in the car and drove to the library. I didn't put the floodlights on until I came home."

"I'll have to ask you—" said Varallo. By all the rules and regulations this was all wrong. But Edward Garvin, an honorable man, wasn't going to be trying to claim violations of rights.

"Yes," he said. "I know. I'm quite ready to come with you." He looked around at his place of peace, where he had been happy in his little peace. "I'm afraid," he said, with the queer fixed little smile, "that this will be—a great shock—to the children."

It was just after eight-thirty when Delia turned onto Waverly Place. She had had pot-luck dinner with Vic and Laura before they had gone to see Garvin. Varallo had taken him down to book him in. She felt remotely sad for Edward Garvin, the man caught in a trap. But as she was driving home through the steady rain, her mind was mostly concentrated—reluctant, groping, unwilling but honest—assessing those little—happenstances? Facts? You couldn't, if you were honest, shut your eyes and deny that they had happened, because they had happened. And simple things they were, too—very simple—but unknowable?

A dream about an apple tree and a little girl. A pair of initials and an old gray Mercedes. And nineteen coincidences happening within an hour, to preserve the lives of twenty-three quite ordinary people—well, twenty-two ordinary people and Dr. James Barlow—and that was too many coincidences altogether.

It could be a different sort of universe than she had thought, maybe not blind and random. Maybe a plan going on in it, too slow and vast for fallible human creatures to understand. Maybe there was a planner arranging things—in the end, a benevolent planner.

And she had a sudden, shocking, most original idea. She thought perhaps some Sunday she might go to Dr. Barlow's church service.

She went in the back door, switching on lights, and went immediately down the hall to the phone and called Hildy. "Oh, Delia, it is such a bad rainy night, but he has been so anxious and asking for you— I'm afraid he will not sleep unless you come—"

"Yes, Hildy," said Delia. "I know. I'm coming." She hadn't taken her coat off, and she picked up her handbag, getting out her keys, and went out again into the rain.

Lesley Egan is a pseudonym for a popular, very prolific author of mysteries. Her most recent novels are *The Miser, A Choice of Crimes,* and *Motive in Shadow.*